THE LAST WEEK END

D1557114

Also by Nick Mamatas:

Novels
Move Under Ground
Under My Roof
Sensation
The Damned Highway: Fear and Loathing in Arkham
(co-written with Brian Keene)
Love Is the Law
I Am Providence

Collections
3000 MPH in Every Direction at Once
You Might Sleep…
The Nickronomicon

As Editor
The Urban Bizarre
Realms (co-edited with Sean Wallace)
Spicy Slipstream Stories (co-edited with Jay Lake)
Realms 2 (co-edited with Sean Wallace)
Haunted Legends (co-edited with Ellen Datlow)
The Future Is Japanese (co-edited with Masumi Washington)
Phantasm Japan (co-edited with Masumi Washington)

THE LAST WEEK END

Nick Mamatas

Night Shade Books
New York

10 9 8 7 6 5 4 3 2 1

Library of Congress Cataloging-in-Publication Data

Mamatas, Nick.
    The last weekend / Nick Mamatas.
      pages ; cm
    ISBN 978-1-59780-842-2 (pbk.: alk. paper)
    1. Zombies—Fiction.   I. Title.
    PS3613.A525L37 2015
    813'.6—dc23
                              2015013630

Print ISBN: 978-1-59780-842-2

Cover illustration and design by Jason Snair

Printed in the United States of America

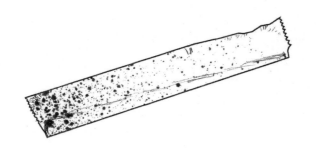

For Oliver Panagiotis Borrin Mamatas, a real California boy.

There's a story so thoroughly circulated that it really isn't even worth telling anymore, except that it *is* so common there's no other way to start.

San Francisco is . . . okay. The Board of Supervisors for the City and County of San Francisco barred new graveyards, and closed down the cemeteries, way back in the early twentieth century. Successive governments exhumed the dead, moved them to Colma where the dead outnumbered the living 1000-to-1, and to elsewhere in the Bay. It took decades to get every corpse out of town. In the early 1990s, long before I landed here with nothing but a laptop and a suitcase full of aborted novels and stillborn short stories after washing out of Emerson, 700 corpses were found under the municipal golf course at Fort Miley on the southern corner of Golden Gate Park; all '49ers, or largely '49ers anyway, some still clutching rosaries. They were dragged off too, eventually. Almost like someone in

 City Hall knew what was to come thanks to an opium dream from the days of basement dens full of sweating, thrashing Chinamen. Is there a yellow notebook in a file

cabinet somewhere, pressed into the hands of every new mayor, photocopied and distributed to each new crop of supervisors? Is that why they killed Harvey Milk, because he threatened to tell the world?

But we're okay. There were some bodies under the ground in the Presidio, but some working weapons there as well. The tiny graveyard in Mission Dolores wasn't a problem either. The last burials had been in the 1880s or thereabouts. Nothing came up. Or if anyone did, maybe the old Spanish of Upper California fell upon their Anglo and Celtic neighbors and the dead did one another in, just as they had when they lived. One of the epitaphs on a crumbling stone in that dump of a yard was repurposed as a pretty common graffito:

> Remember, man, as you pass by,
> As you are now, so once was I.
> As I am now, so you must be;
> Prepare for death, and follow me.

I've recited it myself a few times, for drinks, or to impress a girl.

The rest—the everyday dead of chicken bones in the throat and panicked shootings and hearts that seem to explode— sure, it was a problem. They don't explode, you know—hearts — they just run down and the brain *feels* its own death from quick starvation. But San Francisco is okay. The animated dead don't move quickly; bones are still weak, muscles still necrotized. It's a hilly town, San Fran is, and our dead just snapped their ankles and floundered at the bottom of our hills. You remember the footage, right? The new militia of police and criminals commandeering cable cars and hunting the dead the way their great-grandparents hunted bison—from a slow-moving rail. Down Powell, up Hyde. Google it if you've forgotten.

The Mission is on the other side of the streetcar lines. Here in the Mission District, death is still a worrisome acquaintance. I've heard the story so many times. It takes place in an old man bar. The kind where nothing's on tap and nobody orders a wine till after midnight, and then only for the flavonoids. The body demands nutrients, not the consciousness. Old men, some young but old enough, watering down their bellies full of scotch and bourbon and vodka with some of the grape. No food, not even wings. No flat-screens silently showing a Giants game, no radio, no women, no gays except in a moment of stumblebum opportunity in the men's room.

A regular asks for a refill, grunting more than speaking. That's always part of it. The old man bar isn't a place for a bartender who happily traipses across the barback, keeping everyone fresh in their cups. The last thing anyone wants is a conversation or a smile. Just a stool, a place for two elbows, and a glass to stare into. And the old man is nursing his drink and breathing hard. Hard like a car on the other side of a street, getting closer, louder. His skin is already gray, but so is everyone else's. Awareness comes like a wave across the room. The help steps back and plants himself by the exit on the far side of the bar. Nobody calls out for a drink, but they wouldn't even under other circumstances. A bark or a yawp is enough to get these old juicers chucked out onto the concrete. We could take him, probably, but this isn't a place for brave men. A dozen cowards watch a man die on his stool, evacuate himself, and slump onto the counter. The wheezing rattle of his last breaths take on a different tone. Deeper, chthonic, something older than life. A shoulder jerks, his back straightens, fingers tighten around the tumbler. We can hear the glass crack in his hand, and wordlessly he presents his glass and the bartender, his limbs herky-jerky from autonomic responses more than anything else, pours the new dead another glass and the dead man puts it to his lips and takes a sip. Some of it spills down his chin and onto his pants, but that's nothing new in an old man bar. And that's how we spend the night. Finally, someone manages to get a driller on the phone and he comes out to do his job. He can't believe what he's seeing. He's afraid, just like everyone else. Drillers don't deal with the dead, only the dying, only the human. It's a fat guy, usually, or else a spidery skeleton of a man—there's not many people left who aren't one or the other—and he almost comically tip-toes over to the dead patron who is still running up a tab that won't ever be repaid and places the drill to the back of the old man's head, running the bit through with a *vzzvvvzzz* that ends in a gurgle and the sweet smell of gray matter oozing down the dead man's back. Nothing to do after that but keep drinking.

I hear that story a lot, for three reasons. The first reason is that I am a driller for the City, and always on duty. The hardware is strapped to my back, and I have a brick of an old phone hanging off my belt. The second reason is that I am a functional alcoholic, also always on duty and I thus spend a lot of time in bars. *My* bar is the 500 Club, but I'll go anywhere for the sake of business. Drilling is a purely commission-based small enterprise, and my contract is exclusively with the City, so I'll lurk at the Attic Club, Mission Bar (which has a jukebox and a pool table, and that can attract the wrong kind of crowd), or City Bar (which is at least full of Mexicans and has a sense of humor)—the claw machine is full of porn DVDs (fatties, gay, interracial). I'd even patronize the Elixir, which used to be a saloon and after that was a certified Green Business with a make-your-own Bloody Mary station on Sunday mornings. The return of the dead put all that shit right off, though, and now the Elixir is somewhat acceptable.

The third reason I get told the story of the dead man and his drink a lot is because sometimes I bring a pad of foolscap and an assortment of pens with me to try to get some writing done, and people want to talk about what they've seen, and what they've heard.

9/11 is easy to remember. I was in Youngstown, in college. My folks are Greek, so I didn't *go away* for college—my mother still did my laundry and cooked what I liked, and my father got a kick out of telling his friends that his son Billy (for Americans) or that *Vasilaki* (Greek friends, my zillion cousins) is in college, and that I'll make a living with my brain one day. I majored in English because I liked to read and—why not?—I'd go ahead and be an English teacher one day, though for most English majors that job looms in the distance like an electric chair at the end of a lonely death row corridor. Summers off, union work, sleepwalk through Salinger and *Hamlet*, grade papers—everyone gets a C—on the bar top till last call each Sunday night, and that's that.

I was in the parking lot outside Fedor Hall, just pulling in, when the news broke through on the radio. I sat in my car and rolled down the windows and blasted the volume. "Blasted" is probably the wrong word both for its unfortunate  hint at the nature of the events, and because my car was a piece of crap with no speaker system to speak of. But it was loud enough and as other students passed by my car on their way to class or breakfast, I'd watch their faces melt. People I'd never talked to before came around the car—the black kids, the homely girl with a face like a shovel, hefty blondes and their cuter friends, barrel-y boys who'd rather be working down at the mill already except that all the mills in Youngstown closed in 1977—and listened.

They asked questions: "Was it an accident?" Or answered them: "Fuck no!" or "Maybe it was, you don't know!" if they had been standing there long enough to hear the news already. Then the second tower was hit and we all knew what was up. Someone said they were going inside to find a TV. Most people thought that was a good idea.

I didn't say a thing to anyone; I just drummed my fingers on the steering wheel and rubbed my lip with the side of the forefinger of my right hand. It was a habit I started that day, just to have something to do so I wouldn't have to talk. My lips are always chapped now, from the rubbing. The crowd dispersed in ones or twos, with more than a few people declaring that they were going to their dorms to watch CNN or get drunk. Nobody wanted to go to class and someone started a rumor that classes would be canceled. I decided to drive back home. On the radio, the towers collapsed in a cloud of atomized concrete.

At home the footage was on TV and the candles were lit. My mother, frantic, rushed up and hugged me. My father was home too, on the couch.

"Oh thank God, Vasilis!" my mother said. "I was so worried about you."

I made the joke too soon: "Ma, nobody is going to blow up Youngstown. Terrorists only want to destroy something of value." She slapped me right across the face, then burst into tears. Really, I could have put my fist right through the woman but papa was right there. He got up, and he was a big man, with hands the size of frying pans. We both thought we were in a lot of trouble. He'd never been violent, except the usual shouting and pounding the table. It was always under the surface somewhere; he used to reminisce at the dinner table that my *papou* used to beat him with a chain and lock him out of the house back in the *chorio* for any old reason. My kindly papou?

My father raised one meaty finger. "The CIA did this," he hissed, his accent and his rage lengthening the consonants. "The CIA is responsible."

A couple years later, as a senior, I wrote a short story for my creative writing class. It was about aliens coming down to Earth and this guy who watches the spacecraft on TV; he wonders why he doesn't have any friends. The idea of aliens so dominates his thoughts that almost every sentence the guy thinks—this was first-person narration, mind you, like these words I am writing now—ends with *but the aliens!* I got an A on the paper and the teacher encouraged me to submit it to *The Penguin Review*, a local literary journal run by two poets-cum-wedding musicians he knew. I did and they rejected it because "sci-fi" was against the journal's "mission statement" and also its "vision statement."

The story was called "1/19" because I was a kid and thus an idiot, and also the nineteenth of January happens to be my birthday. I changed the title to something else and sent it off to *Asimov's Science Fiction Magazine*, and I got a formal rejection letter suggesting that my story was a *Star Trek* rip-off, or had a lot of typos, or that I should subscribe if I really wanted to publish with the magazine. Then thanks to some Googling I found a little online magazine called *Infinite* and sent the story in. They accepted it four weeks later and told me my story was worth fifty dollars. I whooped it up around the house and my mother laughed and clapped. The check didn't come for another three months because *Infinite* was a quarterly publication. When it came out, I printed some copies of the check, and the story, and gave them to professors. I had a dental appointment and put a print-out in my pocket so I could use *I'm a writer, I'm a writer, I'm a writer* as a mantra to block out the pain while getting my teeth drilled. It almost worked.

My father calculated that I'd have to sell one thousand stories a year to keep a roof over my head, and that didn't even include all the money I owed him for the last twenty years of room, board, and "other investments."

I don't remember anything about the day the dead began to rise. I didn't even notice for the first few days. Most of my memories are borrowed from barstool chatter, what's left of the Internet, and a few essays I've read. We have some good printers here in the city, and a burgeoning zine scene. Sometimes we even get trucker mail from outside, with a length of gold chain wrapped up in paper as a form of hopeful pre-payment for one of every zine in stock.

It was four days into the end of the world when I was woken up by the door to my apartment falling to the floor and the shouted demand, "ALPHABET!" I opened my eyes. A rifle, pointed at my head. I was on my back, on the sagging couch that had long since warped to fit my shape.

"A..." My mouth was so dry. I realized that I had a strong chance of dying right then and there. I was tempted to let him just fucking do it, but the request was just too strange—

like the last few lines of a Kafka story without the preceding twenty pages of wind-up. So I lifted my hands.

"I can do it," I said. "A, B, C. Alpha, beta, gamma. Whatever you want." The rifle came down. "What's going on?"

The . . . police officer? Soldier? They had become one and the same, I was to find out, and you could add National Guard, militia kook, and aging Black Panther remnant to the mix too, depending on neighborhood and time of day.

"He doesn't know!" he shouted. "Bring in the social worker." And just like that, a social worker walked in. She was also in camo, but only had a pistol strapped to her leg, and a gas mask balanced atop her head so her face was visible.

"Young man," she said, "the unthinkable has happened." She found my remote control and markedly ignored the empty vodka bottles and the sticky puddle of booze. "It doesn't work," she said after a few unsuccessful clicks. "Did Comcast collapse too?"

"I just let the bill slide. Next week, maybe. I'm expecting a check."

She glared at me, then turned thoughtful. "Do you have a clock radio?"

"Yeah, yeah. Something like one, anyway." I said. I went to get up, but the couch held me down somehow, in my little groove. The social worker glared at me. "'Turbulent and dangerous lunacy!'" I fired at her for some reason. "That's *Hamlet*, act three, scene one, ma'am."

She found the radio without my help—I had one of those clunky flashlight/radio jobs on the fridge, earthquake stuff, and the radio told the story. Reanimated dead.

Zombies, as impossible to believe as it seems, President missing, Power grids off line in major urban areas, the usual. On every station. In Spanish, too, and Mandarin and Cantonese. With the last two I only heard the word *zombie*, of course.

"We're evacuating survivors in certain neighborhoods. San Francisco has been spared the brunt due to . . . circumstances. Do you want to come with us?"

"Want to?" Now there were six people in my little room, a place where I used to joke with dates that if we wanted to have sex I'd have to step outside. All were armed. "I can say no? You'll put the door back and leave?" "We'll leave." That was from the guy who woke me up. "It's a free country."

"Thank you, I'll stay." And without a moment's negotiation the social worker dropped a business card on my coffee table and they all left. The radio was still on and I heard the same ten minutes of news for another three hours. I knew I had another bottle somewhere, and it was a good one. Aberlour, twelve year.

Everyone has their own stories of those first few weeks. The funny thing is that the very worst survival trait in those early days was an expansive social network. Friends and family all but guaranteed death and an inexplicable mockery of resurrection. Whatever the cause of resurrection is, and "the cause" is the precinct of the sort of long-term planning nobody has time for in these latter days of society anymore, it's very contagious. You have to be hard to brain your children, to keep from tying up your grandmother and trying to get her to the hospital, where rooftop snipers would just cut you down anyway. The social isolates, the outsiders, the third-shifters—we are the ones who lived. I'm not above quoting Nietzsche: "What is the greatest thing a man can experience? It is the hour of great contempt." Contempt of the self, that is.

The syphilitic old proto-Nazi was right about that one thing. Forget guns and canned goods. Dog-eared paperbacks of Dostoyevsky, Henry Miller, Colin Wilson, these were the best survival tools or at least the best marker of a survivor. Call it anti-social Darwinism. Looters and heroes were among the first to die and then die again when Canadian bombers took out whole cities to bury the reanimates.

The rest of the world had a different response to America's peculiar malady: pointing and laughing.

I am, in general, not a fan of single-sentence paragraphs. Even worse are one-word paragraphs. And yet our national dilemma lends itself to the poetaster strum of that one tedious chord:

Soldiers.
And from the darkened corner of the room, I heard an unearthly groan.
She wasn't my mother anymore.
It was all I could do to keep from holding out my arm to the nearest slavering mouth, to offer myself, to join this brave new world of the dead.
Dear Reader, I ate him.
Twitching.
Then Emily's body began to twitch.

You know exactly the sort of asinine bullshit I mean. The zines are full of it, as is the Internet and all the mimeographed and hot-glue-gunned "novels" that anyone can publish these days if they want to put the work into it. All the greats are dead, and that was so even before the outbreak. "Zombies" are ubiquitous these days, as overwhelming to auctorial understanding of America as was the Vietnam War or the settling of the West. The rise of the dead was so inexplicable, and yet down deep in our cultural DNA. It was so universally anticipated that it has created immense problems for American letters.

But you want to hear a zombie story? Fine, I'll tell you a zombie story.

Drilling is essentially a welfare program; something right out of the New Deal. Of course, the job itself is vital and in an ideal world would be handled by trained professionals according to minutely designed protocols created after years of field testing and results analysis. Instead, we have a bounty system and a network of localband mobile phones—not true cellulars, those networks have long since failed—and ordinary power drills liberated from hardware stores. The job's a simple one and any able-bodied individual can have it for the asking. Find the dead and before they reanimate destroy the brain with the drill.

Firearms, it was quickly discovered, were more trouble than they were worth. San Francisco didn't have much of a gun culture, and the best way to deploy a brace of fascists to the streets is to arm a bunch of milquetoast liberals and explain that they are responsible for keeping civilization intact. Six-shooter fiefdoms sprang up on every other block, but luckily none of them lasted very long. Neither bone nor drywall stops most bullets, and armed morons ended up simply increasing the number of dead and thus exacerbating the local reanimate problem. The first generation of civilian security joined the ranks of the undead.

Then there was the issue of sheer cowardice—City Hall simply couldn't pay people enough to hunt the dead. Nor was it even necessary, so long as the reanimates could be quickly isolated. Bodies still decompose, even if driven by whatever force or infestation leads to dead men walking. A week after reanimation, the danger passes, even if the groaning continues for several more days. Is she not your mother anymore? Just push all the furniture you own in front of the door to her sickroom and let the bitch pound her desiccated hands to jelly trying to get to you. Soon enough she'd fall apart and it would be over; just like drowning a bag full of kittens, except it takes three days and you have to listen to it the entire time. Thus, drilling—destroy the brain and the body will not stand. Preventative—though slightly posthumous—medicine, after a fashion.

The trick is that death is not an event. It is a process. When I put the bit to a forehead and squeeze the trigger, am I mutilating a corpse or killing a human being? Most doctors didn't want to find out—they still believed in "do no harm," or claimed to with a unanimity that bordered on the conspiratorial. So a driller with a folding chair could make a few hundred dollars in goods and government scrip over the course of a week in an ER. Nurses draw curtains and turn away with pursed lips. The other patients pretend to hear nothing, see nothing—just as they did back when vomiting, raving, and death in a puddle of black blood was the worst thing one might see in an emergency room.

I signed up for drilling because I couldn't get down to Mexico. I needed to experience life, to find something to write about. I needed pocket money. My credit score was immaterial, my landlord dead, and as electricity only worked fourteen hours a day PG&E just let the grid run and stopped billing. But the agora bloomed on Market Street once again, and most anything could be had for the right combination of trade goods, favors, scrip, and foreign currencies.

Not Canada, not Mexico. Not even Hawaii and Alaska. Just the lower forty-eight. No one took responsibility for the events, and anyone who *could* reanimate the dead probably would have had a better plan than "Go for it!" And a disease doesn't vector within national borders. What did they know in City Hall? That was the other reason. I dreamt that there was some Masonic hand charting the course of events, or competing elites drawn to some endgame. The chessboard was flooded with pawns again, as if a player had overturned a bucket of them onto the field. But we're okay here in The City. If I worked for The City I might hear something. If I did well, I might be invited into a smoke-filled room. "Kostopolos!" a man in a gray suit would bark at me. "Come with me. We have plans for you. Big plans." It wouldn't be a job interview so much as an initiation complete with oaths and handclasps. William Randolph Hearst, reanimated and hustled out of Colma through a BART service tunnel that hadn't been sealed up, would preside with a great wooden paddle in his hands. Things would get weird, but I'd have finally joined the fraternity of men. I would be one of Them. All I had to do was climb the ladder, and the rungs were largely free of competitors these days. This wasn't an era for bureaucrats or brown-nosers and surely the Star Chamber would recognize my skills. I'd grown fond of the City and wanted to do my part for it. Compared to Youngstown, of course, San Francisco may as well have been gilded Babylon, rich with fruited whores and perfumed vines. In Ohio, there's nothing to do but drink and die, but in San Francisco there's life. The irony in the fact that I had nonetheless found myself drinking and dying, and that that strategy took hold as if it were genetically predetermined even before the return of the dead, does not escape me. It never has, not even for a moment.

Intake and orientation for new drillers was held once a week at the Moscone Center, in the great exhibitor hall where in better times I'd sold my old baseball cards and comic books for rent money. I got there early, as when they run out of drills they run out of jobs, and by early I mean after the 500 Club closed. I decided I'd walk to kill some time. There's a *de jure* curfew in place within city limits, but it's rarely enforced in the Mission, and it struck me as very foolish that I should miss my chance to join the drillers, a squad of brave men who prowl the night in search of the dead and dying, due to such flummeries and mummeries. I'd be facing plenty of danger, and soon enough. It's easy to get lost in the city, especially if one doesn't have a terrain map. The shortest path between two points is hardly ever a straight line given the hills and the collapsed buildings often stretched across a street as if right after a dramatic yawn. It took me a few hours to pick my way over; once I found Howard Street the walk wasn't bad at all, except for some reason I felt entirely turned around and dyslexic, and in need of a nap, so it took me forever to find the main drag.

I sobered up in the pre-dawn chill and waited at the ragged end of the line. Nobody talked except for a few of the agitated and toothless sorts who hunched and shuffled about the line, trying to strike up conversations. There was a time I'd seek such mental defectives out for any wisdom that might emerge from their word salads, but I was dry and nervous that morning. My bravado sweated itself out of my body and smelled of beer and I was in no mood for deranged bullshit. Neither was anyone else. One guy, who had been going on about Oakland and its gigantic Mountain View Cemetery and how the dead were walking under the Bay and coming to take the City back for the famous Folger family of coffee millionaires, was jumped by three machos and kicked across the street. He rolled to the relative safety of the curb and made some submissive-sounding noises, and finally someone else on the line shouted:

"That's enough! That fucker dies, we're all in deep-ass shit." And deep-ass shit was just the sort of wisdom I needed to hear.

The line inched forward, and it was almost 10 a.m. when I had my intake interview; a long table with a woman and two men. It was the usual sort of Department of Motor Vehicles-style event—vacant looks and affectless bleats, though one of my interlocutors was at least some sort of queer and thus amusing.

"Oooh, Greek," he said when I responded to the honking prompt of the woman next to him: *Name*. Then age and residence and current situation. "*Work* situation, that is!" he explained, and I said:

"Writer."

The woman next to the queer said, "Don't put that down. Put down unemployed." I was already beyond arguing.

"Martial experience?"

"Really?"

"Have you been in the military or received military or paramilitary training?" the woman recited. "Do you have experience as a law enforcement officer, a licensed security professional?"

"Martial arts?" the woman asked.

"Maybe some sort of active criminal?" the third person, a white man, suggested. "Can you handle a firearm? Would you call yourself street smart? Perhaps too smart to have ever been successfully prosecuted in…the old days?"

"Oh no, nothing like that. I'm a passive criminal. A lifestyle criminal, really. The state arrays itself against people like me."

"Any alcohol or drug abuse problems?" the woman asked. "And mind you we hear, 'Oh it's not a problem' forty times a day around here."

"I was three-year varsity on the wrestling team." The woman just stared at me, then both turned to the queer.

"Yes, I'll write that down."

"Does that count as a martial art?" I asked.

"You were a wrestler?" the woman asked me. She looked me up and down over the rims of her glasses.

"There are weight classes in wrestling, you know." I'm tall and lank, an oddity in my family, the men of which mostly looked like fire hydrants who for breakfast each morning ate slightly smaller fire hydrants. I hadn't heard from any of them since—how did junior over there put it?—the "old days" and that's just as well. I often wondered who went first, my father or my mother. My mother had a weak heart, or so she always said, but she was essentially a pack mule in a flowered housecoat. Sad though, as after me there were two miscarriages and then she lacked the heart to try again. Or was it papa, who would probably do something stupid like nail all the doors shut from the inside and then blow a gasket thanks to the machinations of the intelligence community, or perhaps just accidentally shoot himself with the rifle he never used or cleaned, only to rise up and finally consume my mother with his black blood-smeared teeth?

"I bet at your size it wasn't so much two men in tight little onesies grunting on the mat as it was a couple of kids squeaking," the man said with a laugh. And I'd pegged the other one as a campy homosexual. But my observational acumen had been blunted as of late and the ever-shifting sexual and performative politics of San Francisco had been under significant pressure these past few years.

"One last question Mister Kastas." *Kastas?* I was used to that sort of instant Ellis-Islanding of my name by now, but in this moment it rankled. "Why do you want this job in the Infection Control department?"

I honestly wasn't expecting such a question. After all the deaths—perhaps one hundred million people, followed by maybe half that many corpses possessed by hungry idiot spirits who live only to feed and savage all that lie before them—after all the chaos, after the jury-rigged society we managed to hold together by cannibalizing shopping malls and launching basement factories; in a city where it never quite gets dark enough to sleep soundly, as Colma is to this day still smoldering, "Why do you want to work here?" is the bit of madness we preserved from the ruins of civilization. Bile rose and it tasted like rye on my tongue.

"I don't want this job for the Infection Control department," I said, so they'd understand. "I don't want anything to do with anyone here. I don't want to look in the faces of dead people. I don't want to hurriedly mutilate them, while hoping their eyes don't snap open and their fingers, like withered tree branches, don't start reaching for me." I held up my own hands and choked the air in front of me. "Really? What the bloody blue fuck do you expect me to say? 'I've always wanted to help people'? 'I want to walk to work every morning'? 'It's my way of giving back to the community'? What did you soulless pus-sacks say when you applied for your jobs? What a lunatic question. What a goddamned monstrosity."

The woman struck a pose I thought fairly manly—hands behind her head, she leaned back and put her kicks up on the long table, all over the assorted paperwork and doodled-on pads before her.

Then she said, "'How weary, stale, flat, and unprofitable seem to me all the uses of this world.'" She said, "That's Hamlet." Then I recognized her as the social worker from the first days after the outbreak.

My friend Jay, whom I'd met a number of times through different mutual acquaintances—at house parties, poetry readings, movie nights, and of course always down at the bar—quipped, "The City only seems large, but really there are only eighty-five people living here." He died from the usual mix of HIV-positive and health insurance–negative status and was cremated before his joke very nearly came true. I wouldn't see Jay wandering around the streets while out on patrol. I had nothing to say to this woman. For a second my mind was filled with the image of an urn in a vaguely Chinese style, white with blue floral designs—rattling and shaking and buzzing like the last moments of a rung bell. Jay's ashes, animated and trying to be free.

"Well, we can make our decision now," she said, looking at me but addressing her colleagues. "What do we think? What *do* we think! Mm-mmm." The man on her left, the one I'd assumed wasn't gay, checked his notes.

"He mentioned wanting to give back to the community—"

"I did not. That was an example of what . . ." I realized that I was talking myself out of a job, and that I was arguing with insane people. And that I very likely was just as mad as anyone else here because I'd stood in line all morning for the opportunity just to keep myself in enough liquor to die and not care at all about what happened to me next.

I was handed a ticket and told to go collect my drill and contact phone and do my on-the-job training. In a kiosk set up elsewhere in the exhibit hall I was handed a drill and some bits in a case, told not to swap out the drills for cheaper ones or try to pawn them, then I practiced on a bowling ball. I didn't quite get it right; the bit wouldn't bite properly and my hands were shaking, so I engraved the side of the ball with a series of jagged scratches before finally getting the drill to push through. I was good enough. The guy I was with, who was perhaps my age though he looked much younger—it was his voice that betrayed him as a forty-year-old, it was deep and thick like a pool of syrup—told me to practice at home. "Drill other things."

"Like what?"

"It doesn't matter. Just get the hang of it. You can put a hole in anything you like now, so long as nobody else is using it. Drill the whole city; make it look like Swiss cheese. It doesn't matter."

I wanted to pat him on the back and tell him it was all going to be okay, but decided instead to take my drill and find a bar. The Chieftain wasn't far off—I'd passed it when walking up, and already tired, I was ready to lower my standards. Outside the battered man from earlier was still stalking the streets, still ranting, but now the ranting was about how he had a knife and was going to kill his own nigger ass and then when he rose from the dead as God's vengeance, he'd kill us all, turn us all, and we'd flood the city with drills and meat-stained teeth and kill all the motherfuckers left in the shitburg town of white faggots. I supposed that was an open possibility.

The Chieftain is a pub that claimed some link to Ireland, or at least Irishness, despite the Liverpool flag and the food and the handsome servers and the goddamned juke box. At least it was before noon so I hoped the assholes with jobs wouldn't be slithering in for their lunch. I put my new drill on the bartop and ordered a Guinness, which I usually don't drink, and a burger with a fried egg cooked in it because I didn't want to make conversation with anybody. Most people know better than to chat up someone who doesn't care enough about life to order likely expired meat. It didn't work, as the bullshit started immediately.

"Well, if it ain't a hero?" the bartender said, declaring open season.

"A city employee, dedicated to service and diversity!" someone else chirped.

"Get that fucking thing off the bar," an old woman, almost all of her jaw red with poorly applied lipstick, said of my drill case. I had my foolscap with me in my bag and took it out.

"Ooh, are we on report?" That was the chirper again. "Writing all our names down? Everybody always wants to write my name down. I don't let 'em though. You can't reduce me to a scrap of paper." I could have sworn I'd seen him lined up outside the Moscone and told him as much. He lit a cigarette—as an emergency sanity law we were allowed to smoke in the bars again.

"A moment of weakness," he said. He launched into his theory of life and work and labor and the futility of it all and even the bartender sighed.

"Does the TV work?" I asked, but it wasn't going to work until 4 p.m. today, when the news came on. I ate my burger and gargled my beer, then ordered another one.

"We don't take city money here," the bartender told me, but I put a piece of scrip on the table anyway.

"Why don't you fucking take it somewhere else then, eh Mickey Fuck?" I didn't even have a quarter of a buzz on, but what the hell was he going to do? Beat the shit out of me, risk that I might crack my head open on one of the brass fixtures or on the concrete outside and come roaring back in five minutes later, cold and angry?

"I said we don't take it." He stabbed the cash with a finger.

"Well then why don't you find someone who does take it, and then trade it for something you do take—maybe a dog for more burger meat. Wouldn't you like to have a puppy of your very own?"

"Now that would be the same as takin' it, don't you think?" he said, too angry for his own good. I took the drill case off the bar. I didn't want him grabbing it as payment, or taking a chance on smashing my face in with it. He went on: "You're just talking market exchanges now. I mean, I could take some euros or pesos as well and try to trade them on a bourse, do a little arbitrage maybe? For I've got nothing better to do than to take your city money and then spend the next day or three trying to find someone that takes it."

"The city takes it. Pay your power bill with it. The TV. How about garbage removal? It can be a new thing you try around here—having it carted away instead of frying it up and serving it."

"Billy," the old woman said. Both the bartender and I turned to look at her. "Is your name Billy?" she said with a sneer.

"Yeah," I said.

"Oh. Anyways," she said, then she looked at the other Billy. "Put it on my tab. You two machos are giving me a sick headache. Anything to stop the yammering. You're worse than my kids." Then she turned in her stool and looked outside. Her shoulders heaved a bit. Billy frowned and began aggressively wiping down some glasses. He hadn't even rinsed them. The other bar patron just pursed his lips and looked at me, then intently at a photo of a rugby team nailed in its frame to a pillar a few feet away. I wanted another beer and certainly had no problem about ordering one and, yes, yes, putting it on that woman's tab thank-her-kindly, but then my phone rang and I froze.

The reanimation of the dead is less a matter of science than it is a matter of Freytag's Triangle. There just aren't enough research institutions left in the United States to determine exactly which variables inform the time between the moment of death—as though death were often just a matter of a moment—and reanimation. Sometimes it takes hours, at other times it takes no more than a few seconds. This is why drillers are loathed; we almost never show up on time. Either one ends up sending splatters all over a perfectly nice living room while desecrating a corpse or one jumps out a window because one's client starts growling, muscles start shifting, fingers flex, lips peel back and death itself rises, just as it did all those times on television. Dramatic irony rules the day; bad luck has washed over the nation like a wave and we're all soaking in it.

Relatively few people depend on drillers, but San Francisco is a large city—seven miles by seven miles, with a few 900-foot-high hills in the fucking middle of it. Families either wisely crush the skulls of their dying relatives on their own, or at least lock corpses behind heavy doors in windowless rooms and let their favorite uncle howl and beat himself to pieces against the walls. The dumb ones hope against hope that

Grandma isn't actually breathing her last, or that she might have some revenant affection or memory in her brain when she rises from her sickbed with a new posture. Then there are the homeless and the insane who wander the streets alone and need someone to take care of them. I didn't know who my call was from, or whether the person on the other end of the line would even tell me the truth—did Joe die just now, or did it take his grieving wife an hour of sobs and shrieking to get it together enough to call 311 and ask for me. The bartender's face melted with sympathy. I took the call. Fucking North Beach, and without even a quarter of a buzz on.

I'm the sort of person who is normally very comfortable in a bar. It's where I go to feel warm, a tiny world with all its citizens and subjects stretched out before me, and I'm Old King Log at rest. Even the Chieftain wasn't so bad, not compared to my new job and the great unknown at the other end of Columbus Avenue. I've sat through other calls from work, text messages, deadlines, tremblors that made tumblers sing in their holders, fights, raids, you name it. Like my father in his cousin's chrome diner back in Ohio, or timid librarians in their bubble-filled bathtubs, a bar to me is more than home. It's an embrace I never want to leave. But I decided to go. Call it pulp fiction, or the imp of the perverse, or just plain ol' *Todestrieb* but I took my drill, hailed a pedicab, and headed over to the gig. My only thought in my head was that afterwards I'd like to pop into City Lights or get a drink at Vesuvio. The corpse I was to attend to wasn't even dead to me, it was a gap, a blank.

I was met at the entrance to a squashed old row house by an elderly man. Asian. Excellent posture, I noticed, which is unusual among the desperate.

"Please," he said, "she's upstairs, in the apartment. I didn't want you to ring the bell."

"Is she——" I stopped myself because it looked like he was about to cry, and I followed him up two flights of crooked steps to his apartment. It was not quite a hoard, but there were enough cardboard boxes and stacks of newspapers and even couches—two in the same room, inexplicably facing one another from opposite walls—to make for a tight squeeze through the apartment. The smell was of mold and cats, though I saw no animals or kitty litter or even toys. And of rotten beets; the *umami*-sweet smell of the recently deceased.

"Why didn't you want me to ring the bell?"

He opened a door to a darkened room and reached inside to flip the switch. "It upsets her."

She was hanged. A small woman in a housedress with a floral print, her neck cracked and face purple. She growled when she saw me and her limbs activated. Clawed hands, nails long, reached for me. Her slim ankles fluttered and shuffled about. This was the closest I'd ever been to one. Then I saw the cats—three of them chewing on pieces of skin that had flaked off the woman. The ceiling was fairly high. Still, I didn't think at all.

"I know it's too late," the man said to me. "I just can't bear to wait anymore. The kitties scratch at the door all day until I let them in. It's hard, very hard."

"I'm a driller," I said, more to myself than anyone else, though the corpse on the rope thrashed a bit. The disused fixture from which she had hanged herself creaked dangerously. "This isn't something I can help with. Just nail the door shut and move. Take the cats or leave them. Get a shotgun and blow her head to pieces from here."

"She's *my wife!*" His grip was suddenly strong on my right bicep. For a moment I had the terrible flash—he was going to push me inside, close the door and lock it. Then his woman would drop down from the ceiling. How many drillers has this man called? Is this how he feeds his wife and his cats? I dug my heels in instinctively and was ready to brain him with my drill case, but that might kill the old man, and then maybe I wouldn't have time to destroy his brain, and what if the woman dropped from the noose anyway and scuttled toward me on her spider-limbs? That would be the end of me. How many other drill cases, other skulls and femurs were hidden in the mess of the apartment?

"Oh, the kitties . . ." he said, sounding like a balloon slowly deflating. I asked for a broom. He asked why I wanted one and I realized I didn't know. The childish instinct of poking at a carcass with a stick, I suppose, but I had to do something and I certainly wasn't going to get on a chair and try to drill with her limbs still flailing. Then a tactic occurred to me and I didn't care at all whether I lived or died. I ran to the middle of the room, scattering cats, and then grabbed the woman's legs. I pulled my knees up and left the ground. I wrapped my limbs around hers, clinging like a monkey. For a few seconds I swung and hoped that the rope was stronger than the rot in the sternocleidomastoid muscle, and—*lo, verily!*—it was. My ass slammed to the floor and her body followed, cold but fast. Her head hit separately, and bounced once, leaving a splat of grue that I accidentally put my hand in as I slid out from under her torso. Removal of the head works as well as destruction of the brain, just as it does with any vertebrate. I screamed like a pressure valve going off, then took a few breaths to calm myself. I was shaking, but not much more than usual.

"Okay," I said, but the man, on his knees now, didn't answer. I wiped my hand on some old magazine, but the paper flaked off and stuck to my palm in clumps. "Well, okay," I said again. He started weeping. "WHAT?" I finally demanded. "What did you expect to actually happen here? I blow some air up her cunt and she comes back to life? Slice open the cuts, find her heart, and put it in a store window mannequin? Jesus Christ, you make me sick." There was something in my hair; it felt like when I was a child and my father would shout "Eat it or wear it!" and turn a bowl full of pasta with the wrong brand of sauce upside-down on top of me.

Then the man was strong again. He snatched up my knapsack and flung it at me. Then he kicked the drill case in my direction. I dodged, fell to my knees. The case clattered against some furniture behind me.

The man could only say "You! You!" I stumbled after the case and picked it up.

Holding it in my hands, I realized something and said it aloud. "Goddamn, you know what? I didn't even charge this thing. I'm such a stupid piece of shit."

"You…" But the rage was gone. He recovered my knapsack and handed it over, extending a single arm. I didn't say thanks, but I took the bag and nodded. He followed me to the apartment door. On the borders of the rooms we passed, the cats scooted and shuffled, nudging over little piles of crap and treading on crinkly old papers on their way back to the lady of the house.

I conspicuously—to myself anyway—went to City Lights first. I didn't even really need a drink, I decided. Plus, perhaps I'd find something I wanted to read along with my drink. My drink, as in the one single drink I'd have at Vesuvio that I wasn't even thinking about. Bookstores are almost as good as bars when it comes to me feeling comfortable there, except in bookstores it never lasts, and there's almost never anything new. Every bookstore is a used bookstore these days. I didn't have much money—I could buy an old New Directions paperback and even had *The Colossus of Maroussi* in my hands—but what if I spent too much in the store and then didn't have quite enough for my drink? Nothing's worse than a bar patron who just sits around waiting for someone he knows to show up from whom to mooch a drink…clearly I had Henry Miller on the brain. I put *Colossus* back and looked at the books I already owned on the shelves—some just cleaner versions of my own, others in new editions. Soon enough my eyes passed over the Ks in the Fiction section on the first floor where my books, which I'd not actually written anyway, absolutely weren't. I nearly choked myself to death; I clenched my teeth that severely. Maybe some Muriel Sparks or, no, the magazines; the little ones especially— the fanzines and the hysteric broadsheets even City Lights knows to keep in a tight corner of the room. I found a Xeroxed bit of nonsense about Folger and the Oakland cemetery. It must be turning into some sort of thing. I bought it to look at in the bar. Damn, it was rye time.

At City Lights I kept my drill case by my feet, but it didn't matter. They knew me at the bar, or knew how to act how they did by giving me a wide berth. I'm sure they saw me come out of City Lights and step on over, and at the bar I drank and I drank and I wrote and I wrote. Just sentences and fragments. How to describe how that woman felt when she landed on me—a nylon stocking full of cold Jell-O? No, ridiculous. A bundle of soggy sticks? That's a bit better. I underlined it. And the husband, I certainly shouldn't call him "a little Chinese man"; he was as tall as I at any rate, and haven't the words "little" and "Chinese" been placed together too often already? Scratch that out then. On furious nights like these, after a day of pummeling by the fists of indifference, the centimeter difference between an underline and a strike is the gap where God still lives, or so I hoped.

We usually got a brown-out around 9 p.m. so I quickly wrote down on the margins of a page the things I had to look up when I got home: the name of the muscle on the side of the neck, who was really buried at Mountain View in Oakland, the official DSM definition of "hoarder." Frank Norris, as it turns out, is buried there, as are a couple of the Folger coffee people just like the zine and the crazy said. During a not-very-lucid moment I turned to the bartender and told her a fantasy I'd just spun about getting a boat from a disused store along the Embarcadero, rowing to Oakland, finding the zombie Norris amidst the ruins, and asking him what to do. I could be a disciple, an apprentice, growling at the world at his side. The bartender said she didn't know who Norris was but if he really died back in 1902 he certainly wouldn't have reanimated, except maybe he'd be a pair of chattering teeth, like that old plastic wind-up novelty.

"I tell you I don't want your cursed opinion," I told her and she guessed it was from one of Norris's books as it didn't sound at all like how someone would talk, and I'd just come from City Lights and spent all night writing until the lights started flickering. Then she had no more time for me. In the mirror I caught a glimpse of my hair, matted to my head from the various fluids of the reanimate from my first gig; my shirt was a slaughterhouse as well. Just as well the lights were very nearly out.

With just a few other patrons and almost no ice at all and only a handful of words spoken between us, at Vesuvio I drank virtually alone all night in the dark.

I write in longhand when out and about because at home the solitude just gnaws at my stomach and I cannot think unless I drown it. Notes are preliminary, little more than individual sentences, full of arrows and cross-outs and little doodles of cubes and spirals. I do write at home, on my computer when electricity and Internet access allows. On screen is where I turn sentences into paragraphs, cut and paste to destroy the vestiges of workaday chronology that I've always found so tedious. I don't have a computer printer—toner ink is one of those things nigh impossible to come by these days—and as revision is only ever abandoned rather than completed, I retype final drafts from the screen onto paper with my Olivetti M5 Premiere Plus, a portable manual typewriter. There is where the final polish takes place, in a medium where too many errors means a whole page retyped. Working the manual is like seeing the text again with new eyes. I love the thunky click of the keys, the tactility of it all. And when the power goes

 out, it doesn't matter. While everyone ran to office supply stores to stock up on cartridges and USB drives and cheap photocopiers in the days after the reanimations, I quietly cornered

the local market on carbon paper and typewriter ribbon. I'm playing a long-term game here.

I am running out of printouts of my one published fiction, however. I'll have to hit the library again and run off some more on the one day a month when it's open. Before the outbreak, I had the URL for "1/19" in my email sig, and would often leave it up on the screen when I had guests over so that it might be nonchalantly discovered. It's both easier and harder to publish now; easier in that since most everyone is dead there are no more Joyce Carol Oateses and Stephen Kings filling up the shelves. On the other hand, most everyone is dead, including the agents and editors and bookstore employees. So publishing is back to where it was at the dawn of the nineteenth century—mostly UK and Commonwealth imports, and often semi-legal at that, or wrapped up along with blankets and emergency high-protein food powder. Domestic publications are small fanzines, regional presses run from a basement, some online stuff but that comes and goes with the power grid on a near-daily basis, and the occasional touring company of poets and actors, though such tours never get very far. *Infinite* is still up somehow, though it's long since a ghost site, like most websites and social networks are.

In a way, I expected this. I got my Olivetti back as a college freshman in 1999. Ten of them actually, from a compact man named Bram Tolbert of the shiny blue suit and happy patter. He stood behind the folding card table and in front of a small white truck of the sort that items frequently fell from so to be resold at deep discounts. That sort of thing was a major economic driver in Youngstown in those days.

Tolbert was going with the carnival barker schtick: "Are you a writer? Are you interested in the end of the world? Come see what you need to survive the apocalypse! Smart college kids are gonna need what I got when the end comes, especially you fancy writer types!"

It was as though his slogans were written just for me, so I had to see what he was selling. I stepped up to the table and Tolbert, with a huge smile of oversized synthetic-looking teeth, lifted a plastic case onto the table and asked me what I thought was inside.

"Is it a gun?" I asked. "Is helter-skelter going down one day soon?" I needed to make it clear that I wasn't taking him seriously, not even as a kook, for the simple reason that ultimately I'm pretty credulous. I'll sign up for any stupid thing just to have the experience of *experiences*. Life is material, but there's not much living to be had in Youngstown except for television and books and alcohol. So he popped open the case and showed me the typewriter. I laughed hard.

"You laugh *now*," Tolbert said, practically shouting that last word. Then, conversationally: "What are your New Year's plans?" It was April, right after Spring Break. I'd not gone to Florida or anything like that, but spent my time mixing cement and carting bricks for a local contractor.

"How the hell would I know?" I asked back, already agitated.

He said, "I'll tell you what you'll be doing. You won't be out having a party. You won't be drinking champagne and singing 'Auld Lang Syne,'" he said. "You won't be playing with your Christmas toys, but you might be wearing your Christmas sweater. Every one you ever received. Every one that still fits." His anaphora was a well-practiced chant, with pantomime gestures for partying—index fingers twirling in the air—drinking—the obvious glug glug maneuver—and sweater-wearing—this last invoking the pull of a sweater over one's head with raised arms and a shake of the shoulders.

"You know why you won't be having a party? Martial law! You know why there won't be any champagne? Nothing to celebrate but years of misery to come, my friend! You know why you'll be wearing three sweaters and struggling to get into a fourth? No heat!" He slapped his hands on his hips. "You know why? It's—"

"This is one of those Y2K things, isn't it?" I said.

"It is, yes." He pulled a business card from his pocket. Bramtolbert Solutions. "Tell me, do you use a word processing program to type up your essays and term papers?"

"Of course I do," I told him. "But you know what? If it came down to martial law, I think I'd take a leave of absence from college. They go after the college kids first, you know."

"Oh I do, I do. 'Four dead/in O-hi-o!'" Tolbert sang. It wasn't exactly a hip song in the late 1990s, but Tolbert looked even older than some ex-sixties radical might. Seventy maybe, but vigorous in his own way. "But there won't be any computers—they'll be the cause of the whole mess. Nor any Internet, of course. You'll be darn lucky if the phone works."

"Not really. Phone calls always bring bad news in my experience." I was feeling morose that day. I hadn't been laid all semester—living with my parents had cramped my style around campus so bad that I couldn't even consume the appropriate amount of pornography a boy my age needed.

"You know what perks a man up?" Tolbert asked. "Receiving, or for that matter sending, a thoughtful paper letter, freshly typed."

"Fine, how much."

"Twenty-five for one, two hundred for ten."

"What the hell would I need ten typewrit—" Then I got it. "How many are you on the hook for, buddy?"

Tolbert stopped smiling, but he wasn't done with his cant yet. "That's proprietary information. These are factory models; no middlemen. Right out of the warehouse, but you know the economy, a vendor doesn't pay rent and they have to liquidate the inventory. There's a significant price break at one thousand units. This is my living, son. Today typewriters, tomorrow napkin holders, the day after that former best-selling novels, now remaindered and selling for a nickel on the dollar. Ever read Rosemary Rogers? She really broke some new ground in the romance genre a few years ago. My wife was all atwitter about it at the time. Rogers let her heroines . . ." he leaned in close and finished *sotto voce*, "invite guests in through the back door."

Tolbert finally revealed himself as creepy enough to get tangled up with. "I'm sure your wife is a lovely woman. Good cook too?"

"The best, my friend, the absolute best. Her name's Aija. She's a lovely Latvian woman. Ever have gray peas and ham?"

"I don't think I've ever seen a gray pea."

"You will, my friend, you will." And I stepped around the other side of the card table and shook his hand.

Selling Olivettis was good for two things—I reserved a pair of them for myself, and it opened me up to a lot of random abuse I otherwise would have only experienced in a genuine correctional or psychiatric facility of some sort. It took Tolbert a few days to realize that I was not exactly a big man on campus—virtually nobody knew me at all as a freshman, a commuter student, and I didn't participate in any extracurriculars. Nobody wanted to buy a typewriter.

Nobody wanted to talk to me except to shout a name or two: "Faggot!" was a perennial, of course, but I would have been called a fag even had I been laying a woman right on the card table. "Grandpa" was a common enough one. "Scoop Brady" I only heard a couple of times, and really had to admire it. Certainly nobody cared about Y2K.

"Why the hell would I care about my term papers if every computer in the world clicked off at midnight?" a girl who recognized me from freshman composition asked.

"You should be selling shotguns and canned goods," her boyfriend offered. "Hell, I'm ready already. The only thing I can see myself doing with *this*," he said as he slid my display model onto his palm and hefted it up like a serving tray, "is putting it in a burlap sack with one or two others and swinging it over my head as a weapon once I run out of ammo."

"Oh, Craig—" the girl, Yvette or something, said. Yvette, yes. Then and there I decided I would fuck her one day. Just to fuck with her, I told myself.

"I don't plan on running out of ammo though." He put the typewriter down. "Good luck to you."

"Yeah. But really, if you think the world is going to end in a few months, why even care about money at all?" She flashed me the smile women generally reserve for children and men in wheelchairs who want to prove that they can still fuck, and walked off with Craig.

That was about as friendly as it got, and they were right. So I chucked the Y2K shtick and decided to just sit and start typing. I practiced in the evenings—it takes a bit to adapt to a typewriter after a few years on a word processor—to make sure I didn't look like even more of a goon than I already did, elbows akimbo, tongue poking out the side of my mouth, pecking away with two lunatic fingers. I got a little faster at it anyway, and decided not to write papers or stories, but quotations. I'd been keeping a Moleskine full of them—some aphorisms, others just turns of phrase I'd stumbled across and wrote down out of admiration.

"She would have been a good woman," The Misfit said, "if there had been somebody there to shoot her every minute of her life."

Who's that? What did she do? I got a fair number of lookie-loos as I typed up the quotes I'd committed to memory the night before. I laughed, because that line was actually from standard assigned reading.

Once you accept A is A, you're hooked. Literally hooked, addicted to the System. The one sweater vest–wearing obnoxio who neurotically read and re-read *Atlas Shrugged* hated that quote. Wonder whatever happened to him. Dead, probably. Good.

I thank thee, Barrett—thy advice was right, / But 'twas ordain'd by fate that I should write.

That sort of thing. Though in college, I was ninety percent autodidact, ten percent passive learner. I had a mind for memorization. The college library wasn't great, but it was good enough for me. I loved nothing more than finding a reference to a primary source in some textbook, reading that, following one of its footnotes or references to another book or journal, and digging my way through the history of the written word, or at least English as she was writ in the nineteenth and twentieth centuries. Then there was Goodwill, and I always had quarters enough for rotten old paperbacks, mostly shit, but some gems. It was a strange ecology—eating garbage and diamonds as raw material, and then shitting back out…what? I'd crank out the quotes on individual pieces of paper and leave them to the side. People would come over. I even sold a few typewriters. I was becoming a fairly good typist, which pleased my mother who—being old—was sure that typing was still a rare skill owned primarily by women but of use to anyone who "wanted to have a good office job." She'd worked for six months before getting married, after all, at a home insurance company.

A favorite, though one that is hard to work into everyday conversation, even now: "...the nausea is not *inside* me; I feel it *out* there, in the wall, in the suspenders; everywhere around me. It makes itself one with the café; I am the one who is within it."

But now I had my first story in a long time, didn't I? That bar—Vesuvio—was not one of my usual haunts, so easy enough to experience as an outsider, and without even a moment's worry about the potential for betrayal it had a complementary *genius loci*. It made me a little sick anyway, as did the encounter with the undead woman. I would have been perfectly within my rights, and certainly within the realm of common sense self-preservation to just leave and call the police. But I dove in anyway, without much more of a plan than "Go for it!" And there was some grue as well, and despite or maybe because of the terror on the streets, grue equals green. The story could sell. I just needed to dig a little deeper than usual, and given the state of publishing in this post-reanimation times, I wouldn't have to dig all that deep at all. One of the current "best-sellers" is an online serial called *I Ain't Killed Me a Nigger All Day*— about a racist "zombie hunter" in the ghetto. But will his black girlfriend be able to make him a good liberal with the power of "the tightness between her thighs"? People send the author money through the website when they can, goods and even obscure "services" when they can't. I can sit here and steam all I like, but in the end that guy is a finisher, and I'm not. Until today, I couldn't manage to "go for it." I had the impulse, but I learned to anesthetize myself.

Stupidly enough, it wasn't a high school coach or a sports drink commercial that inserted *go for it* into my backbrain, like a bit of steaming shrapnel. It was Tolbert. I sold a few typewriters—some to professors, a couple to students. The year turned over and I still stuck with the typewriters. Tolbert was right with most of his predictions; there was no martial law and the lights stayed on, but our heating system gave up the ghost, so I did spend my New Year's at home, wearing three sweaters. A few weeks later I was back in school and got to take my first creative writing course. Like a fool, I volunteered to be the first to bring in my work. Yvette was in the class. My story was pathetic, as most first stories are—it was about a young college kid with a collection of pithy quotations from various sorts of outsider literature. He goes unloved, sees his girlfriend hook up with another boy in the dorms and then, a page and a half later, kills himself. Every young freshman's first short story, in other words, except for the ones who write sci-fi or stories about shooting up their writing workshops. I was flayed alive by my fellow students, of course, and even the professor got his licks in. All well deserved, mind you, but who could help but cringe when a dozen people gather round and chant *cliché, cliché, cliché!* We live out our clichés, it's true.

Near the end of class, when I was finally allowed to speak again, I said, "Well, I've just been reading a lot, you know, and it just feels like…it just feels like there's nothing big to say anymore."

Yvette, that little chestnut colt, raised her hand. "That's postmodernism, right?"

The professor clapped his hands once and said, "Yes, yes it is! Postmodernism. All the great things have been said and have been found wanting. So everything now is partial, contingent, and open to revision even as it is being written. But," he added, with a piercing look at me, "that doesn't mean we have to fill every story with disconnected allusions and then end with a protagonist suicide."

I told Tolbert the story afterwards and he just laughed. He didn't even offer to read the story. Then he finally asked me to come sample that famous Latvian dish so we could properly discuss my future. I'd expected either a blonde mail-order bride in the Barbie mode or an ox in a housedress, but Aija was neither stereotype. She was in her mid-forties with maybe a bit of extra weight, but that made her about half the size of the usual high fructose corn syrup–fed Ohioan. Where Tolbert was hyperkinetic and a jabberer, Aija had a deep and quiet laugh, and when she spoke it brought the conversation to a stop, or would have if Tolbert had come equipped with a pause button. If there were any bookshelves in Tolbert's house, they weren't in the living room—Tolbert called it "the TV room"—or the kitchen. The bathroom had a few issues of *Consumer Reports*, but that was all. Did Aija read in bed while her husband snored away?

"You see, you're not going to learn anything in college," Tolbert told me over our plates of gray peas with cream sauce and bacon. We were halfway through a bottle of red Chilean table wine, and I was relieved to see two others on the kitchen counter, waiting for us. "College is an opportunity to network, to meet people. You think anyone from YSU is going to end up editing the *New Yorker*? Do you need a degree to send a story in to the *New Yorker*?"

"Well, I don't know. I haven't looked into it. I'm not really into the *New Yorker*. Honestly, I kind of consider that magazine to be the enemy."

"That just makes it easier, doesn't it? No ego at stake if they say no. You want to write, just go for it. If you don't like that pretentious crap—"

"Pretentious," Aija interrupted. She made us wait while she took a sizeable gulp of her wine. "What exactly is that crap *pretending* to be?" Aija and I laughed.

Tolbert took the jab like a pro, then ignored it. "Just write a good story and find someone to publish it. Forget the mysteries of life—you think anybody cares about that nonsense? Nobody does. Beginning, middle, end. A little t&a, a little moral, and you're good to go."

"Moral t&a," I said. I shot Aija a look and she returned half a smile.

"Yes, a little moral. 'Good fences make good neighbors.' That sort of thing. And you need to have some cheesecake, too. It's only natural, after all. The procreative impulse makes the world go around."

"We have no children," Aija announced.

"Why do men strive? For women! Why do women put up with all the crap they do—for men!"

"Lesbians are notorious laggards," Aija said.

"I'm the first person in my family to go to college. I want to do something with my life."

Tolbert leaned in. "Major in business," he said in a hoarse whisper, as if imparting some great secret. "That's the ticket. Write your own future that way."

"Did you major in business?"

"School of hard knocks. Self-made man." He was loud again. "I knew when I first saw you that you had some curiosity, not like those other cud-chewers out there. And you made it work. Literary stuff; much better than Y2K. You didn't learn that in a classroom."

"Actually, I did—"

"Bram, please. Don't badger our guest." She went to get the other bottle of wine. I had taken to thinking of the female derriere as "cans"—stupid Updike phrase—and Aija had a good one; round and apple-like. She came back and topped us all off and told Tolbert that there was a message on the machine for him. Tolbert said he had to take the call and I thought I knew what would happen next. We were all buzzed, and Tolbert and Aija clearly had some kind of kinky weirdo relationship. If all media had taught me anything, it's that housewives were all always horny. Was she going to suck me dry, driven mad by her husband's borishness, his refusal to understand her continental sophistication? She swung her hips at me and leaned down to whisper in my ear.

"Get the fuck out of here," she said, her voice a knife. "I'm not saying this to help you; I'm saying this because I'm tired of Bram dragging drowned puppies into my house."

I wanted to turn around and kiss her, grab a fistful of her hair. *Go for it*, like Bram Tolbert told me, so I did and she responded with a smoked tongue. Then with both hands on my shoulders she pulled herself free and told me again to go and not to come back. It was a lonely February night and the heater rattled the entire way home. I was up all night, staring at the phone, waiting to see if I'd get some angry call from Tolbert, or a plaintive one from Aija inviting me back. Neither called. Maybe that was their weirdo kink. Bram mentors, Aija tempts, and then they have a good laugh and take a third bottle of wine to bed together and fuck one another silly, Bram with his stocky little body pounding away like an assembly line robot at an auto plant, Aija all sliding curves. And they needed some kid like me as a catalyst.

But Bram was right. He had a horny wife, got business calls late into the night, and for all his bluster seemed to have something I never did: peace of mind. He went for it, and if he hit a brick wall face first, then he knew to go for it in some other direction. Me, all I had was the smell of the dead still on me and three different writing media—foolscap, glowing laptop screen, and blank paper tucked into a typewriter, taunting my silly ass like a middle-aged Latvian woman.

The next morning I got another call for a driller and took it. Russian Hill. Nice part of town, relatively speaking. Even in the old days, privilege and good health was like a river flowing down the curves of the neighborhood. Down Green Street it was all swinging long limbs in tasteful sundresses, with a chesty man playing bodyguard for each girl. It got even better on Nob Hill, but then in the Tenderloin, on old Turk Street, the scene changed. Cripples everywhere, from accidents or CP or other defects, stumping up and down the block. Toothlessness, shouting and barking on the street corners, grimy delis and fortified ethnic luncheonettes. Money doesn't roll downhill, but shit surely does. Needless to say, I spent a lot more time in the Tenderloin than I ever had in Russian Hill.

Funny—Russian Hill is named after a cemetery, a Russian one right atop the hill from back before '49. That's how far south the Russians made it with their settlements of the West in the early nineteenth century. The Gold Rush settlers did what San Franciscans always do—dug

 up the bodies and tore them to pieces, shattered the crosses and tombstones, and then settled down to the business of living without corpses underfoot.

The call wasn't a surprise. In the poor parts of town, people are used to doing their own dirty work. The grade of the streets is so high that the pedicabs won't go there, so I hailed a van and paid for my trip with half a flask of Teacher's. The cabbie was kind enough not to drink it while she drove up to Greenwich Street. The good middle-class people of the world—being the very best sort of person to be, not grimy and ignorant like the proletariat, nor blood-soaked maniacs like the inbred elite—are usually very considerate, so I had hopes that I wouldn't be facing a reanimate.

It was a kid, seven years old or thereabouts, named Tyler. His parents were ever so nice—both white. She a thin little thing with a prominent nose and bleached hair. He mostly bald, wearing a Stanford sweatshirt that wasn't as clean as he would have liked it to be. Little Tyler wasn't a reanimate. He wasn't even dead yet; he was in his sickbed, and except for his face was covered in both gray blankets and tarps. Someone— mother probably—had with a Sharpie drawn a little set of crosshairs on Tyler's forehead.

"We didn't want to call too late," the man, who introduced himself as Jack, explained. "Don't worry though; it's nothing contagious."

"I'm not worried . . . may I use your bathroom?" I was pointed to it and sat down on the toilet and opened up my flask and emptied it in three hungry gulps. I was going for overload, the boozy equivalent of an ice cream headache, but I didn't have enough for anything other than a dull throb. I stayed in the bathroom for a while—there was a window, and the design was all flowery in oranges and brighter pinks. Mother's room, surely, despite the two males in the house. She must have been in here seconds after either one of them came in to use the commode. Nothing worth consuming in the medicine cabinet; I could have gone for a few homebrew Percocets. I did my ears with Q-Tips, real ones thank God, with a firm cardboard stem. There was a knock on the door and a feminine voice asking me if I was all right.

"Be right out," I said. I was crying and didn't even realize it, and she burst into tears when she saw me. That's how I learned her name was Marina, when Jack told her not to cry because Tyler might hear her and get upset. She went to his room to wait, saying she'd call us, "when he was ready." Then it was just me and Jack in the kitchen. We sat across from one another and after a minute or two, Jack went to the cabinet under the sink and came out with some of the okay stuff— Lagavulin, sixteen year. Without a word he poured us each a drink, not in tumblers but in plastic cups, the sort which Marina probably bought for some planned picnic or kiddie birthday party.

The booze warmed my tongue, and helped level me out from my blast of Teacher's. I remembered something from school—new hires at newspapers were almost always broken in by being sent out to write local obituaries. People *want* to talk; that's the lesson a cub reporter was supposed to learn in the first few days of the job. So I started.

"Good kid, I'm sure."

"Pfft," Jack said. "How would you know?" His voice was steady. It wasn't the whisky talking.

I had to tread lightly, especially if I wanted a refill. "I could tell from his room. Maps of the solar system on the walls, the drawings looked pretty good for a kid. Very detailed, actually." And not of grayish, hunched-over stick figures soaked in red Crayola kind, either.

"He's a retard," Jack said. "Autistic. His favorite hobby was the Goddamned history of the ferry schedule. Number two— the moons of the solar system. Jupiter's moons, especially. *Sixty-three* moons."

"That's a lot." Lagavulin makes me stupid sometimes.

"He loved to chant their names; he memorized when they were discovered and by whom. He liked Thebe—it's shaped like a deformed doughnut because of a large crater. Ellipsoidal, that was Tyler's favorite word. Thebe was discovered during the *Voyager I* flyby in 1979. Did you know that, sir?"

"No. Well, I don't think I did. I liked space too when I was a kid, but that was before my time. I remember when the first shuttle exploded, though. I cried all day."

"Me too," Jack said. "Me too." He looked up at the ceiling— it was tin, and painted bronze. The nicest and most interesting ceiling in the world. "So, what did you do . . . before?"

"I was a writer. Still am, after a fashion." This was going all wrong. I tried something. "Were you a lawyer?"

"Still am, after a fashion," he said. Not a bad guess, given how easily he took control of the conversation. "I work for the city now. Foreign affairs, trade agreements. We'll be trading again soon, almost like a city-state might. Like Hong Kong or Singapore."

"Sure, why not? We have a good port. We could sell . . . uh . . ."

"Bodies."

"Bodies."

"Reanimates. Not live ones." He nodded toward my drill case. "All the world powers want to know what makes a body move. Basic research, you know. Medical applications."

"Military applications too, you think?"

Then Jack roared with laughter. He was so loud that Marina came from her vigil with long gazelle strides and demanded to know what was going on. Her face was flush; Jack's too. She slapped him hard across the face, and that shut him up for a second, but he recovered and hissed that they had a *guest*.

"Would it be better if I waited outside?" I asked. My hope was that the pair would hug one another and burst into tears, and through their racking sobs say that yes yes that would be a good idea, and they wouldn't show me to the door so I could take the bottle with me for company while they waited with their son. Maybe he would last the night. I could leave at dusk and even cite curfew. I was a scofflaw, like nearly everyone, but a lawyer and wife—hell, she was probably a lawyer too; that was probably how they'd met, in law school—would have to accept that excuse. And when they called 311 one next, someone else could come out for this shitheap of misery.

"Don't bother. Tyler's ready," she said. I wanted so badly to finish my drink, but with her eyes on me, little gray stones, I knew that I couldn't. I wobbled down the hall to Tyler's little room. He was still, but not any more still than he had been an hour before. Marina followed me into the room and stood by the door, her arms folded across her chest.

"Ma'am, I don't think—"

"I'm not leaving," she said. "I want to see this, I need to witness it. You don't understand. I know you've been doing this for a long time, that you're a professional—"

"A professional," I repeated. She was on auto-pilot now, not even knowing what the hell was coming out of that flappy jaw. Pre-school teachers who didn't understand precious Tyler and his moon-crazed ways were professionals, too; so were the doctors that didn't just kill him with a morphine drip when they had their hands on him were professionals, definitely. I was just another plumber or house painter. Not a Mexican anyway, so I got to be a professional.

"I'd like to turn him over. It would be . . . better that way. For the equipment," I said. "I appreciate the lengths you've gone to here, but . . ."

"Do it where he lies," she said to me finally.

Were I sober, I would have left. They say that booze and money don't change character so much as they reveal it, but I never felt that way. Drunken ego is something else, a shambling mess of desires, pride, and ultimately lickspittle cowardice. She had her arms folded over her chest. Were they at her sides, I would have left. When a woman is firm with me, I just collapse into a puddle. I took out my drill and put it to the mark on Tyler's forehead. Then Jack rushed me like a wind from around a corner and I was on the floor.

"He's not dead!" Jack shouted. His fist was the size of his face. I heard the drill whine somewhere in the room, Marina shrieked. Jack was straddling my chest and dropping his fist onto my head, but I was loose and it just felt distant, like someone kicking the back of a chair at the movies. I bucked him off and stumbled to my feet. The kid's face was ruined, his nose and cheeks chewed up, but the brain was probably intact. Marina and Jack were grappling on the floor somehow. My head throbbed: I was having some trouble breathing, but I didn't think my nose was broken. It was just the blood and the tarp; the smell made my lungs revolt. Tyler was head down, half off the bed. I drilled my hole. His parents shrieked like animals in a fire.

Most people don't stay drillers for very long, which is why there is such a high demand for us. It's also why we're barely trained and paid so little—tons of turnover, so no need for the city to invest heavily in "professionalizing" the gig. I'd done two drills in as many days. According to my online account, I was already in the top quartile of drillers. Most people, as it turns out, end up throwing their drill into the Bay after their first appointment. Except for the workers who stake out the hospital emergency rooms, nobody ever gets the sort of circumstance we're supposed to—a dead person not yet reanimated, quietly being debrained by a drill. It's all bad craziness, teeth being bared and eyes flying open at the last moment, or poor relations not quite dead, or people who just want you to kill them because they're lonely . . . or even horny. You had to be stone cold to be a driller, and anyone that hard could find a better living as a criminal or in the upper echelons of city government. You know, Jack's bosses.

There aren't any driller bars, not in the Mission or the Tenderloin or the Lower Haight or Chinatown, or anywhere I felt like going. Is this how cops used to feel when they'd enter non-cop bars? But the money was good and deep down in my sober ego I had to admit I loved it. I never bought into the Hemingway myth—run with the bulls, sign up for the Spanish Civil War, box stringy Cubans, then write novels about impotency—but I was in the middle of it now. It wasn't the drunk ego fueling my interest in the drilling gig either. Drunken me wanted to curl up and stay warm and cozy in a bar, leave the drill at home, and wait till the world collapsed enough that nobody bothered keeping track of tabs or favors anymore. It was sober ego, that other me with whom I was hardly familiar after years of estrangement, that craved the drill. The sober ego raked the leaves and shoveled snow, set up email accounts for his hairspray-addled cousins, went to school and got on the

Dean's List, kept his shitbox car together back when he had one—drunk ego had wrapped it around a tree in Berkeley and had his license taken away—and didn't worry even for a second that he couldn't really tell the difference between someone dead, someone near death, and a body in the throes of reanimation. Sober me was helping the world somehow, keeping back the waves of death reborn one cranium at a time. It was drunk me who couldn't take it. Neither the sober nor the drunk ego could deal with the easy way out—sitting in the ER, playing doctor with the rest of them.

I started taking what promised to be the risky gigs. The reports of the dying homeless on street corners. When they get up and wander off when I'm still half a block away, are they reanimated or simply recovering from a boozy stupor? More old people in cramped apartments, some of them so frail and wilted there seems to hardly be any blood in their heads— their skulls crumble under the drill. And there are plenty of people who just call to have someone to talk to. Like I said, communities disintegrated in the face of the rampaging dead. Families collapsed in hours. It's the social misfits who were ultimately the fittest, the ones who needed nothing more than a bit of food and a moldy roof overhead. If the Big One ever hit, we'd all be dead under the rubble, without anyone to even know we were missing. But something else hit, and we talk. I keep my foolscap in my bag and take notes and I hear stories.

"I was at work when it happened," one man told me. His name was William. I introduce myself as Billy, but he didn't make any comment about the similarity. William is gay, and alone. One of those slightly chubby gays who probably wouldn't be alone if he didn't insist that he should be. He looked like a less lumpy Hemingway, or Fred Exley right after *A Fan's Notes* made him famous enough to have a beard.

"At first I thought it was a hoax—we all did, after all. All those zombie marches in town and movies; it seemed like a publicity stunt. I was just working for a start-up, database stuff, nothing fancy, so it wasn't as though I was surrounded by bodies emerging from the grave or sitting up on a slab. Oh dear, I can't imagine how it must have been like to work in a hospital on that day…" He drank his tea, then snorted at himself. "I sound exactly like everyone else. But what am I supposed to say? I wish zombies didn't rot so I could find a nice hunky dead boy to do chores around the house? Chores like me?" He laughed. "Oh, I'm so glad my mother's dead. Dead for over a decade, that is. I don't need an unexpected visit from Florida, that's for sure."

I laughed and wrote and William referred to me as his Boswell. He loved holding forth on the city before and after: "There were two befores and afters, truly: the dot.bomb was the first—the zombies came later"; on the best brunch item one should serve a lover after the third weekend sleepover on spring Sunday mornings: "Eggs Blackstone"; and his own little conspiracy theory about the rise of the dead, which unlike the theories of almost every other gay man in San Francisco, involved neither the federal government nor AIDS: "The universe is a teleological phenomenon. There is something that is *good* that the world must become. We'd hidden away death for too long, painted it up like a working woman."

"Working woman?"

He laughed. "That's what we used to call street whores in the 1990s. It was a solidarity thing. Identity politics. It was all crazy—where was I?"

"We painted death like whores."

"We painted death like whores!" William roared. "I like that. We, as a species, have always been close to death. In parts of Greece, the families of the dead disinter the bodies of their loved ones and wash the bones every few years. Ah, but look who I'm talking to."

"Actually," I said, "I didn't know that."

"Well, it's so. And of course until the last hundred and fifty years ago or so, anyone who wanted to have a chicken dinner decapitated, plucked, gutted, and butchered their own chicken. Isn't it odd that vegetarianism and veganism came into widespread vogue only after animal death became an industrial practice, a bit of mass culture handled by an underclass and by soulless machines?"

"That is odd. Well-said." One had to prime the pump a bit occasionally with folks like William. "I never noticed that at all before. What an interesting and trenchant observation."

"Humanity was on the verge of something naked and profound—ever hear of the Singularity?"

"Let's say I haven't. But it's when computers become smarter than people or something."

"Or *something*," William said. His voice grew colder and lower. "The human brain would no longer be the brake or drag on technological progress. An 'intelligence explosion.' primarily artificial in nature, would lead to a post-human reality where people like you and I," he said, and he put a hand on my wrist, "as bright as we are, might have no place. The post-human experience would be as inexplicable to us as tweeting, 'Catching the 38L to see *Wild Strawberries* at the Kabuki' to our thirty-eight followers or whomever would be to a bonobo."

"So, the dead . . . ?"

"So the dead arose, recent history itself cleared its throat, to stop the species from taking the wrong path. I don't know if I believe in an anthropocentric universe, but I do believe that somewhere, somehow, humanity knew of its own potential fate and something happened to make sure it was forestalled." Then, on a dime: "So, how about you? Got any dark secrets?" William leaned in conspiratorially. "I have to say, my own theory would probably go over a bit better in Berkeley, but I didn't want to haul ass all the way out there when people were alive!"

I didn't really have a theory as regards the reanimation of the dead. None of the usual theories sounded all that feasible, but of course the most intelligent and socially minded individuals were the first to go. A foreign attack, maybe, like the neutron bombs that wipe out the people while leaving the buildings intact? Except that tons of buildings weren't intact anymore. Postcolonial *voudon*—has America finally paid for its role in oppressing Haiti? That's another pretty big theory, but it only has currency locally among liberal weirdos. There are other versions of the same, with American slaves or dead Indians implicated. Maybe some sort of catastrophic and cyclical natural phenomenon that last happened in pre-history? A dead zombie looks a hell of a lot like a dead person when nothing is left but bone and pottery shards.

William looked at me hungrily, as though he had well-practiced answers for all the usual crap people spout. His own personal vintage of crap—fermented in a tiny Western Addition apartment for the last couple of years, while William sat alone and traded in foreign currencies when the Internet was up, and brought home boys to make Eggs Blackstone and talk about the intrinsic finality of our species-being—would surely be proof against anything I might say.

"I agree with you. I mean, even practically, it makes sense, right? Perhaps there's another alternative reality where the Singularity did take place, and some bonobos, wanting the opposite numbers in other universes to keep us from making their mistakes—or even challenging them one day—raised the dead to keep us in check."

William stared at me for a long moment. "So, you agree with me?"

"Yes."

"About the Singularity, the *telos* of the universe, the physico-theological proof of a cosmic divinity . . . ?"

"Yeah, it makes perfect sense."

"But your version of it just happens to sound like the plot of *Plan 9 from Outer Space*?" He stood up and scratched that salt-and-pepper beard. "Or like a big-budget remake, in fact."

"Well, I was just trying to ground it a bit," I said. I didn't give two shits about my theory which I'd pulled from my ass—a place William should have liked!—just to please him and keep the conversation going, but now I was ready to die to defend it. "It's like Kant said, 'If man makes himself a worm he must not complain when he is trodden on'."

"Kant!" I for the first time noticed just how large William's hands were as he'd made them into fists and held them up to his chest, ready to box Kant for three bloody and lopsided rounds. "Kant was very much against what I'm saying. With what you," and he sneered these last few words, the way a drunk does when it's time to throw down, "agree with."

I stood up. I had my drill case. I could brain him with it in a second if I had to, and I had the drill to to finish him. I was on a call; my location had been recorded. Not a jury in the city would convict me.

"Faggot," I said. "You fat old fucking queen."

"Get the fuck out of here," William said, his voice soft and reasonable again. My dreary old Midwestern insult was a shot to the liver. Both his and mine. He sounded just like deep-voiced Aija when he said, "Get the fuck out of here" and it made me desirous of a surreptitious kiss that tasted of ash.

Then there was Alexa. She'd called for a driller early one afternoon and I answered. A colt, like Yvette back in school, and Greek too; American, but Greek. Greek enough to ask me:

"So, what did your father come to this country with?" She didn't seem agitated at all, or eager to usher me toward a dead husband or dying child so I settled in for an afternoon that might actually lead somewhere. A little retsina maybe, and a nooner with a friendly stranger with the kind of body I liked—tight ass, little tennis ball breasts, and limbs that looked like they would break under me, but which first embrace would reveal to be rebar wrapped in silk.

We talked for a bit, in the hallway of her apartment—she had one of those L-shaped numbers with a kitchenette and one other room off the side. The financial district was full of them now that there was little commercial finance going on. Her father had come with a cardboard briefcase, two bottles of Metaxa, fifty dollars, and a change of clothes. She grew up in Brookline, MA, and smiled when I said I went to school in Boston for a year, then frowned when I said "Emerson." Then Alexa laughed again when I told her that I went there to study creative writing. "Too bad there's nothing to write about anymore, eh?" I could have told her about the girl she reminded me of, from back in Boston, but that would have made me seem even more pathetic, I'm sure.

"Well, I did drop out and move here to drink myself to death, so I guess it was kismet." And with that she finally let me in and went to her kitchenette to pour us a couple of screwdrivers, albeit weak ones. "The patient is in the bedroom," she told me. She was wearing stripey socks, no shoes. "In here." In her bedroom, which was the sort of Ikea spartan one used to see all the time before barricading doors in a hurry became *au courant*, was a small aquarium and in it three fish and a body of a fourth, floating. A little black and yellow stripey number. I turned to look at Alexa, and her top was already off, and a black bra—not lace, that would be too trashy, but with a shine—was waiting for me. Her belly was white, a bit like a fish's itself.

"Please don't make a joke about drilling," she said. She held out her arms, almost in the manner of a child wanting to be carried. I stepped forward and walked her right onto the bed. There's always a moment in a book when I cringe—it's just at these moments when a writer recounting or contriving a scene has a choice. Did Alexa and I actually *make love* or is the event of physical coupling better handled by the Anglo-Saxon bark of *fuck*? Should the male gaze take it all in— Alexa's stubbly cunt, her thick nipples too large for her small breasts, the ribs visible like wings? Or should we just move to afterwards when she shows me the gun—some 9mm of the sort cops generally have—and tells me that she salvaged the apartment the hard way.

"I'm a really good shot. My father was into guns. From Crete, you know, where they still have blood feuds. He was like a Greek Republican hillbilly redneck. I moved here just in time for the reanimation—I was supposed to have a roomie and live up in the Oakland Hills."

"East Bay, ugh," I said. That joke was one of the few that was always still funny. Alexa had a piggy, snortful laugh. I made a vow at that moment to be one of those serious-minded men who were kind to animals and who dourly read the news about the rest of the country while muttering *What a waste, what a waste* under his breath. I hoped Alexa didn't like cut-ups.

"Yeah. Anyway," she said, "I just thought you should know. You must have seen a few reanimates up close. Don't you just want to destroy them when you see them? I have no idea why anyone would try to keep their relatives 'safe' by locking them away, and plead with them as if a personality or a soul were somewhere in there. It's something deep, Billy, deep in me. Like my ovaries are demanding I assert some generative impulse by wiping out the dead. It's just that sense of the uncanny, you know, that makes me want to strike out." She put her tongue to the barrel of the gun, then turned on her side and rested the end of the gun barrel on my chest.

"Please don't shoot my nipple off."

"Are you getting hard again?"

"Uh, I was."

"I want to go on patrol with you." She held the gun up, pointing it to the ceiling, and kissed where it had lay on me. "I bet we'd make a great team. You must have come too late to certain calls and had to deal with a reanimate. More than one, probably, and more than once."

I laughed. "Mostly, people just call for company or to, you know…for relatives who may not actually be dead. I mean, I'm not a doctor or anything."

"Do you fuck a lot of girls this way, *Vasilis?*"

"Define a lot."

"When was your last before me?"

Sober ego took over—*lie!* Alcohol is truth; it takes a sober mind to lie effectively, to chart the minds of the people one must lie to. Drunk ego wanted Alexa; sober me knew a woman with a gun was always trouble. So I told her two days before. Another woman, absolutely. In Pacific Heights. Slightly older, but well-preserved. Did she have big tits, Alexa wanted to know. Yes; a sizeable rack.

"I could have rested my gimlet on it. She had a dry bar in one corner of her apartment. It was a real ring-a-ding-dinger of a place. Like something out of an old men's magazine." Alexa stopped smiling. "She was a good cocksucker too—the way I like it. Mouth only, her wrists in my hands."

Alexa knew I was lying now, which was part of the lie, of course. She was wild enough to want to be titillated by the idea of a wandering driller sexing women left and right while zombies march down the streets below, unmolested and free to breed in their own peculiar way. She wasn't wild enough to be treated like one of the guys in a locker room somewhere, not while we were cuddling in a pool of our own sweat.

"I think," *you should leave.* But no. Alexa said, "I think you should help me break into City Hall."

When women ask me for something, I have a tendency to obey without hesitation, unless it involves the bedroom.

I'm enthusiastic, but not generous as far as love-making goes, I admit it. The first woman to tell me this was Yvette, who was also the first woman to phrase her requests with "I think you should…" instead of in the form of a question. It's a jejune thing to notice, but in Youngstown in the early 2000s such forwardness was rare. If Youngstowners were ever a scrappy bunch of proletarians who made the country great, it only took a generation or so after the mills shut down to turn everyone into giant blobs of high-fructose corn syrup, fueled by inchoate rage. The 1950s era reasserted itself—girls got pregnant early and married quickly, everyone ate TV dinners and gratefully consumed plastics, and men ruled the town for no other reason than they had greater upper body strength and more enthusiasm for shouting.

Yvette was different. She was going to get her degree  and then leave town to become a Big Deal somewhere on the East Coast. When I met her in college in the same town she grew up in, she was starting to break away. Like every other dumb first-year, she was going to college while dating her high school boyfriend. But she dumped her Craig when he joined the army, to the open-mouthed disgust of her high school girlfriends. She was a whore after that, a slut. Practically a member of al-Qaeda itself, and a stuck-up bitch, too.

When she finally hooked up with me, it was on her own initiative. The typewriters were long gone, but I still saw Tolbert occasionally; he was selling some semi-dubious local Internet service now, for $9.99 a month, and hoping to be bought out by AOL, "Or one of the other big boys," he said. "It's all about the flip. No need to build a business anymore; nothing will ever be long-term again. Today, a business or even a sales line is like a suit. You wear it till it falls out of fashion in a year or three."

Yvette told him, in that very same parking lot where I'd sold typewriters more than a year earlier, "Well then, no reason to pay attention to this, what is it, lifetime warranty on this CD-ROM you want me to buy?"

Tolbert gave her that little six-gun point—index finger forward, thumb up. "Sharp!" Then he turned to me. "She's a keeper, so keep her." I wasn't even with Yvette, though with her triple-digit IQ, her newly single status, and the denim miniskirt she had worn to class that day, I was amenable to the suggestion.

"I think we should go now," she said, and walked off without waiting. I gave Tolbert a shrug and trotted after her.

"Sorry," I told her, when we were halfway across the parking lot. "He always has some scheme."

"He's a good judge of the human condition, I think," Yvette said. "He has me all sorted." Yvette tended toward Britishisms, though she had the same accent as any other local. Even her stories were often about the *neighbours*, and involved people wandering through museums and remarking on the *colours* of this or that famous piece of modern art that somehow perfectly captured the emotions of the characters. Then they realized that they weren't happy, but indeed, neither was anyone else except perhaps the long-dead painter of the art that so loomed before them.

"Sorted how?"

"He's right. I think we should date," Yvette said. "Let's date."

"Well, all right." And my fascination with wiry young women, blunt ones who just blurt out what they want without prevarication or even subtlety, was born. Our dates mostly comprised of enthusiastic fucking—we were like a pair of loggers operating one of those long saws on the first day of work. And like that, it got less fun as time went on.

Yvette lived in the dorm though she was as local as I—I'd went to Rayen High School but she had attended Cardinal Mooney, but had managed to convince her folks to spring for room and board to "complete the college experience." Like any Catholic school girl, she instantly became a wild cocksucking pagan who stood naked before Wotan two nights a week and thought the new moon was sufficient cause for a holiday. Yvette's clothes reeked of patchouli, but at least she had a stylish wedge haircut instead of the common long hippie 'do that said, "I have the same haircut now that I did in the third grade" that most of her cohort wore. And she shaved her legs and armpits, thank God and all the saints that mama lit candles to in our kitchen *ikonostasis*.

"I think you should date other people," she said three delirious weeks later. We were in bed. I'd been watching the clock so I could get home by midnight. I needed a mattress I could stretch out in, and Yvette's YSU-issue twin bed wouldn't do it. Generally, I bent her over with my own feet on the floor, or she played cowgirl. The clock turned over: 11:11. *Make a wish.* Here's the thing about Yvette—she was a psychology major and prone to provocations. She loved to taunt and tease. But gin and bile filled my mouth anyway.

"What? What do you mean—are you breaking up with me?"

"I think you need more women. Don't you think you'd benefit from living a little, seeing other women?"

"And come back to you later?"

"Not necessarily."

"Christ, Yvette," I said. "Then *what* necessarily?"

She smiled for a moment—Yvette had an upper lip that turned up when she did, and I loved seeing it so close. I wanted to kiss her hard and make her swallow what she had just said.

But she turned away from me and said, "I fucked nine guys this month." I raised my fist. I didn't think I was the kind of guy to hit a woman, but in that moment I was. The moment passed. "Ever hear of polyamory? That's what we should do. I mean, we never agreed to be exclusive or anything. I don't even believe in monogamy. It's oppressive."

Anger left me and was replaced with an intense desire to kick open the door of some other room in the hall and empty my balls into the first girl I found. If she could fuck around, I could fuck around. I was hard again, and Yvette gripped me, rolled over onto her belly and did my favorite trick. She talked with her mouth full. Through slurping and murmuring—and she'd swirl her tongue around my head when I guessed right—she told me that we were animals, meant to fuck all the time. That we'd be better fucks if we both fucked a lot. That I'd be her something. Her what? *Something.* Finally, I took a fist full of her hair and pulled her off me. A line of drool stretched from my hog of a member to her lower lip.

"My *primary*," she said in a snarl. "My 'main man,' like the hippies used to say. We could come back here, compare notes. I'd even help you pick up other girls. We could be total sluts together—try everything, try everyone. But we'd be committed to one another."

Yvette needed a slapping. Hell, she needed to be back home with her parents. Back to those Catholics and their terror of what's between a young girl's legs. "Where the hell did you even hear of this crap…Oh, let me guess. That 'pagan' guy, right? What's that asshole's name? Stag?"

"Yes, it was Stag's idea. He lent me books. *The Ethical Slut.* There are websites too. Do you want to see?"

"No, I want to wash my cock off and go home."

"You leaving mad makes me horny," she said. A hand slipped under the sheets. "Come back at 3 a.m. At one minute after, I'll be asleep and you can spend the night outside or drive on back to your parents'."

I grabbed my clothes off the floor as we chatted about pleasantries. With Yvette, one had to develop that skill. One second she was talking about the forty-year-old man who ran the school's Dungeons and Dragons club and convinced her that she should suck every cock she meets; the next it was on to whether or not I'd ever seen *Twin Peaks.* Had I read "Araby" yet?

With one leg in my pants I said, "Gazing up into the darkness I saw myself as a creature driven and derided by vanity; and my eyes burned with anguish and anger." Then,

"No, I haven't read it yet." I found the other pant hole in the dark and pushed my naked leg in. "I'm not coming back."

"I hope you do."

I was home in ten minutes, leadfooted all the way. The TV was on in my parents' room—infomercials already, but the murmur of Chuck Norris was hard to make out over the rumbling of snores and occulted Greek mutterings. We were a family of terrified sleepers; something was always roiling under the surface. I only found out that it was unusual to have two or three nightmares a week because of my creative writing class, where my stories were critiqued for the inevitable dream sequences that ended in a twist and shout. *So much blood, so much blood*…that's how my last nightmare had ended. I risked a quick shower, then went to my own room and stood with my finger on the light switch for two minutes. Then I sat down to write.

If there's a story more tedious than the dorm-room affair short story, I've yet to encounter it. Then again, I knew nothing but the raw and bleeding scab of my whole life; Yvette didn't just go for the heart—it felt like she had dug her nails into the flesh of my forehead and yanked the skin off down to my toes. I was exposed, nerves on fire, viscera knotted. And I poured out a story that, oh no, wasn't about her and wasn't about me. Bob and Elaine. Of course not! And in my story, it was the guy who had heard about polyamory and experimented with it by arranging for all his friends to come by and pull a train on his "newly wedded wife, with the raven hair in a thick thatch between her legs and ice-blue eyes." So different—if I had to describe Yvette's real hair, I would have said "the underside of a nuthatch" or something, and I liked that turn of phrase so much that I took it as a title. "The Underside of a Nuthatch." Maybe some of the students would think I was making a reference to insanity. Fodder for future critics and bibliographers, oh yes. I didn't even spellcheck it. I printed it out—all eight pages—and saw that it was a quarter to three. I found a bottle of retsina downstairs and took it with me, for Yvette if I made it back on time, for warmth if I didn't. Any other girl, the 3 a.m. deadline would have been a bluff, but with her I knew it was serious. But her little icicle of a body next to mine or a night in the car would both be fine with me.

I waited outside Yvette's dorm all night, snoozing in my car and occasionally waking up—as always, with a start and often with some kind of yelp from the hands narrative ideas around my throat, the fissure ripping open the city— to add a few words in the margins of my story. In the car, it was as though everyone were dead, and only the buildings and automatic systems remained. Yvette liked to run in the mornings before her 8:30 class—she was a go-getter that way. The sun rose slowly, if inexorably. I sunk under the dash of my car with the bottle to try to get a few more winks of sleep, but before long it was too sunny. I'd have to move soon, as I'd parked on the grass in a little traffic island. I revved the engine just as Yvette happened to come out of the dorm in her running shorts, and she turned to me, then jogged off, taking a path through the greenery I couldn't follow in the car. The retsina bottle was empty.

Our writing workshop wasn't Iowa-style—we didn't get stories to bring home and read and mark up between sessions. The teacher read the stories aloud in a strangely affectless voice; shades of Stephen Hawking. We couldn't take notes, but instead just had to respond to what we were most viscerally affected by. So I had a story, and it was more or less a moment-by-moment re-enactment of the night before, and it was an absolute piece of shit. I handed it to the teacher, whom I don't think had ever even managed to publish anything other than a poem or three in some saddle-stitched journals (and this, before the apocalypse that made saddle-stitched zines the center of the literary universe), and he decided to read it first. I laughed the entire way through it. *The Ethical Slut*, hahahaha, and 11:11 was hilarious too, a big belly laugh. And the ending was a real laugh riot—none of the usual undergrad histrionics or stapled-on epiphanies. I just ended it mid-sentence, so it looped around back to the first paragraph, which started mid-sentence.

"It's a haiku of sorts!" I announced, though talking while one's story was being considered was against the rules of the class. "Please read it aloud again. Haikus are recited twice. That's also why the story loops back around." The professor frowned at me. I smiled over at him and with my hands shooed him on a bit. He knew I'd just bark and bellow more, it would be a festival of enthusiastic and ridiculous demands. So he read the story again and I whooped it up at all the killer lines, nudged my seatmate with my elbow, and occasionally glanced over at Yvette. Her face wasn't red, her eyes not watery, but she did seem very interested in a stray molecule off to her left and on the floor. Her neck tilted oddly, as if she were broken.

Finally, we were done again and without raising her hand or even waiting for a prompt from the teacher, Yvette responded first. "I think it's a pretty good character study of a young alcoholic," she deadpanned, "who is constantly afraid of everything and possibly even impotent. I thought the worry about getting home to his mother, even when his girlfriend encourages him to have all the sex he wants with anyone who'd have him, was a great little implied plot point. Sort of like Hemingway."

"Who was also an impotent alcoholic, right?" someone else said. And the worm turned on me. The story was praised more than any other I had submitted to the workshop.

"Men don't often write about utter losers that way; very refreshing," one of Yvette's cronies said.

The older woman whose stories were always about her grown children not wanting to visit her got her licks in too: "I was ultimately very pleased that the story was read aloud to us twice. It was a good technique, since the second reading made it clearer to me which parts of Billy's story were intentionally incoherent, and which he'll actually need to work on during revisions." Then she listed virtually every paragraph as needing revision.

Even the freshman who wrote movie scripts about serial killers and the Devil, but all in prose form—"Cut to . . . an abandoned warehouse that smells of brimstone and fear"— praised me with faint damnation. "I could really identify with the inner turmoil and madness of the main character."

Yvette never looked up, never flashed anyone a smile. She was a few heartbeats away from needing to be strapped to a chair to be kept upright. Between the two readings and the effusive and extended comments from everyone, the theme of the session was me and what a drunken cretin I was. And that's what I needed. A solid rhetorical beatdown; a half-dozen hits to the face with a lead pipe, just to make Yvette frown. I was drunk enough so that the bruises on my psyche wouldn't surface for hours, maybe even years. She was really hurt, though. Despite the concerted if unconscious efforts of all our classmates to block me by surrounding her, I managed to exit shoulder to shoulder with Yvette.

"What do you think?" I asked her and she told me:

"I think we should talk." We went back to her dorm and wordlessly fucked, or tried to, as both booze and the endless accusations of impotence weighed heavily on me. We found some other pleasures for Yvette, and finally we started talking after silently deciding to cut the rest of our classes for the day.

"The reason I said I thought you and I should see other people is because—"

"You want to fuck Stag."

"No, it's because I'm going to transfer out. YSU sucks. The professors are all morons, the students are only here because the market for crystal meth manufacture is already supersaturated, and the whole town smells."

"How do you know the town smells? You live here and have all your life, just like me. A smell isn't something you'd notice if you grew up with it."

"Remember, I was in Pennsylvania last summer, on that experimental farm. I haven't been able to get the awful smell out of my nose ever since I returned. Also, I'm not being intellectually challenged here. So I want to transfer, to Boston."

"Ha!" I knew absolutely nothing about Boston, except that it was the setting for *Cheers* and even there it existed only as a gray and shadowed ocean from which Norm and the others came to sit at the bar and drink. That, and one could not park the car in Harvard Yard. I suspected that there was something about Boston that was still very much like the eighteenth century, with thick wooden furniture and men in white wigs plotting genteel revolutions—themselves to be the only beneficiaries—in the scratches of their feather quills.

"Ha," Yvette repeated.

"Where in Boston?"

"There are lots of colleges out there. A lot of culture. Maybe BU, maybe Boston College. They're a Catholic school. My mother would get on board. Emerson. All sorts of places."

"So you're just toying with this idea, then." Yvette was going to go to Tanzania last year, got as far as Pennsylvania. Then there was the dropping out of school to apprentice to a Japanese tattoo artist, and culinary school, and South Africa. She'd also "tried" to go to New York to volunteer at Ground Zero, but her attempts had been limited to some late-night Googling, and a glance at the Greyhound map.

"No, I got into all three of those schools." Yvette slid her hand between her bed and the wall and came up with some torn envelopes, acceptance letters still inside. "I'm going to move this summer. Boston's crazy; everyone leaves right after Memorial Day. You can furnish an entire apartment just on the cast-offs left on the streets. It's like a neutron bomb hit. And then September 1 is Moving Day. The streets are packed with Ryder trucks and U-Hauls. I even found a website that offers odds on how many trucks will be stuck under overpasses. It sounds like a riot. And there are a ton of bookstores, lots of local music, arthouse cinema, it's a major market for events. The Charles River!" That last she shouted like she was at a geography bee. "Did you know that it is entirely devoted to recreation?"

"Isn't Boston Harbor supposed to be gross and disgusting?" I'd been a kid during the Dukakis run for President, but just seeing a real live Greek on TV, with the eyebrows and the surname and the great helmet of hair like my uncle Yianni's, was electrifying. I couldn't believe he'd demanded a waiver of the Clean Water Act. My father blamed the Mafia on this act of cowardice, and the Irish Mafia was also implicated somehow in my father's Formica countertop rants about the election back then. I'd eat French Fries and catch only every eighth word of the rapid-fire Greek of the unofficial Dukakis Brain Trust of Youngstown, Ohio. On Election Day, my father stayed home and waited nervously for the returns to start coming in, though he never even thought to register to vote himself. He was worried the FBI would be able to find him more easily then, and that this would somehow lead to the diner being torched.

"Everything's clean now," Yvette said. "Everything's perfect. I always wanted to take up rowing."

"I'm coming with you," I told her.

She snorted. "You're half a semester away from graduating. You can't transfer now."

"I'll go to grad school. I'll get my MFA."

"*MFA!*" Yvette was the queen of this masculine gambit. Forget the relationships and emotional connections people have, and just move right into the bald practicalities of a situation. If she hadn't been an unrepentant Nader voter, Yvette probably just would have married the gaptoothed chinless son of a steel magnate. Was that why she was going off to Boston, for a superior pool of dorm-room fucks?

"You hate MFA students. You rant about them all the time," she said. She sat up on her elbow, tucked her chin in a bit and deepened her voice. "Did Bukowski get an MFA? Did Celine have a master's degree? Harlan Ellison even failed freshman English, and at Ohio State too. Blah blah, I'm awesome like them so I don't need an MFA. Also the *New Yorker* can suck my balls, not that I'd ever submit, because technology hasn't found a way for me to email my balls to them so that they might more efficiently suck!" Then, back to her natural voice. "Plus, you can't apply now; it's already too late for September. And your parents would kill you. What would they do without their prince?"

"Do you get why I suddenly decided to try for an MFA?" I asked her. "It's just a reason to go with you on Uncle Sam's dime. I'll take out loans and write whatever I was planning on writing anyway, and maybe I can end up teaching community college instead of high school. Look at it this way, you convinced me. Boston's great! We can drink the water, and they have movies there . . . strange and mysterious films that nobody in Ohio could ever imagine."

"Oh, Billy," Yvette said. "I think you really just don't get it."

I didn't get it, but neither did she. I didn't want to make it easy for Yvette, I didn't want her to win by palming me off on someone else. In that moment, I only thought *Let the acid of my anger corrode me more than it does her; let me dig two graves on my mission of revenge.* Boston ruined me for years afterward. How many nights did I spend awake thinking about debt and disaster and wishing some quantum tunnel into existence that could bore a hole in time just large enough for me to whisper, "Back down! Don't do this!"

And I did hear just those words, in my own voice, in my head, at that very moment. In my less lucid moments I even dreamed that old sci-fi dream that I would one day happen upon a method to communicate with the past. I'm no scientist; never took more than the usual Physics for Poets class and two semesters of calc, but anything could happen in the future, I thought. A freelance journalist gig, a stray particle too small to be held in the amber of time sliding through a half-mile of cement and lead and cementing itself in my brain . . . too many comic books as a kid.

My father would growl, "That junk is for the *retarded children*. Are you telling me that you are *retarded?*" But so much of it stayed with me—knuckled fists with a starburst and pow beneath, the narcissistic audacity of the villains. I still doodle muscle-bound men on the margins of my foolscap when the words won't come. For a long time every long walk I took home from a job was fodder for the daydream of finding a magic ring and using it to fly to the black tar roof of whatever crappy little apartment building Yvette had been living, when I decided to join her in Boston. After the troops had woke me on my couch, four days into the new world of the walking dead, I left behind my ridiculous little daydream. Surely, I would have warned my past self in that post-coital haze not about Boston, but about the living dead and San Francisco's great secret.

I soon discovered that Alexa was paranoid, like many Greeks, and also a wreck, like many alcoholics. She had all the zines and books and print-outs one could want about the reanimates, which she kept in plastic garbage bags in her bedroom closet. It took her almost twenty minutes to sort it all out, on her hands and knees on the floor. The crumpled papers looked a bit like an avant-garde form of carpeting.

She spoke rapidly while she worked. The gun was on the nightstand. I briefly considered picking it up to feel its heft, or just tucking it into my pants, which I had slid back into as the night grew cool. Alexa probably had another firearm somewhere, but that was also the problem—Alexa probably had another firearm.

"Look," she said. "Don't you think it's odd that there aren't any cemeteries in the city, and even when an old off-map burial ground was discovered, the settlers almost invariably exhumed the corpses and put them somewhere outside city limits?"

"I do think it's odd. Everything's odd. I've read all this junk, too."

"What I've been doing," Alexa said, "is boiling down all the information, all

(6)

the theories, to find out what elements and narrative strings they have in common. And I think I have a semi-useful theory as to why the events of the past few years have occurred."

The events of the past few years—what a phrase. It reminded me of 9/12, when I went to my local bank branch as my father was screaming that we needed to get all our cash out and convert it to "wearable gold" immediately because martial law was coming and coming soon, and the bank was closed, according to the handwritten sign "due to circumstances." That just set papa off even worse. He nearly took a hacksaw to our heat registers in a mad drive to sell the copper pipes within for folding money.

Alexa went on with the same sort of frantic energy I'm already so familiar with, the sort of passion that heats up my brain so fast and so hard that I have to douse it in gin, in beer, even in wine by the jug. She was sure that the '49ers had known something, and that whatever they had discovered either in their mines or mills or just in their wandering of the city's hills had been hidden in City Hall. Even thinking about rye was enough to get me in a poetic frame of mind.

"You know, City Hall was destroyed in the big quake in 1906," I told her when she finally caught my attention by saying *City Hall.* "Why would anything from before that time still be in there, like in an old Hitchcock film where the drama always unfolds around a landmark?"

"Because the city just seemed ready, somehow. For all of the twentieth century. So we should do something." Alexa had the endearing habit of blowing her hair out of her eyes with a twisted lip and a *ffft* noise. She did that then, and it worked.

"Kidnap a bigwig and make him talk? Poke around in the basement? Climb the underside of the rotunda?"

"Whatever it takes."

"It's not going to take anything, *girl*," I told her. She bristled at girl, but that was the sort of thing I liked to say. "Your theory is just another thought-fox; you convinced yourself it's real with a few details, but it's nothing but scribbles on a page."

"Thought-fox?"

"It's a poem by Ted Hughes?" If Alexa had said *Who is Ted Hughes* I would have left just there and then, even though Greek girls usually surrender the anal sex on the fifth or sixth date.

But she said, "I don't know the poem, but Ted Hughes . . . world's worst husband, right?"

"And father!"

She laughed for a moment, then swallowed the rest of it to say, "I need to know what's going on in the world, and in the city. It's just too neat. I *have to* figure it out." She spat the *out*, practically.

"Why?"

Alexa said, "I want to do something with my life. I want to be remembered. I want a statue, Billy, what can I say? And for a long time there was nothing I could have done at all. My dreams got smaller—from ballerina-astronaut performing the first ever *Swan Lake* on the moon–"

"Ha! Really?"

"Shut the fuck up," she said. "And yes, really. From that to being just another one of the world's B-minus students. Ooh, maybe I could be a project manager at a non-evil environmental clean-up firm." She threw up her arms. "Well, the Great Recession killed that dream, too. Maybe I could dress up and stick my tits out and keep my cunt waxed and maybe meet a nice dot.com CEO and just have babies? It turns out they mostly like blondes and girls who can shut up on command. And then the world ended and the game reset. What did Chairman Mao say? '*There is great chaos under heaven, and the situation is excellent.*'" People in California loved quoting Chinese Communists for some reason. I told myself it was because they weren't clever enough to memorize quotes from novels, like I did. Nobody reads anymore.

"Excellent chaos? I'll buy that," she continued. "Now I have a chance again to do something nobody else ever has. Find out what happened, for real, and maybe even do something about it."

I had nothing to say but what I always say. "I'll buy you a drink. Do you know a place around here?" I wanted out of Alexa's apartment immediately, since we clearly weren't going to be going another round that night.

"Schroeder's; used to be a German place with schnitzel and everything. Now it's just a German place with beer and electricity 24/7. They have solar batteries. They're a smart bunch."

So we went. Beer isn't often my drink, but six o'clock is my hour. Schroeder's was a social place, with long tables and bright lights. It was a chatty bunch. The social worker I'd seen in my home and then again when I applied for the driller job was even there, drinking schnapps and holding a tiny court. There were a few small plates featuring actual food as well. She saw us and waved us over to join her table, which we did. She even raised her glass to me. With German efficiency my drink was served and I broke out a little Bernard DeVoto for the occasion.

"'Nothing stopped us from sea to shining sea," I said, "nothing could stop us, the jug was plugged tight with the corncob, and we built new commonwealths and constitutions and distilleries as we travelled, the world gaped, and destiny said here's how.'" I got applause and nods. Not quite the usual bar experience, but I was on a date of sorts with Alexa so I was almost able to relax.

"We're talking about our theories," the man sitting next to me said. He was an ordinary fellow—going a little bald, getting a little fat, his smile hinting at little wrinkles to come. The nice sort of guy one hopes one's sister marries, because he'll be happy to mow his in-laws' lawn. "It's our weekly meeting."

"Wonderful," I said. "Alexa has a theory." With the bear trap thus sprung on her little brown ass, I leaned back and relaxed.

Alexa started recruiting for a raid on City Hall. There was something there that could have been apprehended even in the nineteenth century, which she said was why the City was still relatively safe today. The usual objections were raised to her goal and her theory. Why did the dead arise only in America, even to the point of respecting the borders with Canada and Mexico? Had to be a foreign force—the North Koreans, the Chinese, al-Qaeda, "Haitian voodoo."

Makes no sense, though someone else asked what sort of technology could possibly do this, and ruining America ruined the world's economy more or less indefinitely. Not that the *bokor* of Haiti would have noticed worldwide economic collapse, but if they had the power why wait *two hundred and fifty years* to unleash it? That was the ordinary fellow on my left. Pollution, or Jesus Christ simply offering a Revelation unlike any we'd have ever expected. An ancient yet recurring and cyclical catastrophe that we were just unfortunately alive to experience though ageless history is too young for any record of it. Harvey Milk, now that was a strand of conspiracy pretty much unheard outside the Castro, but there was that old gay specter haunting the table. The teleological blather I'd already heard from that guy William—that must have been catching on somehow, probably through a zine I'd not yet read.

I liked Schroeder's a lot, I decided, because a waitress in Oktoberfest garb whisks away one's glass the moment it is dry and replaces it on a nod. One drink in front of me all night long, it's like I wasn't indulging at all. How many was it, eight or ten? We were long past DeVoto's famous hour of six o'clock, when a man should never be alone, and deep into a Bukowski evening. Was I keeping pace with everyone, or outdrinking them all? Nobody seemed to care; they were all intent on rearranging the contents of the minds of their tablemates. As if apocalypse were a matter of consensus.

"May as well blame Cthulhu," I said finally, but nobody got the joke so then I had to explain what Cthulhu was and how it wasn't a real thing or even really mythological, and how in the old days Cthulhu ran for President every four years— remember *"Why vote for the lesser evil?"*?—and how he and his tentacles were even put on pairs of fuzzy slippers worn exclusively by nerds.

Then Alexa said I was a writer and had even published a science fiction story. The table erupted in semi-interested murmurs and grunting, as if I was surrounded by extras in a film. *Rhubarbrhubarbsciencefictionrhubarbscifirhubarb* . . .

"Why Mister Kostopolos," the social worker said, "you didn't mention your artistic inclinations when we screened you for your city job. So, what do you think about this brave new world and how it works?"

In a flash, a theory of my own was poured into my head like a pitcher full of milk. It wasn't about the reanimates, but about the normal workaday human being. Nothing there but us little wind-up toys.

"Figuring out how the world works in an old bar, eh?" I said. "Isn't that always the way? The Sons of Liberty met in taverns in Boston, New York, and Philly, hashing out a revolution and a new kind of government like they were computing a tip. Lenin probably knocked back a vodka or two with Trotsky and Stalin too, I bet. I'm sure Socrates—a cousin of mine, if you believe my father, and I don't—passed around a wineskin between philosophy and buggery.

"But it didn't matter, none of it did. Are the reanimated dead inexplicable? Of course, as are the unanimated living. We never knew how the world worked. Was Freud right that we were just all little personalities bobbing on the black sea of the unconsciousness, not knowing where the routes and winds would take us?" I was on a roll.

Schroeder's felt so warm. I wished they still served food; I wanted something we could all tuck in to, like the Harvard boys used to in the bowels of their secret societies. I could almost taste the breading of a schnitzel on my tongue.

"Or Marx, or the Frankfurt School or game theorists? That's all the stuff we learn in college and then we forget all but five minutes worth of conversation about it, because none of it is useful in our daily lives." This being San Francisco, somebody muttered something about postmodernism. I snorted at that. "*Postmodernism*. Postmodernism, that's just the no-it-ain't-so-times-infinity of politics—*Ah, maybe we're all determined by economics, well, uh, conversations about economics. No, no, thinking about conversations about economics.*

Well, okay, maybe nothing determines us at all, but anything you can possibly conceive of has some little impact on us, and now here's a list of my personal favorite conceptions. So nyahnyah, I win for losing!"

The social worker smiled. "Zhou Enlai—first premier of post-Liberation China—was once asked about the French Revolution, and what he felt about its impact. He said, 'It's too soon to say.'" Zhou Enlai's job description was surely for my benefit only. Everyone else smiled knowingly. Ah, the wisdom of the Chinese Communist Party! The perfect *bon mot* for a San Francisco dinner party.

It was too choice a quote. Nobody at the table could think of anything to say to keep the conversation going. I didn't think the social worker got that quote right, and had no idea what she was hinting at. If anybody else at the table did, they found silent contemplation of the remnant food on their plates more interesting. My jaw felt heavy now, my head elongated. I'd never felt like this, not from drinking anyway. I was a cruiserweight if not a heavyweight; I knew how to nurse a drink, and when I decided against doing so I knew how to keep oblivion at arm's length, like a handy banister down a flight of steep steps.

I looked up at the ceiling. Schroeder's had high ones, criss-crossed with decorative wooden beams. Then I just remembered something I'd read once on a flyer wheatpasted to a lamppost a few blocks away.

"It's probably something with the fault lines and whatnot. Some old Indians wandering the fissures and the white man's muskets couldn't kill them, but we know the reanimated are no good for climbing. Why it suddenly started spreading, who knows? Diseases hit a tipping point like anything else."

"That's it!" Alexa said.

"No chance in hell," said an older woman. "We were just talking about that one." Not the social worker, who steadfastly refused to introduce herself by name even as she traded on her passine acquaintance, but a woman next to her; a leathery prune who may have fought her way here from Los Angeles. A tough old bitch; she probably wanted to brain me just on general principles.

"Maybe a chance," I said. "Maybe hell."

"How can we go about proving it? It's not falsifiable," said the reasonable fellow. Then I noticed that the social worker had left her seat and on the table half a glass of peppermint schnapps. How I wanted it so badly at that moment, that old lady drink. Ol' Leathery was looking toward the door with a frown. I was a pile of desires. I leaned toward Alexa, aiming to kiss the nape of her neck—a purely proprietary gesture, with no affection involved—when I slid off my chair. I went down easy, like a little cloud had been under my butt the entire time. Then Alexa was next to me on the floor and it rained glass and shouting. Two hands on my ankles pulled me under the table and that's when I realized that there was a pretty bad earthquake hitting us, and it wasn't stopping.

Earthquakes were usually hard for the Midwesterner and I was still a stupid Ohio boy, experience of the world notwithstanding. Quakes just felt to me like a truck rumbling by, most of them. This one, though, was like a truck hitting the building, and then another truck hitting that truck, then backing up and quickly slamming forward again. And again. It smelled like schnapps under the table, and other liquors besides. The lights didn't go out. Schroeder's had a generator.

"Will there be a fire?" I tried to ask, but my voice had been separated from my body by the vibrations and buckling of the floorboards beneath me.

I'm still missing some time. The next few days were ash and chaos. I remember walking down a wide street, probably Market. Buildings, façades covered the sidewalks like dirty slush. Drillers were called out and deployed as part of "rescue squads," but the most efficient thing to do was to simply wait for people to die under the rubble, then crush their heads with a handful of concrete or a piece of wood. Fog City was under a thicker shroud than usual, a burial shroud. At sunset the sky burned red, but for much of the rest of the days that followed the quake—and those weeks were a montage of sameness, like a Warhol film I'd read about but never seen—I felt like I was trapped in a single black and white frame, mostly shadows and grays, with one flaming bright spot just on the edge of my vision. That was probably just from a concussion or hemorrhage.

The drillers were a motley crew; mostly drawn from the pre-animation underclass of desperate blacks and Latinos the city had always seen as their great and untamable enemy. When the dead began to rise, they'd been recruited. Folks like me—flâneurs I'd call them when feeling generous to myself, white vanilla losers on most days—came and went. It was the Youngstown boy in me that kept me going. I was a proletarian without a dark satanic mill to serve, but now I had a whole city full of the dead and dying, all writhing and reaching for me. Like the work processes at any day job, the hours blurred together. There was sunset, and that meant a break in a bar, and other than that there was not much at all to disrupt the monotony.

Our phones didn't work. There was some vestigial impulse, like a twitch of a tail looking to burst through the flesh of, I don't know, municipal pride? We had tools, we had to be good for something. So we showed up at City Hall and waited for orders. Most of us were hung over, a couple still crusty with blood from minor wounds. I was both, and somehow I'd lost a tooth. I couldn't stop probing the gap with my tongue, wincing whenever I hit the nerve. That just excited me; I'd jab and jab at it, trying to get used to the thud-sting of pain. Someone finally came out and set us in "squads," though the squads were really just a direction to go back to our own neighborhoods.

San Francisco is like a bunch of little islands. Had I ever been to Parkside or Dogpatch, to name just two bits of town that I only even bothered to think about after they were destroyed? Hell, I didn't even know anybody who'd ever been to those neighborhoods. Whoever lived there, whatever demographic that was, they hadn't ever been recruited into the drillers. Half the squad went back to the Mission and that's only because we left a lot of them behind in the Tenderloin or SOMA. Most of my crew went to City Bar—I couldn't even bear to see if it survived the quake, the ramshackle old piece of shit. I swallowed my pride and I think I went to Elixir. I remember approaching the bar, my gut on fire, my jaw throbbing, but then nothing.

Once, I was walking alone and came across an overturned MUNI bus right by where Buena Vista Park meets Haight Street. The dead were animated, but they stayed near the bus for the most part. A couple, on their hands and knees, were on the grassy hill at the edge of the park, slowly crawling toward...something. One slid down the hill as I watched, and just started crawling slowly back up like a determined baby. The reanimates on the street milled around the bus, ignoring me. I'd felt like I was visiting the zoo and peering past the bars at an extended family of howler monkeys or bonobos who didn't register my existence. Nine of them altogether. Perhaps the first to reanimate had consumed the corpses that were a little slower to revive, or those too mangled to have their lidded eyes flip open with that familiar burning idiocy. And they were sated, for now. Maybe, but maybe it was something else.

In the old days, when the buses were almost always on time, I'd wait like anyone else on the corner or in a Plexiglas kiosk, not saying a word, with a crowd of people also not saying a word. And the climbers—well, this is still San Francisco, there are always climbers. 5 a.m. pilates, in the office by six to be able to pick up calls from New York on the very first ring, salads and lean chicken breast for lunch, back to gym after work, then off to save the whales or do performance art or build a giant fishmobile for Burning Man. And those were the minor functionaries, the walls of flesh deployed to fill up space in meetings, the men and women whose only role was to stand between the rest of us and answers.

I heard the roar of a motorcycle coming up behind me, but didn't turn around. The reanimates didn't look up or past my shoulder, not until the very last moment. Then I saw it, or thought I did. Not the baring of teeth and the wild lurching, no jerk stepping or feral glare, but fear. Eyes wide, mouths agape, a shiver from one, arms up from another, and then the motorcycle tore past and from the sidecar a man in black leather threw a pair of Molotov cocktails, one at a reanimate, the other at the carcass of the bus. And the dead howled and screamed and stumbled and thrashed into the flames. I ran onto the sidewalk and stepped up onto the hill proper. The reanimates on the hill had turned to watch the flames.

It was hard to tell the living from the dead. Only the living drank, but other than that, I wandered the valley of *Das Unheimliche*. Were the reanimates slowly learning how to learn, were their emotions and feelings chained to the walls of the rotting cages of their brains? Or was I just shellshocked and confused?

My apartment building was uninhabitable, but there was still plenty of real estate going spare in the Mission. I missed my books, but whenever I tried to read a paper or a zine I couldn't focus my eyes. I couldn't sleep either, not at all, which was hard because great swaths of the city were entirely without power. In my neighborhood, only trash can fires lit the streets, but the bars stayed open. I drank by candlelight shoulder-to-shoulder with the other ash-soaked survivors. For once I didn't get grief for being a driller, though I don't remember ever taking out my drill at all during those dark weeks. The case was a passport.

I drilled a couple. They were young. I don't remember how I got the call, or if I did, but they were living in Golden Gate Park, on the eastern end in a mews off Stanyan Street. They'd salvaged a nice tent, or maybe even had just owned one in the old days, and they must have made enough friends to go unmolested. I saw a light on, but no silhouettes.

"No wonder they mistake marsh fires for light, or when they find a light believe that it is the only one," I said to myself. It was courage, as Bernard DeVoto had said about the supporters of inappropriate cocktails. Like Manhattans. Ah, Manhattan, the city I'd truly wanted to live in, but never could. The pair were dead on either side of a kerosene lamp. I was at my most efficient. It was eerie—for a moment I wondered if they were the first dead to stay dead. Should I have waited to find out? Of course not. Too many marks did that already; the lucky ones had been consumed so thoroughly they only existed as the subjects of poorly sourced rumors. *How do you* know *that's how Jimmy died? Just because you never saw him again?*

I saw Alexa again, but she didn't speak of her plan to infiltrate City Hall. Not with all the tents set up in the United Nations Plaza and that crazy park with all the artificial trees right in front of City Hall. She said instead—and this is strange; as I write, I cannot picture where we are at all, but I imagine her standing before a foggy black and white street in a film noir—that she was sad and that she knew that the world was really near its end.

"Do you know, Billy," she said, "did you even notice at all, that we don't have a name for the earthquake that just happened? Not the Hayward Fault Quake, or The Big One, or Five-Fifteen or M-Fifteen or whatever little dating nomenclature we've all been using for more than a decade. There's no more mass media, so no more instant mass language—"

"And that's a bad thing?"

"It's history, it's important. You're not going to give me one of those San Francisco, 'We don't need The System anymore' lines of bullshit. Big deal, CNN got to name disasters. Manufacturing slogans to manufacture consent, but at least we all had something to agree on. The way the world worked is better than the way it doesn't."

"History's written by the winners," I said, "and there ain't any winners anymore, so it's the end of history. Welcome to it."

My mouth tasted of whisky; Teacher's or some other blended shit. Was there a bottle weighing down one of the pockets of my overcoat? Alexa was wearing a business blazer of some sort with lapels that could carry her to Angel Island if she jumped off the pier. I took hold of one. It just felt important. "I haven't slept, or don't think I have, in days. How did I even get out of Schroeder's?"

"I don't know—I came to outside. We were pulled out; the building didn't collapse or anything. The Financial District is still in pretty good shape. You were long gone by the time I was on my feet."

"Could it have been...a reanimate? That pulled us to safety, that is?" I asked. I told her about the bus and the faces I'd seen, and the other things too that I had forgotten till then. The reanimate I stalked for three blocks, because I noticed it waited for the light to change at the crosswalk. Rubble that had been removed so quickly and then piled in the plazas at the old BART stations on 16th and 24th Street in my neighborhood— there weren't even enough people left in the Mission to move the tons of concrete and steel, much less to fill the multi-story escalator and staircase wells with the stuff. The dead had to have had a hand in it.

"They're regaining their consciousnesses, somehow. Maybe just the most recently reanimated, maybe because we're still challenging them, so they have to evolve here even if everywhere else in America they're just a shambling and slavering horde. They're going to *win*," I told her, "because they're getting smarter." Alexa pulled herself out of my grip. "Soon they'll be able to blend in, maybe even talk!"

"Oh, don't start," Alexa said. "And you said I was credulous when I showed you my files. You're just a hupper." Hysterical uncanny perceptions—HUP. Lots of people saw a glimmer of recognition or experienced a moment of confusion when faced with a reanimate, especially when it wore the body of a relative or friend. It also happened when men were confronted by the moving body of a woman, or when women encountered dead children or teens with wide eyes and high growls. It wasn't a real disorder or psychological thing, just a three-letter acronym coined in some broadsheet or website somewhere that took off because it still happened every day somewhere or other, because humans were hardwired to try to find a spark of life somewhere in the dead. It used to keep us sane, that impulse, now it was very strongly selected against by evolution. God, we were all dying. I knew there was something different about what I had seen, though.

"I'm not a hupper. You need to have had a relationship with the reanimate, of some sort, to be a hupper. I'm a student of human nature, a trained observer. A driller. I've seen a thousand faces—"

"And you rocked 'em all?" Alexa laughed at her own joke, a harsh sea lion bark. She must have been drunk too, but I don't remember buying her a drink or passing her my bottle. My bottle, yes, of course. I dug out the Teacher's and took a long swig. Alexa went on. "You haven't bathed in days. You've been out all night, every night, probably. HUP and alcohol-induced delirium. It's a disease of the night, you know? Delirium is a disease of the night," she repeated. Then she smirked and told me she could quote from fancy books, too, but I couldn't place her reference.

"And why," I asked, "does the sandman always appear as a disturber of love? Freud!" I was so excited I dropped the bottle and it shattered. I don't remember anything else of that night;

I know my memory is at least somewhat accurate as my pants smelled like Teacher's for a few days after that and every time I stole away to a secret place to disrobe and take the pants leg to my nose, I remembered something else about what I had wanted to tell Alexa.

I wanted to tell Alexa about the moment I first felt like a normal person, a person inside someone else's point of view, in the center of things. I had a habit, ever since I was a kid, of saying to myself *This moment I'll remember forever.* Naturally, I rarely remembered the actual moments, or what I had been thinking about just before making my little declaration. One time in the dark backseat of my father's car, full of cigarette smoke coming in from the front, I was in a scratchy blue suit— Easter? Some cousin's christening? Were we returning from a visit to a great-aunt who only spoke Greek and pinched my cheeks and cut me slices of halva? Another time I remember it being so hot that the acrylic carpeting I was lying on top of, in front of the TV, smelled like it was about to break down into its component chemicals. But dozens of other times, dozens of solemn vows that this or that moment was something I'd remember forever, I forgot most all of them.

I got to Boston only a couple of months after Yvette. The  MFA programs had long since made their decisions, so all I could do was sign up for a certificate program at Emerson. I was going to get a Literary Publishing Certificate. Even then I knew it sounded extremely fucking ridiculous, and I laughed every time those three words marched out my mouth, all in a foolish little row. My mother wept for three days, then told me that I couldn't have any money. My father did slip me five hundred dollars in wrinkly twenties and told me I could call if I needed more.

"For food," he said, "only for food." He made jokes about me meeting Mike Dukakis and told me not to drink the water in Boston.

I found a room in Somerville the easy way—scanning copies of the *Globe* till I found an ad for housing with a Greek surname. Papatheofanis, that suited me. Then I called and said *Vasilis Kostopolos* properly with no American accent, and dropped the other few Greek words I knew. I wasn't going to Emerson or to college, but to *skolio* and would love to see their *spiti.* It worked. I sold the car for two months' rent and was otherwise stupid—I thought I'd write a short story a week, just like Ray Bradbury, and sell them for money. More than fifty dollars too, I promised myself. *I'll even write gay porn if I have to*, I promised myself. The room didn't allow a hot plate, but I packed one anyway.

"Writers are desperate people and when they stop being desperate they stop being writers," Charles Bukowski once said. He probably said it more than once. I was desperate in Boston, but I wasn't really a writer. I guess Bukowski's little aphorism isn't commutative—desperation doesn't make the writer. I was desperate for Yvette, and also desperate not to seem desperate. We were in different workshops at school. I would trail her around the city, hoping to be nonchalantly discovered by the right shelf at Commonwealth Books, or just happening to be attending the right film in Kendall Square's fancy arthouse theater, or in line at the Abbey Lounge. Abbey Lounge, that was the death of me. Yvette had a little page on MySpace, and on it mentioned wanting to go see Lyres—a pretty famous local band that never got anywhere but old. The vocalist/keyboardist was notorious for playing with only one hand. I decided I'd go as well.

Yvette wasn't talking to me much, really. She wasn't all that polyamorous either, so far as I could tell. She was seeing a guy named Colin. He was short where I was tall, as fair as I was dark, local and loaded rather than Midwestern and broke like myself. He wore suit jackets with patches on the elbows, like he was seventy years old. His wardrobe had belonged to his grandfather, who had a men's room at Harvard named after him or somesuch, but Colin still felt oppressed by the specter of white Protestantism that haunted "the Square." You know that line Gore Vidal supposedly leveled at Dominick Dunne at the sort of party I'd be able to attend only if my uncle Stelyo was catering the thing:

"Why do you suppose Irish Catholics are all such social climbers? Is it because their mothers were all maids? Oh, I don't mean you." For Colin, that was all of American society laid bare, its seminal racism on display.

I know all this because Colin turned out to be the nicest guy on the planet. I saw Yvette in the pile outside the Abbey Lounge. To call it a line would be an insult to Euclid. She smiled at me; her brown eyes widened. She looked authentically happy to see me, after several weeks of hugging herself when we spoke, of keeping three feet between us in the halls at Emerson.

"Billy! How great!" Yvette said. "The Lyres are supposed to be awesome."

Colin materialized next to her with a quick correction. "Lyres, not The Lyres." And then they kissed, hard. Yvette was the initiator, actually. She threw her arms around his thick neck and pulled herself to him, her tongue out of her mouth before even making contact with his lips. She kissed with her eyes closed, but Colin kept his open. He was looking right at me, suddenly aware that he was a pawn in some asinine game. Yvette's enthusiasm seemed authentic enough; she broke away from the kiss at the right time. Colin looked like he was about to die of embarrassment. I stood there watching, a giant pervert. Had she gone down on him right on the pavement I wouldn't have been less entranced. All the little things she did with her kisses with me—the hard squint, the sucking on his tongue in her mouth—she did with him too. Yes, I was watching that closely. All three of us went in, and I headed straight to the bar.

I drank, of course. I'm from Ohio, of course I drank; in the 7-Eleven parking lot, while someone else's car stereo blasted "Sweet Emotion"; with my folks, slurping down sweet Greek wine my father pressed himself and fermented in big clear carboys; on my twenty-first birthday, thrilled to be legal and ready to try everything in the bar in alphabetical order. Alabama Slammer. Bourbon, neat. Collins, comma Tom. The bartender even snorted at my little joke. But that night at Abbey Lounge, I really drank. Not to forget, but to remember forever that ineffable mix of betrayal and hunger I felt. The bar felt good under my elbows. I slouched like the guys I'd seen muttering to themselves and flexing their fingers around longnecks in the bars of Youngstown. That's when I decided—I'd be one of those guys, a guy with a wound that could never, ever heal. I drank till I liked the taste of the cheapest beer they had. The band went on, but it was all just high-pitched buzzing to me.

What did I want? Yvette to sidle up next to me, put a hand on my shoulder, lean in close and tell me simply and succinctly what a total loser I was? Then I'd be satisfied. I could saunter up to Colin and have him beat the shit out of me. He looked like one of those slummers who pretended that being Irish in the Boston area still meant something; maybe he took boxing lessons. He could break my nose. I'd wake up stretched across three plastic chairs in an emergency room. Some billionaire resident from Harvard medical school could give my schnozz a nice clean jerk and snap it back into place. I'd be happy again.

But that didn't happen. The Abbey Lounge was a two-room club—the bar in one, the bandstand in the other. There was a window cut into the drywall, so it was easy enough to see Yvette and Colin bopping their heads along with the music, along with everyone else. It was like an assembly line, and I was the drunk peering in from the other side of the factory gates, wanting in yet knowing I couldn't ever hack a day job. My hands began to shake. I wanted to smash a beer bottle over my own head, be a riot. I knew I had to say something, to confront Yvette. I took a step forward. My tongue felt hollow.

I woke up in Somerville, on the saggy couch that some Tufts girl had left behind a few weeks prior. It smelled terrible. It always had, but I was sure I'd soiled myself. Now it was my limbs that felt hollow. Then the thing I'd always remember— Colin was sitting on the edge of the milk crate and balsa wood coffee table, looking concerned. He had moved some of my books onto the floor so he'd have a place to sit.

My mouth opened and an exhalation fell out. This was the first time of so many I'd wake up on my couch, or some couch anyway, not quite sure how I'd gotten home or who helped me out of my clothes, or how long it had been since booze last hit belly, and it sure wouldn't be the last. You never forget your first, not ever. After a while, you start to crave it. It's like teleportation—blink your eyes, and you're home. Or like being a baby again. Someone carries you where you need to be.

"'A woman should be an illusion,'" I told him.

He looked around, eyes suddenly everywhere. "Henry Miller?" he guessed. I didn't have the heart or mind to tell him Ian Fleming, so I just pretended I made it up myself.

Colin brought me soup. He cleaned up the room a bit. The bathroom was suddenly spotless. He was the nicest guy in the world, really. For a long moment I even contemplated bisexuality—my own, not his. No wonder Yvette wanted to crawl into his mouth and set up housekeeping by his molars back at the Abbey Lounge. How else could she tell me that it's over? I wouldn't have believed that she really did find someone better in every way. So much better that even I couldn't stay mad at him. I could only stay mad at myself, and I have, forever.

Colin and I actually started hanging out. He never said anything about my drinking, which I guess was fueled by his presence in those early days. I still wanted to punch him, then maybe flip Yvette up on the bar of wherever we were hanging out and wale on her ass with my belt, just like the abusive redneck fathers in half the stories we had to read for our workshops. It was a fashion for a few months, actually. A competition. Each class the fathers in the stories would get drunker and more violent—spankings turned to strappings turned to crude fingering. Finally, in one of the stories where the girl character died, the professor declared the story "genre fiction, horror really," and the workshop reset itself.

I mostly saw Yvette over Colin's shoulder when the three of us would go out. Women were always a mystery to me; that was my problem. My problem with her, with myself and the great idea I had to drag myself halfway across the country to live in a bedsit half the size of my room at home, and with the nonsense I tried to write for class. How sad and pathetic I must have looked, tagging along with them all over town, like a foreign cousin already bored with America. They didn't even bother trying to set me up with any friends. Yvette knew it would be a waste of time, and Colin's friends would find me utterly inexplicable.

"What do you *mean*, you don't go sailing every summer," they'd say through congenitally clenched teeth. "Surely you do. You're just being contrary."

Colin also rolled his eyes when I did that impression. So I was the third wheel, the date-ender. When I passed out, it was time for everyone to go home.

But Yvette wasn't a mystery anymore. She was just one cute girl in a city full of them, who had a ready smile and enough quirks to make her seem attainable. Every girl likes to think she cleans up well, likes to think she gives a great blowjob. What other kind of feedback are they going to get from the free market of men, anyway? The only reason I thought she was special was because she had once liked me, and I hated me.

Drinking became a problem pretty quickly. Even as I write these words, on some level I am still aware that I have a problem. I keep drinking because there's no reason to even contemplate stopping anymore. The world is ending because America has ended. My marginal Greek might fly in overcrowded, broiling, desiccated Athens, but I have no way to get there. They say that one can kick alcohol only after it becomes a bigger issue than everything else in one's life, but that will never ever happen. The times have caught up with me. But the little core of my interest in drinking is just what I said—Yvette used to like me. Colin, for whatever reason, was breathtakingly nice to me. Every day I'd wake up in my dumpy little twin bed in a shoebox-sized room in a town I hated, away from my parents and my few friends, and want to split open my own sternum, dig my fingers into my chest, and yank my black heart from my body and throw it against the wall.

I made it through the semester. It got so cold, so quickly, in Boston. There's a bite to the city that we don't get in Ohio. Another reason to stay in a bar till closing time. The walls in my little room were paper-thin. I didn't love alcohol at first. I could nurse a whisky for hours. But then I started to crave it. The way whisky filled the sinuses. The candy flavor of cheap wines. Martinis that taste so weak on the tongue, but leave the stomach bruised. I was punching myself, and like anything a person does often enough, I got used to it. Got to like it. And writers drank. They didn't drink as much as tyros and wannabes, but they *did* drink. I was going to drink myself into torpor, into genius. Colin would often drink with me, even if Yvette was off somewhere else. Once, he asked me about her.

"Why do you care so much?" he said. "This is friggin' Boston. You can whip out your dick and trawl the streets for women just by being here, young, and able to speak decent English."

"Is that your drinky-poo talking, Colin," I asked, "or are you *practicing* slumming so you'll get good at it?"

"I'm working on a story."

"Is it about a Harvard guy who slums in the bars of Somerville, picking on proletarian Midwestern ethnic types?"

"It's about a proletarian Midwestern ethnic type," he admitted.

"You're buying this next round," I told him. "WASP tax." I whipped up a theory on the spot; I'm sure it's full of holes. "Lots of people out in Ohio, or wherever, just marry the first girl who's nice to them—"

"So 'girls' aren't people?" Colin interrupted. He even flicked his fingers to make visual quotation marks around the word *girls*. I just went on. Colin was obviously just engaging in reflexive critique anyway.

"One handjob under the bleachers; one flash of leg, and painted nails, and pink cotton panties from under an oversized OSU sweatshirt, that's all it takes. We're hooked, see? Because men drink with men, and women only drink at parties. There's an artificial pussy scarcity in the Midwest. The old 1950s morality is gone, but the supply of vagina hasn't increased. Withholding sex is just a mercenary thing. That, and being gay is still looked down upon, so . . ." I just trailed off there. I forgot what I was thinking. The whisky was heavy on my tongue. "Why are you even writing a story?"

"Yvette is always talking about her workshop, about her stories, about you—"

"Me?"

"Well," he said. "Yes." Colin often said *Yes* rather than *Yeah*. One of those class markers he was given to subtly displaying whenever he got the chance. "She thinks you'll make something of yourself one day." There was a lot to unpack there. Yvette didn't think I was anything now. Colin apparently agreed. She thought that might change in the future, and was comfortable enough to share this insight with Colin. And that Colin was jealous of me, and needed to share his jealousy with me, likely in the hope that I would start sweating, lick my lips, blush so hard I'd nearly pass out, and decide that no, no, I won't ever make something of my fucking self. And that's what happened. I stormed out of the place, into the cold of a Somerville December. I bought myself three 1.75 liter bottles of vodka, locked myself in my room, and decided that I'd have myself a merry little Christmas all on my lonesome, all on my loathsome. Let Colin win. He can have her. He won't ever marry her or anything; the Boston Brahmins do arranged marriages, to keep the money in one place and the kids bright-eyed and bucket-chinned. He'll get bored with her soon enough. Then I wouldn't have to make anything of myself, prove anything to anyone. I drank till I pissed the bed. It kept me warm, at first.

"Hurhm," Alexa said. She rolled her tongue around her teeth whenever she said it.

We'd run into one another again, in a boxcar crowded with freight, and a few passengers, headed up to Berkeley. BART service has been permanently discontinued, the ferries had all sunk thanks to an ill-conceptualized takeover by enthusiastic Burning Man types who had no idea how to pilot them, and too much of the Bay Bridge had collapsed thanks to sub-par Chinese bolts, so a repurposed freight train using the CalTrain tracks down to Santa Clara and then Union Pacific tracks back north was the best way to get over to the East Bay. We were going to a party by the new fissure that had opened up near the Cal campus. The school itself was no longer a state university, but had become a weird collective of intellectuals and hackers, bringing it into harmony with the rest of town. The reanimated dead roamed the hills and took over most of the south part of the city, where Berkeley  bordered Oakland. But the college was in okay shape. Unfortunately, the freight line's Berkeley stop is on 3rd Street, about a mile and a half from the edge of campus. So we had baseball bats, issued by the jovially named One-Way Dead-End Transport Cooperative. Alexa rolled hers over in her hands. She had a pistol-grip shotgun too, strapped across her back like a girl in a movie. Her wifebeater T-shirt was almost supernaturally white though, not gray and stained to match the sweat on her biceps. I sweated enough for the two of us.

"Don't hurhm me," I said.

"Well, I didn't think you were the type to come out to the East Bay," she said.

"Free booze."

"There's plenty of free booze in the city, if you know where to look."

"And if you get invited. Drillers tend not to be. Especially when they actually stick with the job for more than two days."

"Really? Is that it?" Alexa giggled at herself. "Man, it's like I can't believe a word you say. I'm so suspicious!"

"Yesss." I hiss sometimes, especially when it's hot and I'm thirsty.

"They don't want to be reminded?"

"They don't want to hear our detailed anecdotes about drilling the dead."

"Well, I don't either."

"So, let's be sure to stay at least fifty feet away from one another during the party," I said. The exact opposite of what I wanted to say. Even as the sentence left my mouth, I thought of saying, *Well, in your company, I wouldn't grow maudlin* and wanted to stab myself in the belly for not saying it. And for even thinking a phrase like "grow maudlin."

Alexa didn't say anything.

"What?" I said.

She set her jaw. The bat in her hands was still. She looked out through the slit we were standing near at the ruins of the neighborhood passing by.

"I was just joking. I'm happy to see you. It's a great coincidence. This is my first time here. Even before the big zombie apocalypse, I never made it out to the East Bay. Weren't you living here?"

"I was supposed to. And it's not a coincidence." She poked with the thick rounded end of her bat. The aluminum was hot. We were all sweating. "I've been trying to track you down for days."

"So, you're a stalker, eh?" That almost sounded promising. Alexa looked good, armed and sweaty.

She leaned in close and said, "City Hall. Remember?" I turned to look out the slit. "Here comes the stop," I said.

There comes a time between a man and a woman when the man can cut loose with no regrets. As I'd already had sex with her, which apparently made her comfortable enough with me to demonstrate some severe mental issues, the time was now. But I was never one for doing something just to avoid regrets, or to cut a girl loose. I let them do it, after long seasons of sucking every bit of affection and attraction from their spines. Even at the fork of the road, where I can see the road less traveled, the one normal people take, I can't help myself. I took Alexa's hand, and squeezed it hard.

"Let's go." The problem is that the normal people are all dead. I don't know what I do that helps me to survive, but I decided that I'd better keep doing it.

The walk across Berkeley was fairly uneventful at first. University Avenue was the usual row of low storefronts, windows smashed, goods torn to shreds or rotting. We all spread out, us party-goers; couples mostly, taking one block at a time, partially to keep the noise down in case any revenants were about, and partially because the boxcar had been pretty tight. Alexa was anxious, so we took the vanguard. She handed me her baseball bat; it felt ridiculous to carry two of them. We were in sight of the campus, which loomed over the street on a dark hill at the end of the avenue, when they jumped out at us, howling and screaming.

Alexa was quick with the shotgun. It was off her back and balanced against her hip in a flash.

"Wait!" I shouted. I dropped both ball bats and slammed into her. The gun roared and lit up the night. Then the kid she aimed at spun around and shrieked, much of his arm disintegrating into meat.

The others stumbled away hands up, quickly articulating, "Don't shoot! We were just messing around! We're human, we're alive!" Their friend moaned in his fresh puddle on the sidewalk.

"What the fuck!" Alexa shouted. It wasn't a question, but she repeated it when she didn't get an answer. "What the fuck, what the fuck!" She didn't drop the gun, but she did stagger and nearly fall to one knee. I retrieved the bats.

There must have been eight of them, all white kids. Older than teens, dirty like the slumming homeless punk rock kids. With a glance, I saw that the rest of the boxcar crowd had vanished off onto the side streets or empty buildings or just ran back to wait for the returning train, having been scared away from the idea of free Berkeley booze. I stepped in front of Alexa and brandished both bats. Someone giggled, so I dropped the one in my left hand and hefted the other, ready to swing.

"What the hell is wrong with you all! When the fuck did jumping out at people become a good fucking idea? Especially armed people!"

"Hey man…" one of them said, but he ended the sentence with a confused shrug and a look at his bleeding friend. They all wanted to run on their skinny legs, dreadlocks and nearly visible clouds of stink waving in the breeze, but they stayed, loyal to the kid moaning on the sidewalk.

"I totally bruised my hip. Jesus fucking Christ," Alexa said, an open letter to us all. She raised the gun again, nearly stumbled, then pointed the barrel at the sidewalk. "Are you guys here for the party?" she asked.

"Can we please—?" one thick kid, who I suddenly realized was a girl, said. She nodded toward the wounded one. She had some kind of fabric ready, spilling out of an old military-issue bag of some sort.

"Yeah, do," I said. She ran to comfort the kid, wash his wounds with the boozy contents of a canteen, bind them with torn sheets. The kid was awake, sweating. The moon was big and low. I walked up to her and snatched the canteen from her hand, took a swig. Didn't recognize it.

"Homebrew stuff."

"Yeah," she said. She had a pudgy face, plastic glasses, and a big dirty hand outstretched. She took back the canteen and helped herself to a swig.

"I said," Alexa said, "are you here for the party?" She had the gun leveled at two guys, including the shrugger. The others must have run off.

"We live here," the shrugger said. "They don't let us on campus."

"But we manage to sneak in all the time," the other added. That one was tall and thin. I thought he was just another dirty white kid at first, but he had the slightest sing-song Mexican accent..Maybe he was mixed, or had an immigrant parent.

"Names?"

"Thunder," the girl said. I just laughed at her. Poor thing must have been named after her thighs by her cruel crustypunk boyfriends. But then the others topped her.

"Spaz," the shrugger said.

"Man-o," said the Mexican-seeming kid.

And then the wounded kid gurgled a bit and said, "Louis… uhm, Magpie."

"Listen, we were just messing with you," Spaz said. "It's safe around here. Cal takes care of everything." He meant UC Berkeley, of course, but it sounded like an individual. Cal, a mean hombre who eats zombies for breakfast and shits vegan burritos for brunch.

"Will they take care of him?" I asked, pointing to Magpie with the tip of my baseball bat.

Alexa stiffened up, though she still winced when she moved. "This is ridiculous. He jumped out right in front of us. It's not like he couldn't see my gun."

"You're pretty cold-blooded," Thunder snapped. Alexa muttered something along the lines of *fucking Berkeley*. "Thank *you*," Thunder said directly to me. "I saw what you did. That's why he's not already dead." That's when I realized she was the leader of the crew, not any of the guys.

"You do a good job keeping these guys alive off-campus, eh?"

Thunder frowned down at Magpie, then shifted on her knees. Her fat jeans were sticky from the blood she was kneeling in. "Until fucking now I did," she said. Then, "Jesus."

"May I be excused to get a cart?" Man-o said. "It's a shopping cart with an end cut out. We can put him in and get him to campus sooner." He addressed the gun pointed at him, not the woman pointing it.

"Go," I said, before Alexa could say anything. He hustled off.

"Do you think he'll be back?" I asked Thunder.

Alexa answered, "Doesn't matter. We're leaving now. It's not like they need us to get to Cal."

"But wait—"

"Go," Thunder said. "You've done enough already."

"Not nearly enough. There's a world to save," Alexa said. Her voice was steel all of a sudden.

"'You begin saving the world by saving one man at a time,'" I said. "'All else is grandiose romanticism or politics.'"

From the ground, Magpie, weak but enthusiastic, said, "Hey, that's Bukowski." And then Man-o reappeared, with a dirty shopping cart lined with somewhat clean-looking towels. Alexa tugged on my arm.

"What?"

Her eyes blazed. Through clenched teeth she said, "Come. On." She sounded like my mother, like every angry Greek woman I'd ever met. The old shriekers at church, the fist-shakers on the city bus, the table-pounders and hair-pullers and catfighters. Greek girls are a sheet of skin and hair draped over a bonfire. She had her bat in hand again. Alexa had come to some kind of decision, and my choices were comply or join Magpie on the asphalt.

"Walk!" she said, like a cop. We walked. The kids loaded Magpie up; there was some wailing.

Alexa limped a little bit, but held herself erect. The kids didn't seem to care about making noise or attracting revenants at all. Magpie was probably dying, and not because he was bleeding, but because he was a dirty, undernourished teenager who was bleeding. Would Alexa be upset if he died? Would she blame him, or me, with all the intensity and righteousness of a President launching a war, or my father railing at the television? Probably.

I decided to daydream about the party instead. Nobody ever comes to Berkeley from San Francisco if they could help it, and it was always easy for me to help it, even before the country collapsed. So I suppose I imagined a lot of tie-dye and girls with hairy armpits and jazz-listening longhairs with crazy pipes and tweed jackets. And lots of Asian kids.

I was all wrong. The party was held in the midst of a collection of shattered eucalyptus trees. They're not local to California. Some genius brought them over years ago to turn them into railroad tracks, but the eucalyptus wood is too soft for spikes. An invasive species without local predators, the trees spread pretty rapidly. Except for the occasional joke about air-dropping in koalas to strip the leaves, nobody ever looks at the trees and sees anything but California's "natural" environment. In that, the mighty eucalyptus tree is much like the living dead.

The party wasn't much of one. We doubled the size of it when we rolled in, and that's without anyone else from the train following us. They were probably all running down side streets and tripping over revenant nests. No screams in the distance though. It was a quiet party too, with all of eight people, dressed identically in orange jumpsuits. They all rocked the same slick haircuts too, gelled with sharp *sharp* parts; sort of like a New Wave band, or Bowie, from some era I'm not familiar with. A number of tree trunks had battery-powered lights attached to them—big round ones that for all their size didn't give off that much light. They were the kind of thing you used to be able to find in chintzy stores full of off-brand and as-seen-on-TV crap. Grandmothers had them in closets and vestibules. The fissure from the quake didn't look like I'd imagined—not a cartoon crack in the earth, glowing red from deep magma and steaming with hideous sulfurous gases. It was pretty much just a new curb in the grass, or a shelf. There were some few puffs of steam coming up from the ground, but it could have just been busted pipes or something.

I also noticed a table full of snacks. No drinks. No wine bottles, no cooler, nothing. Just crooked homemade pies and pots of green stuff and roughly piled chips.

Thunder pushed past us, even shouldering Alexa out of the way, and called out, "Hey, we need help! This bitch," she said, hiking a thumb over at Alexa, who literally *growled* at that, "shot Magpie." She said it like the partiers knew who the hell Magpie was supposed to be. They probably did. The whole Bay Area is just a small town, now. My mouth felt so dry. I tried to remember if we'd passed a liquor store on the way. But a very burnt out storefront in my mind's eye looked like it could have once been a liquor store to me. I didn't bring anything with me. I never do. I'd discovered long ago that when I go to get some wine to bring to a party or some girl's apartment, the bottle never made it there, and even I was only a fifty-fifty shot.

The Bowies rushed to take care of Magpie. I heard the death rattle in his throat. It was a quiet thing, a gurgle under gurgles, but I'd heard enough of them to know when some divine spark has finally sputtered and blackened. The last dregs of wine and gin from earlier in the day teased the back of my throat, my sinuses. The Bowies pushed Magpie's cart over to one of the little vents in the ground that was puffing steam. I vaguely wondered if I should do something. I didn't have my drill, and Berkeley isn't part of the City and County of San Francisco so I wasn't going to get paid, but didn't off-duty cops often intervene when coming across a robbery back in the old days? I looked at Alexa, whose own gaze followed the Bowies as they set the cart over the steam.

She noticed me looking and said, "They think the revenants come from some formerly dormant bacteria."

"God, this is going to be one of those parties, isn't it?" I said. Alexa made a face.

Thunder stepped between us, her eyes slick with tears. "Can you…" she looked at me, then at Alexa, and specifically her shotgun. "…you know?"

Alexa didn't. She hugged Thunder instead, tightly. Thunder put one arm around Alexa, like a confused man might, and shared a grimace with her two filthy comrades. They stood around uselessly. Then they all started looking at me. I wished I could run off into the woods, though there were really no woods around. The little eucalyptus grove was plopped down in the middle of campus, and the ruined city beyond it.

Spaz finally spoke. "So, what's supposed to happen? Is he gonna wake up and kill us all sooner, or later, or never?"

"That's what we're trying to determine," one of the Bowies said. The others had arrayed themselves around us, casually pretending to chat in pairs by this or that favorite tree or puff of steam. It was all transparent bullshit. How would they know we'd bring a fatally injured person to the party? Clearly, they were planning on somehow killing whoever came, and experimenting on their corpses. Forget about poor dead Magpie. Let him rise up, let him eat his fill of all of us. My head was throbbing. The Bowies, I decided, where the ones who needed to die. I started measuring them up, the way an old streetfighter once told me to. That guy was a prime juicer, arms and legs like rebar, and he loved to shove his tongue through the gap left by his missing front teeth at any woman who walked in. He told me to watch for posture:

"Good posture is bad." Badasses knew how to carry themselves. They wore good shoes; bad ones often split during brawls. Real fighters were relaxed.

"In a situation," he said, doing what they'd do, "they just tuck their chin, put their hands up, and are ready to go. First punch, motherfucker," he'd said. Then he jabbed expertly at the air, and sat back down. He gave that little lecture, or a variation on it, whenever I saw him. He coulda been a contender in his prime, I'm sure.

None of the Bowies looked all that tough. Their glacial art-rock facades had all melted into art-project anxiety as they undid Magpie's multiple layers of clothing. One of the Bowies, shorter than the rest and a little stockier, made eye contact with me. He muttered something I didn't hear, then trotted up to me.

"C'mon," he said without stopping, "I need your help."

Alexa's eyes pleaded something like, *Don't be a fuck-up, just go with him,* so I did.

A few seconds later we were out of sight of the party. The baseball bat felt so good in my hands. One down, seven to go maybe? But the short guy stopped and turned and put a hand on my chest.

"Hey there," he said. He had an accent. A squeaky New York accent; he was a little rat face from Queens. And my salvation. "You gotta help me with this," he said as he unzipped a few inches of jumpsuit and stuck his hand inside. Maybe I wouldn't need the bat. He didn't have his hands up, he wasn't calm and relaxed. I was a foot taller. His chin pointed up at me like he was a little kid marveling at a freakish circus giant. And it wasn't a gun he withdrew from the interior pocket of his suit, though at this point I hardly would have minded, but was the most glorious object in all the world. A flask, and a fancy one at that; round, with a steel shot glass inset. Less booze that way, but classy, pure class. Ah yes, drinkers know drinkers, and drinkers hate to drink alone. Especially not with dead bodies nearby. He flipped the top, poured himself a shot, then slammed it.

"There, now you know it ain't poisoned," he said, though his voice was raspy enough that I wasn't actually entirely convinced. He handed me the flask. "It's a faggy little bottle, ain't it? I was married once, ya know. Father-in-law gave it to me. Had to put my own wife down."

Whatever was in the flask was a lemony homebrew. Neither sweet nor girly; it bit like a small animal. The poor bastard probably just found some rotten Meyer lemons at the base of a tree in an abandoned backyard and made the best of it. It filled my ears and drowned out Ratso's story about the be-yoot-ee-ful girl he met while mopping floors in Atlantic City. The one who wanted to move out to Reno to get away from her crazy family, and spin the roulette wheel, and when the shit hit the fan they took another gamble and managed to claw their way into San Francisco. Then she managed to plant her foot atop a rusty nail and died right away and so he killed her. He came out to Berkeley hoping to be torn apart by the living dead who roam the center of town in the shadow of the Berkeley Hills—the coyote and wild turkeys own those lands again—and instead he ended up wrapped up with the Bowies and their mad scientist experiments.

"I was a vet tech, see?" he was saying as I floated back to the surface. The lemon rot was warm in my stomach, already filling all my booze-hungry cells. Juicers know juicers. The problem is that this guy was the type of juicer who liked to talk to others when he drank; I'm the type of juicer who prefers to drink and just talk. Good thing we had booze in common.

He continued, "So I had a good job out here. I know the campus like the back of my hand. I knew that other people would have the same idea, and then I met this crew. They're real scientists, see. *Real* scientists. Not like me. I just clean cages, dissect mice, you know…"

Lots of juicers, kooks, and imaginary CIA radio transmission recipients believed in the *real* scientists. I did too, half the time. The *real* scientists are the ones who knew what the hell happened when the dead began to rise, and failed to warn humanity for their own purposes—say, because most scientists are hideous foreigners out to destroy America somehow. That's the soft version. The hard version is that the scientists, evil foreigners and fifth columnists all, used some sort of virus to create a change in the infected. Or maybe it was plastics, some peculiarly American form of Tupperware illegal in Canada and unaffordable in Mexico, adding methyl groups to the national DNA, rotting the dopaminergic neurons, and giving us all a very virulent form of posthumous Parkinson's disease. The usual contingent partial story, like all the grand narratives of humanity and theories of history. I did take it seriously, only because I heard some variation on it whenever someone else was buying the drinks. Always sounded more like the real *industrialists* to me, rather than the *real* scientists, but I try not to argue when someone else is buying.

"I mean the *real real* scientists," Ratso McGee—he handn't introduced himself, so I gave him a name—said. "The ones looking for a cure."

I just laughed. I spilled some of the lemony booze. The real real scientists were the biggest purveyors of bullshit left in the United States. They raised money, and then later traded goods, going door to door. They had plans. Flyers and websites explaining the need to weaponize some Winnebagos and make a run for the border. Tales of tanker ships turned research labs, and zombies chained deep in blood-splattered holds. When I was a kid, our next-door neighbors were this family called the Knowleses. The Knowles girls were blonde-haired cuties, a few years older than me, and their mother was an evangelical Christian of an especially gullible type. She hoarded food when Y2K was coming around—but had no interest in buying one of my typewriters, because she "had all the writing anyone would need" in the Bible already. One of the girls, Joanne or something like that, told me that one time her mother had handed over the family vacation fund to two ersatz archaeologists who came to church one Sunday to raise funds to go to Turkey and dig up Noah's Ark from where it rested deep within Mount Ararat. Not that Joanne knew what the word ersatz meant, even after I told her—she'd just told me that the pair were archaeologists. Like Ratso telling me know that the Bowies were the real real scientists.

Ratso read my expression. He made a fist and pumped an enormous, if imaginary, dick down by his waist. "I know,

I know, but these guys really have something going on. Your little pal hasn't woken up yet, has he?"

"No…but, it can take more than thirty minutes for a corpse to revenate," I said. For a moment, I thought about telling him that I was a driller. That I saw two people in a tent in Golden Gate park and used my discretion to put holes in their heads. When I drink I can never quite tell how forthcoming I should be with my experiences. "Well, I mean, you know. In the city we end up with a lot of dead people."

Ratso snorted. "In the city, *you do*, eh? You're in the East Bay now, ol' buddy ol' pal. You should go take a stroll down to the border with Oakland and see what we had to do to keep those dead niggers out." I suddenly lost my taste for Ratso and his Lemon Pledge rotgut. I strained my ears, practically hoping for a scream and the thrashing of an undead corpse tearing through partygoers. Ratso was a small guy. I could have just punched him right in the face. But why did I ever care—it's not like black people ever did very much for me. It was just all those damn survivalists taking advantage of the chaos of apocalypse for their own redneck racist ends, and that I'd just coined a neat term like "revenate" and Ratso didn't even fucking notice. And then the screaming started, just a few seconds after I would have really appreciated it.

The party was in chaos, of course. The Bowies had scattered into the trees, their orange jumpsuits beacons and targets.

Thunder and Alexa were tussling over the gun, Alexa shouting, "Fucking hupper!" and trying to throw rabbit punches. Her hip was still hurting her though, so Thunder had the advantage. Spaz and Man-o were leaning over Magpie, who didn't look like he was reanimated. He had moved, or had been moved, and was slumped over the steaming bit of earth differently now, but he was no revenant.

"Great party," I said. Ratso trotted past me and expertly drunk-weaved through the trees to where Magpie lay. The girls had worn themselves out and now just shoved and tried to upset one another, all sweaty and gulping air.

"Maybe you should just *not* shoot anyone else right now, eh?" I called out to them, and Alexa actually backed off, leaving Thunder with both hands on the rifle, which she in turn shyly handed back to Alexa.

Magpie stayed dead. The Bowies slowly made their way back to his position. One of them, the tallest male who I supposed was the leader because he was tall, and a man with an excuse on his lips. Dead bodies sometimes jerk or move, there's air in the lungs, cellular death comes later. The usual sort of thing someone says right before a body's eyes snap open and arms lurch for a human throat.

"'But, alas? What avails the vigilance against the Destiny of man? Not even these well-contrived securities sufficed to save from the uttermost agonies of living inhumation, a wretch to these agonies foredoomed!'" I shouted, happy I could remember the lines. Everyone turned from Magpie to me.

"Poe, motherfuckers. Edgar Allan Poe." They still just all peered at me, even that semiliterate baboon Ratso. "Count on it," I said, lacking anything else to say. I headed over to the snack table and started eating with both fists, leaving my bat at my feet. The food wasn't too bad. Not stale, or overly rough and "natural" like so much food is these days. The Berkeley crew probably had some decent refrigeration, maybe even some real bakery ovens, buzzing away in the depths of the campus.

Thunder came up to me. She was sweating a bit, glistening like heavy girls do sometimes. She was cute though, doable. The booze didn't make her attractive to me so much as it made me feel confident in my ability to somehow get her to another part of the campus and fuck her quickly, maybe standing up or on a bench, and then make my way back to Alexa, then San Fran, and nail two in one day. Whatever is not forbidden is permitted, and little is forbidden anymore.

"Hey," I said. Some bit of cracker fell out of my mouth. "What do you think about the current situation?"

"Your friend's a fucking maniac, you know that?" Thunder said, her voice a whisper.

"This is a world of maniacs, girl," I told her. "Is there any other way to survive this barren place?"

"Stop hitting on me," she said. She was pretty sharp after all. Had to be, to live in Berkeley, and to run with a crew off-campus. "Listen, she's going to shoot someone else, eventually. Don't you think it's strange that she basically killed someone, even if by accident, and doesn't seem to have any emotional response to her own actions? She's like one of those soldiers in an old movie who goes crazy and becomes a cold-blooded killer."

I looked over the top of Thunder's head. Alexa was pacing in front of two of the Bowies, talking to them, gesticulating emphatically. The tone of her voice cut through the woods, but she had the Bostonian tendency to underannunciate so I couldn't quite make out what she was saying. The party, such as it was, seemed strangely empty.

"Hey, where are your fri—" Then I felt four hands on me. "Oh." They marched me up to Alexa and Thunder demanded the gun, which Alexa raised and pointed at all of us.

"Jesus!" I said. Man-o said it too. Spaz just twitched. I recovered myself. Nothing slices through booze-haze like the barrel of a pistol-grip shotgun in one's face. "Look guys, you can't really keep me hostage." Thunder turned to look at me with one eye, the other still on Alexa. "I mean," I said, "I can kick all your asses. I'm a goddamn driller. I almost kill people for city government." Then I added, for the benefit of the Bowies: "A real goddamn city too. Not a hippie-dippy college town in the fucking East Bay." It only then occurred to me that with my arms in the grip of her comrades, Thunder could knee me in the balls any time she wanted, and that's exactly what she did.

I went down pretty hard, and decided to play dead. The boys let me slip from their grasp, almost as though they wanted Alexa to shoot. The ground seemed to be the best place for me, especially if the gun went off. I noticed that the Bowies were all wearing matching Nikes, which reminded me of that cult of UFO people who all killed themselves when I was a little kid to hitch a ride on a comet. Feet were suddenly everywhere. I covered my head with my arms and waited for kicks and stomps, but I was forgotten. The argument had grown generalized, a Stirneresque war of all against all, except for me. I peeked out at the world again through my fingers, like a child might. Naturally, whatever processes reanimate the recent dead finally hit the tipping point inside Magpie's body and he began to twitch and jerk.

It was Ratso who saved the day. His nasally voice cut through the cacophony. "Hey, you dumbasses, it's back! So much for the anaerobic bacterium vent theory!"

Thunder and Alexa and the boys stopped shouting like dumbasses, Alexa dropped the gun and screamed like a girl in a movie. Ratso and Spaz both scrambled for it, and got tangled up in the mess. Magpie got to his feet and started shuffling over. The Bowies spread out into some sort of weird defensive formation—each of them had picked a tree to hide behind sometime beforehand, I guessed, since the trunks they rushed to were the ones with the lights attached. Man-o had his head about him and rushed to get my bat from the snack table where I'd left it. With a whoop he snapped it up, turned on his heel and swung right at what was left of Magpie's head. It burst like a rotten melon hitting the sidewalk. I reached for the gun and snagged it. Sometimes I love having long arms. Headless, fueled by nothing but memories of memories of walking inscribed in his nerves, Magpie managed three or four more steps. There was still enough chaos that I was able to get to my feet, wave the gun menacingly—yet non-chalantly—at the assembled and smack Alexa across the face to get her to stop screaming before Magpie fell to his knees and flat onto his stomach, black blood and grue pouring forth from his neck.

"Is everyone all right?" Man-o shouted. "Headcount?"

"Minus one!" Ratso said. Then he fell into a fit of boozy giggles. The other Bowies came out from behind their trees, and now some of them were armed with small pistols, or devices that resembled small pistols anyway. The firearms pickings in Berkeley had to have been pretty slim right after the apocalypse, but if these guys were *real real* scientists and not an insane cargo cult of test-tube pretenders, the weapons probably had some kick to them.

Alexa was back to normal, though probably not thanks to my slap. She had her nails sunk deep in my left forearm, and moved to drag me out of the eucalyptus grove.

"Well, we had a lovely time at your party. Sorry the vent theory turned out to be bunk. You know what Thomas Edison once said—now I know ninety-eight different things that don't work. That's progress!"

"Wait," one of the Bowies said. He was large. Not as tall as I, but twice as wide, easily. "You can't leave."

"Well . . . why not?" Then I shrugged, like I was only vaguely interested in the question in an academic sense.

"Maybe you're infected."

"Then we should leave, eh?" Alexa said. "After all, we'd just join everyone else prowling around Berkeley already. You don't let possible infecteds stay on campus, do you?"

"And if you shoot us," I said, nodding at the weird squash-shaped gun in his hand. "We'll just change right now."

He smiled. "This weapon is non-lethal."

I turned my gun to my own chest, awkwardly thumbing the trigger. Everyone took a step back. "This one ain't. I don't care if I live or die, let me tell you that right now. But I do care that I get the fuck out of the East Bay, with quickness. So let us by."

One of the other Bowies said, "Samuel, this really isn't the protocol we discussed." Samuel shrugged and stood aside, his mouth open to say something.

We walked past him and Alexa said, "Thank you, Samuel."

We trudged back across Berkeley in silence. I didn't give Alexa her gun back, and she didn't ask for it. I only had about a quarter-buzz on from Ratso's flask, and all the crackers from the snack table were soaking up the juice in my stomach, so I was still a little twitchy. We passed so many bombed-out liquor stores, and I cringed and sucked my teeth at each one we passed. My mouth filled only with blood, thanks to my missing molar. Berkeley once had a number of ghetto strips, and forty thousand liquor-hungry students to dose, but not one intact bottle remained in the rubble and wreckage. Nobody, living or dead, was on the streets either, so it was a lonely walk, and slow because Alexa was still limping the slightest bit. Finally, at the train stop, Alexa asked for her gun back. The train was waiting on the tracks, just as when we had left it, with the One-Way Dead-End Transport Cooperative skeleton crew hanging around near the engine, passing a cigarette around and chatting about whatever microdrama railroad squatters chat about. A girl named Emily figured large in their conversation. She was a crazy bitch, apparently, but I knew crazier.

"I don't want to ride in the same train car as you," Alexa said. "And if I'm alone…"

"I left my bat back at the party. We should stick together," I said, being reasonable. I didn't want to get into a long discussion of whatever terrible thing it was that I did that made Alexa so upset with me. She was the one who shot somebody, after all. All I did was nothing.

"No, we're not going to stick together. If you follow me, I'll scream rape till someone intervenes. I'll throw myself on the fucking tracks and kill myself if I have to." Alexa clutched the air, her eyes wide. "I fucking killed someone! Those assholes jumped out in front of me, and you let them come along to the party, like they were friends. You—"

"I *let*—" But she barked right over me.

"You know what, maybe you should keep the gun. The way I feel right now, I'll blow your head off," she said. "Or maybe blow my own head off." Then she said, "No, fuck that. Give it to me. Get out of my fucking sight." I gave it to her, calmly, like I was handing over a French bread or something.

"All right then. I know it's hard. I'm a driller…" And with that, I transformed myself into an utter asshole, now and forever.

There's a particular sort of man, one more common back when American capitalism was a worldwide phenomenon rather than a secondary practice somewhere to the south of scavenging, who was expert in every conceivable topic because he had some success in his own career. The greatest orthodontist in Danbury, Connecticut, knew everything there was to know about pitching fastballs—hey man, it takes a steady hand, just like slapping on a pair of braces—or running a war—blood, everywhere!—or writing novels—so many characters coming in and out of the office. Or sex. You know, it takes that steady hand again. And it was the same with writing. What's just like writing? Pretty much anything according to these guys: coaching a Little League team, being a corporate accountant, breeding champion Schnauzers. Anything save reading and actually writing. I'd promised myself back in Boston that if I ever managed to land a good job and make something of myself, that I wouldn't use my expertise as a platform from which to pontificate. Well, drilling isn't exactly a great job, and I've studiously managed to avoid making anything of myself, but "I'm a driller…" still spilled out of my mouth, like it had been programmed into me. I didn't even care about being a driller, and certainly didn't qualify as a good one. I couldn't even imagine what a good driller's working day would be like. Soberly burning through the waiting foreheads of a ward full of kids with measles, I suppose.

Alexa could smell my anguish. "You're a driller…" she said. "And?" That *and* was a long one, stretching to full volumes. *And you're one to talk. And you think you can give advice? And you're the world's biggest cretin, a worthless sack of rank wine and dirty flesh. And you need to get on some other train car, or I'll kill us both right here and it'll be all your fault. And then everyone will know what you drove me to do.*

"...and I'll see you back in the city," I said. I walked down the platform to the first car, nodded to the train crew and slipped in to one of the cars. It was empty of the freight that had been brought over from the city, of course, but there was a surprise waiting for me. Thunder.

I fell in love with Boston's T. Not the buses; the trains. The streetcars of the Green Line especially, that were dual-use subway and street cars. Boston had a token system too during my time there, forsaking the impersonal and authoritarian swipe card regimes of New York and San Francisco.

It was a small system—Colin called it a "wind-up toy subway" as compared to the transit systems of the world's great cities, but to me the trains and their passengers were endlessly fascinating. When not in class I'd take my pocket change and ride all day. To Downtown Crossing and then to the Red Line all the way to the provocatively named Braintree. I still picture cartoon brains pulsing and thrumbing to themselves like hideous apples on the hundred-branched tree from my parents' backyard. Or I'd take the Blue, which led to the water. The lines were color-coded that way. The Green Line cut under the lawns of Boston Common, Red brought passengers to Harvard Square. It was a subtle little thing,  one I was told at some drunken party or other. The secret was knowing that the Orange Line runs down Washington Street, which was once called Orange Street.

I told myself I was taking the train for material. To eaves-drop on people's lives, to record snippets of real proletarian dialogue that surely spilled from the lips of passengers over every inch of track. And I did hear a few good things. One guy swearing that he "didn't never been there today," to his girlfriend, on the topic of visiting the home of his other baby mama, grumbling about "our boy Chucky"—it was another drunken night in a pub when I learned that was slang for the members of the Irish Republican Army, and that I was helping fund the conflict just by ordering another pint; which I was happy to do twice more that night before switching to whisky.

An old Greek lady I followed all the way to Brookline mumbled *Kyrie eleison* for the entire trip. None of this stuff ever made it into any of my stories. Mostly I just spent time watching girls, the unself-consciously sexy Latinas with big hoop earrings and shocking black hair; white girls in cardigans and long skirts messing with their iPods; fat girls in even bigger Tufts sweatshirts. How did they fuck? Did they shave their cunts? Take it up the ass? Lay on their backs, heads hanging off the side of the bed, letting men fuck their mouths? Moan when they come, or whimper like a hurt little girl, or did they not come at all from sex—instead sneaking orgasms later with some ferocious clit-rubbing after their boyfriend rolled over and went to sleep? Did they ever try other girls, or just swap spit when boys were watching? Even older women, with their worn-out old tits and horrid eye makeup, I couldn't help but fantasize about. The ones who were "bad girls" back when there was such a thing. Those who only ever slept with their husbands, and spent their whole lives regretting it. And sometimes those old women would make eye contact with me, and I'd wonder if they were thinking the same thing, thinking of coming up to me and asking for a little phallic charity now that poor old Sal or Buddy or Leon was in the ground.

I looked at men too. I liked to whip up stories about their pasts—one old guy with a limp was a former bootlegger who still had a bullet wedged in his femur. A frantic young kid, who turned his pencil into a spaceship and used its lasers to disintegrate his mother with *pshewpshew* noises, would grow up to design death weapons for the Pentagon, giggling amorally at a spreadsheet full of protected bodycounts; one billion, two billion, three billion bodies—ah ha hahaha! He'd laugh like The Count from *Sesame Street* because that was his, and my, favorite character on that old show. But to women I gave no careers, granted no interesting pasts or compelling futures. They were just holes and tits.

Soon I took to following women along their commutes. Rather than choosing what trains to take arbitrarily, I'd find a cute girl or an interestingly dressed old lady and just take whatever trains she took. It wasn't quite stalking, since I never followed anyone off a train to a workplace or to a home. It was just a way of organizing my day, and saving money. On the T I wasn't in a bookstore or a bar or in a restaurant I couldn't afford. And I couldn't afford any restaurant. I would ride and ride, and stop to eat at the Dunkin' Donuts in the Harvard Square T stop when I found myself at that stop. Chocolate glazed—one in the morning, one in the afternoon. A few tokens a day. Then class in the evening, or back to my room and my eBay laptop, transcribing whatever snippets of overheard conversation I remembered, whatever fantasies I dared share with the workshop.

To pay for my tokens and donuts, I signed up for psychological testing at Harvard. It wasn't nearly as exciting as I'd hoped it would be—no electrodes, no megadoses of LSD or other experimental drugs. I made five or ten or twenty a pop playing boring perception and learning games. See a 7, type 7. See a 6, type 13. See a 5, type 11. Then it would speed up, and I'd lose my place and just frantically mash buttons till the graduate student came to save me and hand me a ten-dollar bill. The business school had experiments too, and those were mostly endless variations on the prisoner's dilemma and other game theory notions. The business school paid well— up to fifty bucks if you did very well against the homeless people and eager Harvard undergrads who comprised the sample populations of virtually every experiment. I tried to read up on game theory on the Internet in order to guarantee bigger payouts, but the games always seemed tilted toward the Harvard kids. I could still make between seventy-five and one hundred dollars a week though, and I had enough money saved from typewriter sales and other shit jobs in Youngstown that I was able to keep up with the rent.

I even got about twenty seconds of free psychological treatment once. I'd answered a question about death and how often I thought of it—my own death, the deaths of others— with a 4 out of 5. The grad student experimenter stood up and closed the door, then smiled at me.

He said, "Four out of five, hmm. Often, but not always, that's a sign of depression. Do you ever feel depressed? We have some resources if you do . . ." He was nervous. Very short too. Tall men tend to make short guys anxious—he was a thoughtful little chihuahua of a boy.

I did think about death a lot. *I should just kill myself* whenever I missed a connecting train, or when I replayed old conversations from my college days, ancient embarrassments from childhood. A dozen times a day, maybe more. Then there was everyone else whose death would be a great relief.

So I said, "I'm a writer. I'm working on a book. It's sort of . . ." I let the rest of the sentence hang there so he could fill in the blank as he liked.

". . . a murder mystery?" he said.

"Sure."

"Okay," he said. And he didn't give me the list of phone numbers or public health department websites or whatever it was he was supposed to do. And that was that. I didn't even want to peel my skin off and leave it on the work desk and run screaming, red and bleeding through the streets, like I often did whcn someone talked to me about me. I did spend the ten bucks from that day on some okay Chilean table wine.

Between the T and the lab rat business, I was absolutely not getting laid. I grew expert at finding the cheap bars far from any of Boston's zillion colleges, and nursing a single pint or shot for an hour or more. These weren't places where someone like me—someone with most of his teeth, who wanted a girl with all of hers—could meet a woman. The old women in these bars were like the old men; chewed up and spat out by life, limbs and jaws moving only so much as needed to get ass to stool, booze to throat. Bags of unironed skin hiding the rusty works beneath. And they were all owned, these old gals. Drinking is not like a Bukowski novel. There are no sexual adventures with vibrant, crazy bitches, or even tedious workaday humping with aging whores who'll spread for fifty bucks' worth of fortified wine. The old women are all paired up with old men, and they don't try to flirt with the young stud in the next booth to make their husband jealous, or care at all about anything but the glass in front of them, and finishing it.

Drinking in an old man bar in Somerville, when the Celtic revival crap was on in the background, was like working in a Youngstown factory. Long hours of mind-numbing work, a trade of precious irreplaceable quanta of life for just enough fuel to continue at it. Our secondary sex organs slough off. We all wear shapeless garb a hard winter away from falling completely to tatters. There's no jukebox, no dartboard, no pub food, not even little bowls of peanuts or pretzels. We don't need the mass-produced fake joy to be compelled to lift our glasses, we don't need the salt to swallow the next mouthful. After last call, we do our grocery shopping at the gas station—a can of ravioli, a packet of two aspirin, and a Mounds Bar. The coconut in it makes it the healthy option, surely. It's a living, but barely.

There was a gas station girl I talked to. Her name was Aishwarya, according to her nametag. Short, light brown, no smile for me or anyone else, but her face was alive and she was paid to make eye contact with customers by her very own father and uncle, the co-owners of the Shell station. I was never a chatty drunk, these pages notwithstanding, and knew that small talk would fail. So I started heavy.

"Do you have a lot of racism around here?" I asked her one night. It was snowing outside. Thick, swift flakes falling slashways across the lights by the gas pumps. Unlike the girls at Dunkin' Donuts, Aishwarya never remembered my usual, which is just as well since she didn't have to fetch the candy bar or canned pasta for me. Instead, she looked aghast at my selections every time, like I was some brand-new asshole each time.

So when she asked, "Is this…it?" in that dubious way, I hit her with the racism question.

"Excuse me?" she responded. She was probably pretty sure I had just said something racist, or called her a racist. Her accent was mostly American, and her English better than mine, so it wasn't a gap in her understanding. I was just a drunk and mumbling freak, and my mouth was maybe a foot and a half over her head, closer to the growling heating vent than her ears.

"Racism. Are you a victim of racism on your job? Do people call you names?"

"Names...like what?"

"Like, uhm..." *Don't be racist, don't be racist,* I thought. "Well, someone might call you a bitch, for example. Don't get me wrong. I'm not calling you a bitch. I'm just using that as an example."

"'Bitch' is not a racist term, sir," she said. She put my can in a little paper bag. I fell in love with Aishwarya in that moment. That bag would be destroyed in a moment out in the wet snow, but she soldiered on with her routine, fiercely refusing to accept the world as it was to keep my groceries dry. "It's a sexist term."

"But, well, a bitch is a dog, meaning less than human," I said. "And lots of dogs are brown . . ." Some sober part of my brain, way down deep in the stem of my spine, begged me to stop talking. Take out my keys and gouge out my eyes and the flesh of my face if need be, but just shut up, shut up. But those neurons were outnumbered. "So, isn't it a kind of racism as well?"

She said, "Nobody has ever called me a bitch here at work. Nor on the bus either coming to or leaving from work. You're the first person to ever say that word in my presence, in this room, in any context whatsoever." She had change for me. She put it on the countertop rather than holding out her hand to drop the money into my palm.

Did I just ruin our relationship forever? My cheeks boiled with embarrassment. But as Aishwarya gave me the bag despite the futility of it all, I felt the need to continue.

"Well, perhaps you've experienced other kinds of racism. Have you ever been called a dot-head? Have people mimicked Apu from *The Simpsons* and said, 'Thank you, come again!'"—and here I did my own impression—"as they leave? Do they ask for Slushees?"

"You seem rather interested in cataloging all the ways in which someone might like to insult me," she said. Then she didn't say anything else. She didn't ask me what my problem was, or tell me to leave, or reach for her cell phone, or turn away and busy herself with the take-a-penny jar or the firearm surely hidden right under the countertop.

"I'm a writer," I blurted out. "I'm an observer of the human condition, an explorer of the world we all live in, but never truly examine. I'm interested in how people live, what challenges they face, how they get out of bed in the morning, and with whom they go to bed after a long evening. It's about life, Aishwarya!" She glanced down at her own nametag for a moment. "That's what I want to know. How do you live like this—and don't get me wrong, I'm not saying this is a bad way to live. It's better than my life. I can barely talk to people anymore. I drink all the time, *all the time.* It's like dipping my overclocked fried-out brain in Nyquil till the pot boils, then inhaling the vapors, you know? It's the only thing that keeps me from melting into a puddle of anxiety and rage. I eat nothing but junk food but look like a scarecrow because of all the nervous energy buzzing away in the very marrow of my bones. And all I want to do, Aishwarya, is capture some authentic moment of reality, and put it down on paper, and send it forth into the wild moronic inferno we call America, so that someone, somewhere, can read it and realize that he—or she—is not alone." I swallowed a hiccup right after. It tasted like sewage and rum.

Aishwarya glanced outside at the snow swirling by the gas pumps and then looked back at me. "Perhaps you should consider that the writer's best subject might be himself, and not some uninterested person who has troubles and concerns, and joys, of her own."

"I'd like to know about your joys," I said. "Tell me about one." I was just thrilled that she was still talking to me, that on some level she had listened.

"I enjoy standing behind this counter all night, mostly by myself. Sometimes the door opens and a puff of cold air comes in along with a customer and brings gooseflesh to my arms. It takes only a few moments for my body temperature, and the heat of the air in this little box of a building, to bring my skin back to normal. But I like it, I suppose. It's the little things. Call that a present, Mister, and take it with you. Come back a bit closer to sober next time, and you can be on your way back to your own nice warm house that much sooner."

That was rhetorical judo of sufficient skill that I left without another word, without even a nod of my head, but with a smile and a backwards step that I hoped connoted respect. She was wrong though—I didn't have a nice warm house. I had a poorly insulated room up a flight of steps in a two-family home. Rear entrance. My feet sank in the snow drift in the backyard up to my shins. The house was never quite dark, as the old Greek lady who lived downstairs kept late hours herself, and when she fell asleep it was on her couch in front of the huge black and white TV that must have cost a mint back when she bought it in 1963. Infomercials, Jesus Christ. At least drinking . . . No, not at least drinking.

My room upstairs was nearly pitch black, as usual, as I had to use one of my two blankets to cover the window and keep out winter. The only light that greeted me was the little green one on my laptop. I turned on the light, peeled off my pants and left them to puddle on the floor, switched into sweatpants and started to write. It was about nothing, really. Yvette had liked to shower when she was cold, to warm up. That never made any sense to me. I dreaded nakedness, both before the bath and after it. Before, I shivered. After, I was resigned, and would just throw open the curtain and step out into the frigid air and reach for the towel. Nothing in the bath ever comforted me, made me want to linger in the tub reading a book or playing with bubbles. I always felt like I was either a piece of meat being rinsed off, or already part of a human stew. There was no joy for anything else either. Not exercise—I hated the smell, the strain, the way my muscles felt dead hanging from my bones afterwards. Not spending money—never had any dough anyway, and there was never a charge in either bargain-hunting or buying something expensive. Even sex was always at least a minor disappointment, more similar to performing some poorly understood magic trick than a communion between two people. It was always better, harder, dirtier, in my head. All I had was books and booze. My two prescriptions for staying alive.

It was enough for a dumb little vignette. Couple showers together; girl loves the water, man shivers just outside of the stream. They fumble a bit to switch places because the tub is narrow and the dude a little portly. No mention of her pubic hair or of waxing—a bit of maturity there, as Yvette rocked what she called the runway and what I called "Hitler's mustache" when we were together, and it would have been so easy to throw in a reference—or anything explicit. Just them showering together, giggling about the awkwardness of it, and then quickly turning off the water, throwing the curtain open, and jumping out into the cold of the bathroom. She howls that she's cold and miserable now. He says that so is he. Being cold and miserable during the writing helped. I grabbed some dry, dirty clothes off the floor and poured them over the one blanket on my bed. I saved the file, emailed it to my web mail account in case my laptop died in its, and my, sleep, and went to bed. I forgot to make my can of ravioli. I was hungry, but colder than hungry, and too cold to get up or even proofread, so I slept. The next morning I took the T to Boston and was the slightest bit kinder to the women opposite me.

Thunder came home with me. We didn't talk about why. It was pretty clear that Berkeley was the exclusive precinct of lunatics and the living dead, that life was better in the City.

In the traincar she asked me about myself, what I'd done before the apocalypse, what brought me to the Bay Area. She was born up in Hayward, and just gravitated toward Berkeley because the street kids seemed friendly and the weather was nicer. Her nickname came from her claim to have never ever heard any thunder. It's true that there aren't many thunderstorms in the Bay.

We didn't fuck the first night, as it took so long to pick our way back to my apartment. We didn't bother pretending that we weren't going to fuck, so we squeezed together on my couch as best we could, with her atop me, my left arm reaching toward the floor. It was warm under her. She woke me with her mouth in the morning, which was a weird and pleasant surprise. I even tried to push her away, though my heart wasn't in it.

(10)

After she finished, she looked up at me and said, "I want to kill zombies. Breakfast, and zombies." She didn't try to kiss me, which I appreciated.

We had shopping to do. The Pill is a remnant of the old world, except for illicit imports from Mexico, which could be anything. Condoms are somewhat easier to find since they last a long time and there's no percentage in adulterating them, but there are plenty of local kiosks that sell prophylactics made from repurposed plastic bags. It's San Francisco, and people will buy anything that promises simultaneous conspicuous social responsibility and the possibility of orgasm. In some neighborhoods, it's like one big stupid Burning Man. We settled on some eggs instead, cooked for us and served in tiny paper cups that would have held ice cream in better times.

"There's a lot of life here," Thunder said. "Why hasn't anyone organized a force to take back the East Bay from the dead? There are so many resources in Berkeley and Oakland alone that nobody can get to."

"You know," I told her. "Snobs. Half of them didn't care about the East Bay before, and half of them are in no condition to help anyone else out anyway."

"Fucking snobs," she said, like she had expected the answer, even though it was oversimplified to the point of inaccuracy.

"You know, if you wanted to kill revenants, you'd have an easier time of it in Berkeley. We don't have too many here."

"That's what you think," Thunder said. "The campus people get pretty pissed when people end a zombie. They want to study their unlife cycle or something, and so they need to go unmolested by the rest of us. Even in self-defense." She slurped down her eggs like it was a jello shot. "We're supposed to run. They have cameras everywhere."

"So they knew we were coming…"

"Well, of course," she said. "It was their party. Anyway, California self-defense laws always worked that way. You have to run if you're at all able to."

"I'm not from around here," I said. "It's just that I think I fit right in. Now I do, anyway." I held my arms open wide. "Now that this place is a fucking wreck, and still the greatest city in the U, S, of A!"

"You Ess of Ay!" Thunder mimicked my voice, aping my baritone. "Yah, I can tell you're from the Midwest. Nobody from the Bay Area would say You Ess of Ay, unless it was a joke. And…"

"And?"

"And you didn't offer to reciprocate this morning. Typical Midwestern patriarchy bullshit." I must have looked appalled, or disgusted, or maybe even bemused—which I was—because she burst out laughing. "Why so serious?!" Then she added, "I like it down here. The population is large enough that it is still possible to be somewhat anonymous. You can hustle in this town. Be the hunter, rather than the hunted. I want to fight back, Billy."

Thunder had strong opinions, and some jewelry. Probably stolen or salvaged, but she claimed that the chains and rings were her mother's, and she knew enough about the precious metals to talk a good game and make some decent trades. By the end of the afternoon, we had bags of pot, two snub-nosed revolvers and a few boxes of ammo, first aid stuff, some MREs Thunder was strangely fascinated with, a set of brass knuckles with a built-in Taser, a car battery and transformer for it, and some new clothes—mostly old T-shirts and hippie dresses. Thunder didn't spend all her jewelry either.

"Portable wealth. It's an old Roma trick. No bank accounts when riding across Europe in a caravan." At home she stripped nude and stood in front of me like she was about to be inducted into the Army. She was a cute pear of a woman, with large tits and a shameless gut. She got sweaty when we fucked on the floor, and went into a stream-of-consciousness mode in which she discussed whether she should trim her pubic hair, the bad spackle and tape job done on the ceiling, how strange linoleum feels against her ass when it's warm, that I could slap her tits and face as hard as I like, and wouldn't I like to do it harder and that she liked pain and the idea of being fucked very roughly, which gave me the idea to plant my forearm against her throat which at least stopped her talking. She orgasmed easily and twice, a datum toward confirming the folk-belief that fat girls come a lot. She smiled when she came, both times, and had the little curl in her upper lip that Yvette did, but more pronounced. I liked this girl. She was somewhat less insane than Alexa. I pulled out and ejaculated on her belly, like a high schooler.

Later, I showed Thunder my drill and pager and told her a few drilling anecdotes, but not the one about the couple in the tent in the park.

"Lame," she said. "We should go out on patrol, like superheroes."

"Superheroes go out on patrol, hoping to stumble across corpses?"

"Police, then. We can get skateboards and make good time. I used to be pretty good."

"Lots of hills; I'd hate to drag a skateboard up one."

She shrugged. "You said revenants never make it to the tops of hills anyway."

"As a driller, I report to deathbeds and make sure people don't become revenants. We're not going after revenants."

"I am," she said. "You can come with me if you want. Do you have a spare key?"

Spare key. There are so many parts and practices of the old world that just don't matter anymore. Nobody cares about Twitter, really, though of course it still works just fine, internationally. The "third date rule" went out the window, as it always does after disasters, except that our national disaster is continually unfolding. School prayer is a non-issue, as is alternate side of the street parking, and what to name next year's hurricanes, and whether leash laws are a good thing. Spare keys are another non-issue. People either don't let anyone near their home, or just leave all the doors and windows wide open. Looting and theft is so supersaturated that for anything still around to steal, scarcity is a thing of the past. Someone takes your bike, walk a block and find another. Come home to a trashed apartment, just kick down the door in a building across the street and sleep there. Half the population is living out of bug-out bags at any given time, and the other half watch the world go by through peepholes and slits in the blinds, never coming out onto the streets themselves except under cover of darkness and armed to the teeth. And then they die and on the way to some bar or other I hear the half-rotted howl of a starving revenant and the slam of dead flesh against the doors as I walk by. But spare keys, no, nobody has spare keys anymore. Take anything you want from me, and good luck with it.

We patrolled the Mission with our handguns tucked discreetly in the pockets of our coats. It gets chilly at night in the city, and foggy, and the end of America took a big hunk out of global warming—and there's another theory that zombism is just parasitic manipulation of humans by some naturally occurring but typically dormant fungus that responded to climate change by waking up—so we were inconspicuous. I never spent much time around guns. I'd done some plinking with a .22, went hunting to no result a time or two. I knew just enough to know that it was hard to shoot a moving target in the head, even if the target was moving in an awkward shuffle. I often find myself attached to women who simply cannot be argued with, though, and thus here I was, stalking the streets for zombies with Thunder, who huffed as she walked and often asked me where the prime locations for zombie sightings were as we marched from the Mission to the Castro.

"This is stupid," Thunder finally decided. I was about to agree with her and suggest a bar I knew nearby when she added, "We can't just walk around randomly. Who dies—old people mostly, and the sick. But hospitals have drillers, right?"

"Well, generally—"

"So where do we go?"

It was about two miles to the Tenderloin, which consistently hung on to its shithole aspect for a century, and when the dead arose, not a lot actually changed. Thunder had a lot of questions about the city, which was pretty odd for someone who was from the Bay, I thought. Was she lying— and it's not as though she magically owed me the truth about anything—or was she just one of those provincial suburban types whose parents never let her come down to the big city? I checked my pager a few times, but the city was quiet.

"Are we going to walk all night?" I asked Thunder.

"Don't you like walking the night?" she said, like a bad poet might.

"I prefer a bar. I like to have a few drinks, unwind, catch up on the local gossip. Do some people-watching. Or stay home and write."

"You write?"

I just remembered then that I had a print-out of my published short story in the breast pocket of the coat I was wearing. It was well-creased and a little faded but still plenty readable. I handed it to her, and she took it and skimmed the first page. Maybe she knew that I was testing her, to see if she'd wave her hands and tell me she'd read it later, or make a face, or just tease me for carrying it around. It's not as though I'd hang on to my print-outs, like little talismans, if the world hadn't collapsed around me. We all need security blankets of some sort. Thunder's were street punk clothing and plastic specs and a mannish posture. Alexa's belief in some conspiracy hidden inside City Hall was her security blanket. I suppose I should add drinking to my list, but it's not like there's any reason not to drink oneself to death anymore.

Thunder snorted as she read. I kept myself from asking, *What? What's funny? Do you like it?* but only just barely. I should have brought a bottle with me.

Then she asked, "Who is Edward Said?"

"Well, he was a literary critic. He had this term called 'Orientalism,' by which he meant that Western writers and social scientists looked at the Middle East through a racist lens."

She read aloud from the story: "The real problem, Jeremy decided, was that the alien problem was the precinct of bad, expensive movies, and bad, cheap paperbacks. Public intellectuals had never bothered with the aliens. Noam Chomsky never wrote anything about the aliens. Edward Said never wrote anything about the aliens. For the last three days, Israeli bulldozers hadn't knocked down any Palestinian houses because of the aliens. If they had, Jeremy hadn't seen it on the news because of the aliens. If there was looting and riots because of the aliens Jeremy hadn't seen it on the news because of the aliens." Then she took a big step to outflank me, shrugged comically, and said, "Lol what? What is this story about? It's all English major stuff. I get that the aliens are supposed to be all 9/11 and stuff, but why are you—"

"It's not *me*, it's a character."

"Oh fuck you," Thunder said. "It's you. You have aliens invade New York and their mother ship is floating around and all you—well, this guy—does is sit around thinking about the aliens and how nothing will ever be the same."

"Right. That's the story. It's a story. So this character read a lot and so he thinks about people like Noam Chomsky and Edward Said."

"Well, it's fucking *bullshit*. I mean, look at what actually happened to America. It fell apart, but people fought. Hell, we're still fighting!" She patted the pocket in which she carried her gun. "I've seen all sorts of crazy shit. Explosions, riots, pirates taking over tanker ships in Oakland and trying to drive them to Japan. And you write about some sad sack who sits in his room all day. This is supposed to be sci-fi?" She handed the papers back to me—she hadn't read the last two pages—and then caught a look at my expression. "I mean, it's well-written and all. Very English major-y, in a way. Experimental. But, you know…"

"I know…"

"It's not…"

"Leisure reading?" I said.

"Right, it's not leisure reading." She turned around and looked both ways before crossing the street. "C'mon, there has to be some revenant out here."

I followed her lead for a block or two, though she didn't know the area. I always seem to fall in line behind aggressive, assertive women. There was something especially out about Thunder, though.

Finally, I asked her, "You realize, this sort of adventure you're after is what led Alexa to Berkeley. She shot your friend, mainly because she was looking for someone . . . something, to shoot."

Thunder turned and sneered. "She's a cunt and a fucking murderer. I'm not after something to shoot, I'm after a revenant."

"You still sound pretty bloodthirsty." She didn't have anything to say to that. She stomped out in front of me, standing straight, legs springy, ready for action. Then I asked her. "Do you think, Thunder . . ." I said, trying to get my words right, since she was both armed and angry, "that the whole disaster with the living dead has changed something about the way women behave?"

"Changed. *Women?*" she said. "Oh yes, oh fucking yes. You don't get it, Billy boy, do you?"

"Let's both pretend that I don't, and you can tell me and I'll listen," I said.

"Two big changes, I think. The first is that the men fucked everything up. They're the ones in charge of stuff like security and law enforcement and science, and something happened. Then they died by the millions. Women have always had to defend themselves from men—from rapists, abusive husbands and boyfriends, you know? But we've never been successful. You know why?"

I wasn't sure what to say that wouldn't get me either shot or screamed at, so for a moment I said nothing. Thunder repeated herself: "You know why, Billy?" She frowned at me. "Well, men have greater upper body strength, I guess, and back in the old days . . ." I didn't know what was on her mind, not at all.

"We've never been successful because there's a whole . . . ideology!" She waved her hands around, trying to encompass the whole crazy wide spinning world. "That men protect women. If you're a Mormon or a punk, men protect women. Even lesbians have bull dykes. Men protect women and prey on them at the same time. Men can prey on women because, socially, their role is to protect women. Well, guess what? Women live longer than men. We don't get into a lot of street fights. Men took care of the problem of men, and in the space that remained, women were able to step up."

"Is that why you're going reanimate hunting?" I asked. "Are you stepping up? Acting out?"

"Yeah," Thunder said. But she was distracted. "Is that one?" she whispered and nodded with her chin. It was a woman—if that's ironic or not, I don't know anymore—obviously homeless, hunched over a two-wheeled wagon filled with the usual detritus of a life on the streets. She was hunched over the handlebar of her cart, her back nearly parallel to the sidewalk, and she was slowly moving toward us.

"Hey you!" Thunder called out. "Hey lady! Identify yourself." She reached into her oversized pocket for her pistol and struggled to draw it.

"Maybe she's deaf," I said, talking quickly. "Or schizophrenic. Just because she doesn't answer, just because she doesn't hear you, doesn't mean she's a revenant. She could be alive and insane. She could be alive and suicidal, or really dangerous in some other way. Don't assume, don't assume—"

Thunder had her gun out now, and pointed it right at the woman, who certainly had the posture and sensibility of a reanimate. I drew my own firearm and called out: "Lady, please! She's not kidding! If you're in there at all . . . Christ, I'm a hupper!" I blurted out.

"Relax, you're just making sure," Thunder said. She cocked the hammer. The old woman glanced at the sound, finally betraying awareness of something. Her skin was dark and rosy, like someone with lupus, or a classic alcoholic with a face full of shattered capillaries. She only had a few teeth, hair like strings, and a significant hunch. Honestly, she could have been alive three minutes ago and turned while she walked toward us. Stranger things have happened, if barstool blowhards are to be believed. Sometimes it takes an hour, sometimes it's over—and begins! in a flash. Maybe that's evidence of some sort of viral contamination that magically stops at the borders. The word "magically . . ." has to be inserted into every damn theory of reanimation at some point or other. As it turns out, nothing is like the movies. No easy answers that one group of scientists can quickly arrive at. No rampaging bands of military rapists or cannibals kitted out in hubcaps and burlap sacks and riding across the open desert on color-coordinated dune buggies. And no obvious moment of transition—the woman shuffled toward us, no, at us really, her head bowed. There was no great moment of revelation when she opens her mouth and roars like a CGI dinosaur, no red glowing eyes burning with rage. We either shoot her now, or wait till she attacks, if she attacks.

Then a voice from overhead. "Whatchoo motherfuckers doin'?" Three stories up, a black guy in an undershirt leaning out the window of his apartment shouted. He had a kerosene lantern or something in one hand. "Don't you be shooting up the neighborhood! I'll call my boys on you." In his free hand, he waved something else. Cell phone? Small gun? Maybe it was nothing but the back of his hand.

"We have a reanimate here!" Thunder shouted up at him. "Do you know this woman?"

"I don't know nobody. Don't you be shooting!" He ducked inside and slammed the window shut. The lantern light danced behind the row of black windows—the guy must have had a railroad apartment.

"Is he coming down? Should we wait?"

"No, let's retreat . . . and wait," Thunder said. We both walked backwards, keeping our guns on the woman, who must have been a reanimate, I decided. No random mentally ill person is so locked off from outside stimuli and still able to walk. Not that I had any psychological training. Not that I myself didn't have a few episodes of waking up on my couch two days after leaving my apartment. Who knew how I acted during those blackout periods? Not me.

A heavy steel apartment building door flew open and out came the guy, lantern still held high in his left hand and a drill in his right. The little object was a battery, of course. "I'm a driller," he said. "This is my gig."

Thunder gestured with a shoulder toward me. "He's a driller too," she said. He glanced at me, expectant.

"Hello," I said. He turned back to the woman and approached her slowly, like a kid trying to catch a wary cat.

"Oh yeah, oh yeah, she's one of them."

"How can you tell?" Thunder asked. She shot me another hard look. "Are you sure?"

"Yeah, I know this one," he said. "Don't shoot, don't shoot. You be shooting, everyone will start poppin' off. I care about this neighborhood." He put the lantern down carefully and stood between us. The lady was moving ever so slowly right toward him. "This lady be screaming all day and all night, all the time. Cunt this, baby that, shouting nig—the n-word." He licked his lips. "If she quiet, she dead. Watch this, y'all." He bounced on the balls of his feet a few times and then swung out his left leg. His shin took the wagon out, sending garbage and empty bottles flying. Lights came on all over the canyon walls of the block. The woman staggered, then fell to the ground. She lurched forward on her belly, fingers scrambling across the asphalt of the street. Almost nobody used cars in the city anymore. It was just the four of us, and an increasing audience of lookie-loos twinkling into existence through open windows. The driller jumped to the right, pivoted, and ended up with one foot on the lady's back. He reared back with his right hand, planted the drill on the back of her skull and only after making contact did he hit the button. She didn't scream, only burbled. Black blood burst from the back of her head, splattering all over the driller's undershirt and face. He didn't mind. He didn't blink. He smiled, teeth still white.

Above us, a small round of applause circulated in the air. The driller yanked hard on the handle of his drill, but it wouldn't come out. He smiled again, sheepishly this time, at me and Thunder. We finally realized that we could lower our pistols.

"It's stuck," he said quietly, an embarrassed grin on his face. "It's got a reverse button." He flipped a switch, and the drill brrred slowly to life, its bit rotating backwards as he eased it from the old woman's head. He looked up at us. "Good spotting, y'all. Good hustle." Then to the people above us, now looking through their windows down at the streets. "It's a'ight! Thank you for your cooperation! Have a safe night!" He switched the drill to his left hand and then held up a fist for a bump. I slipped my pistol back into my jacket pocket and obliged. Thunder and he just hugged, arms wide and with a huge smile. Then he walked upstairs while we waved bye, both of us a little confused.

"Let's go home," Thunder said. "I'm hungry."

Dry goods and canned goods last forever, and are easy to buy down by the Embarcadero from Mexican fishing boats. So I had plenty of pasta and canned tomato sauce. Despite the whole new world for women that opened up along with the zombie apocalypse and the end of America, Thunder quickly volunteered to make us a late dinner. I found a little bottle of something—I keep stashes of miniature bottles around when I remember to buy them. It's like finding an Easter egg out on grandma's lawn, not that my *yiayia* ever had a lawn or believed in hiding Easter eggs. We boiled them and painted them red, for the blood of Christ, and played the traditional game of smacking end against end in an informal elimination tournament around the dinner table. Everything smelled like lamb, back then. I haven't had leg of lamb in years, or avgolemono soup, but I figured I could at least reclaim the Easter egg hunt tradition for my own amusement. It's hard to live alone. I guess I liked Thunder's company, but that didn't stop me from hiding the mini—a tiny Smirnoff—in my palm and then my lap so I wouldn't have to share it with her. I could pass it off as water, maybe.

Thunder even put the food on plates and presented mine to me as grandly as she could, but holding it high in her left hand and bowing slightly. I took it and sat on one side of my coffee table. She plomped down on the floor across from me.

I was pretty hungry, so ate easily, but Thunder just picked at her food.

"This looks like brains," she said finally. "Just like the back of that old lady's head. And . . ." Unspoken, I presumed, was "Magpie's head." "I'm not hungry, sorry. I don't mean to waste your food."

I graciously snatched up her plate and started eating off of it. My strategy was twofold—one, indeed no I didn't want any food wasted, and two, by eating and keeping my mouth full I wouldn't have to think of anything comforting or poignant to say. At the very least I wouldn't say anything stupid that would upset her further. She rambled for a bit about Berkeley, how the dead outnumber the living there, how tough it was to make friends with some street kids just to see them shamble at you a week later. How at first her crew had gone down to the posh Claremont section of town and kicked in the door of a mansion to live in, but then some older people with guns showed up and threatened to kill everyone.

"I slept with a couple of them to get us out of there, honestly," she said, clearly not completely honestly. No wonder she wanted a gun now. Finally I reached down under the table and brought the Smirnoff out.

Thunder sighed happily, smiled and said, "Thanks," and then opened the bottle and drank it one inhalation. "I don't want to fuck tonight," she said, so we didn't. I found another mini and drank that to keep myself even. We went to bed and didn't have sex, and we didn't hold one another or anything like that either. She sniffled a bit, but then got to snoring. Perhaps another reason why she was called Thunder? I was up for a long time, finally in a place where I didn't have to constantly review my day for regrets and minor humiliations.

Maybe it was that someone else, someone pretty friendly, had shown up and solved a problem I was facing. Maybe it was just exhaustion burning out my nerves so I couldn't feel anything more, but I was able to sleep well for once.

Were this a novel, I suppose I'd write "And when I awoke, Thunder was gone." But she wasn't. Actually, she was packing. She had both guns, and had appropriated some Sterno cans, some chili, and a can opener. She also had emptied out a canvas bag of the books—Knut Hamsun, Kathy Acker, Charles Willeford—I'd been keeping in there. It was filled with a few more of my things.

"Is this it, then? Is it over?"

"Of course not, Billy," she said. "Nothing's ever over. I'll see you again. You know what it's like. People always run into one another in small towns."

"Is there anything else you'd like to take from me?" It was all easy-come-easy-go junk, except the guns, which I wasn't too fond of anyhow, but she could have asked. Or woke me like she did the morning before, at the very least.

"You don't want to send me out there with nothing, dude," she said. "I shouldn't have both guns, maybe? I was planning to keep one and barter the other. Except for your computer, which I'd never take because you're a writer—"

I laughed. "You didn't think I was much of a writer last night!"

Thunder scrunched up her face. "Hey, listen. I'm sorry. That story just wasn't my cup of tea. You wrote it before all the shit hit the fan anyway. Keep working at it. Anyway, I know you *like* writing, how about that? And you have all those notepads full of writing." She added quickly. "Don't worry, I didn't read it. I assumed it was a diary of some sort."

". . . plus you couldn't, because my handwriting was so terrible?"

She blushed at that. "You just strike me as a loner. I need community. Like that neighborhood last night. They were all in it together. You ever drill a neighbor, or even look out a window to see what some noise is outside, to try and help?"

"Just take what you need and go. If I see you around, I'll see you around." My throat was also cracked and raspy. I needed a drink immediately, and didn't want to give away any more hiding spots, or any more stuff. "I'm almost always home, you know. If you wanted to come by."

She put down the bag, bent over the couch, and kissed me on the lips, slipping the very tip of her tongue between them, just for a second, to show that she meant it. Then she said, "I will. We'll definitely see one another again very soon," and then she picked up her bag, walked to the door, waved at me, and let herself out.

I stayed on the couch for a while, wrapped up in blankets that smelled like Thunder—baby powder and dirt and sweat and sugar. I barely knew Thunder, so I didn't miss her much. The apartment seemed larger without her. I couldn't help but feel that she was part of some secret of which I was only slowly becoming aware, that she was a single strand of an all-encompassing web of the sort my father would spend hours detailing from misremembered news reports and hearing our neighbors speak of politics. She had come to San Francisco from Berkeley for a reason. It may have had to do with me, or I might have just been some patsy to use and abuse for a few days, or maybe it was some kind of test for *her*. I didn't know anything, but I was suddenly sure.

I never had a big blow-up with Yvette, thanks only partially to the T-riding and the drinking. Whenever I was around the Commons, where I might run into her on her way to or from a class, my hands would shake. Every girl in a pony-tail and sweatshirt looked like her, if only for a second. And in Boston, that was most girls. In winter the coats came out—slick girls in long black wool coats like something out of Prague, practical girls in puffy down insulated things that looked like bright blue waffles, sporty girls in purple soft shell jackets from REI. I grew even more agitated then, as I wouldn't know Yvette till she was right on top of me.

I realize now that I spent a lot of time in those days daydreaming about stories other than the one I was living in. I'd rehearse what I'd do when I saw Yvette. Smile at her and strike up a conversation like everything was still cool; rush past her, hiding my face, and go home and beat myself up for it; or let my heart soar with joy when she called out after me; give a sharp

nod and keep walking if she was with a guy other than Colin. She had agitated for opening up their relationship, which stressed Colin out quite a bit, and me even more.

But he was fine with it because, "Harvard guys get all the pussy they want," he told me at one of the innumerable Au Bon Pains that littered the area around Harvard Square.

I laughed out loud. "Still trying to be 'one of the guys,' eh?" He was drinking tea. I had a cookie and lemonade. Sugar is a good substitute for booze, and it was 9:30 am.

He quirked his eyebrows. "Facts are facts, brother." He smiled. "Is that any better?"

"I'm not really the most 'authentic' guy in the world myself," I said. I even did air quotes over the word "authentic," grinding a corner of my cookie to crumbs. "I can't give you a blue-collar white dude ghetto pass or anything."

"Do you ever stay up nights, wondering about what it means to be authentic?" Colin asked, suddenly serious. "Being an authentic person, an American, an individual? What it means to play a role for parents, or classmates, or just people you encounter on the street?"

"No, mostly I drink and read books." I took a gulp of lemonade. "That sort of thing never even occurs to me."

"I think you work it out in your writing. Have you been writing lately?"

"Uh…not lately." I hated when he asked me about my work, which wasn't going well, and which I didn't like discussing even under the best of circumstances—and what those circumstances could even be was beyond the scope of my imagination.

"Let me cut to the chase, Bill. Want to make some money?"

"Always."

"Sell me a story."

"For what?" I asked. "Starting a magazine?"

"No, I want you to ghostwrite something," he said. "Maybe ghostwriting isn't the right word…"

"You want me to write a story—about anything that sounds 'authentic,' I suspect—and then you can put your name on it and show it to Yvette…? Is that right?"

"And if it's good, publish it."

"Publish it. Under your name," I said.

"Yes, but remember, most journals only pay in contributor copies. I'm ready to pay you five hundred dollars up front," he said. "And! I promise not to enter it into any contests that will pay out more than you'd earn for writing it. I really just want to submit it to—" and he named some journal I'd never heard of. I made a mental note to see if the Harvard Coop carried it on its newsstand.

I wasn't prepared for this at all. Was I being taken advantage of?—well, that went without saying. Nobody makes an offer to anyone without perceiving himself as better off after the trade is made. It's just up to the sucker to accept the deal. On the other hand, lab-ratting was about to end for the semester, and it would be three long dark months before I was able to make five bucks answering surveys about how suicidal I was. I'd rank that ideation as four out of ten, and climbing. Five hundred bucks could buy a lot of oblivion, and nearly as much self-loathing. On the third hand, which I often grow when contemplating alternatives, a deadline is always a good motivation.

"Okay. But you take what you get. No revisions. I'm not going to write a story just to have you give me a zillion notes on it, like 'Make it more compelling' or 'Give the milkman more shading.'"

"There's going to be a milkman in my story?"

My story rankled me. I nearly threw my lemonade at him. "No, I guarantee that there won't be one. There won't even be milk, okay?"

"And no suicides."

"God no." I was so thirsty, suddenly. "I want half up front."

"No," Colin said. "How about fifty bucks up front. That's what that sci-fi magazine paid you for a whole story, right? I mean, with two-fifty, you can leave town…" He must have seen the expression on my face, because he then added, "Kidding! I mean, with two-fifty you can probably get someone else to write *you* the story, and then hand it in to me as your own work."

"I'm not going to leave town, and fifty is fine." Leaving town, yes, that's what I'd do. But I'd need the whole five hundred bucks. That was plane ticket money, or *On The Road* money. A cheap-ass car, bus, the train tickets, fleabag motels. I could make it anywhere.

"I'll have it in a week."

Colin shook his head. "No, no, take your time, I want your best work."

"You'll have it in a week," I said. "That'll be my best work. I'm enthusiastic, excited. I'm a professional."

Colin slipped a fresh fifty-dollar bill out of his pocket and slid it across the table. He had come prepared. "You're a professional *now*," he said. And with that, Colin has purchased me, like an ascot or a yacht, or a highball or a call girl, or whatever else wealthy people buy. And he was the nicest guy I knew. He couldn't help himself. He was born and bred to see everyone and everything around him as a commodity. No wonder he stayed up all night, biting his pillow, wondering about his authenticity…and then he turned around and proved what a plastic, empty shell of a man he was by buying me, to wear me, to pretend to be me.

I headed back over the river, stocked up on some staples— vodka, pineapple juice, rum, and beer, and got started. I drank two PBRs to start, to get me up. I was free, free to write whatever I wanted, since I wouldn't be showing the story to anyone, not to the workshop, not to Yvette. Let Colin take the lumps. It's not like anything I ever wrote got me anything but lumps, and even those were from the omnipresent fists of indifference. I wrote about the Y2K scheme I'd been a part of in Youngstown, and those crazy typewriters. Yvette knew the story, of course; Colin didn't. Nasty of me, eh? But nobody takes a deal without thinking they can somehow get one over on the party of the first part. It wasn't bad, the story. Just around 2500 words, and some of the paragraphs I managed to commit to memory. They're in the pages above. I was enthusiastic, jittery. Not just maintaining, the fluid in my spine was boiling.

So even as the first draft of Colin's story was printing out, I opened my web browser and started looking for plane tickets. They were more expensive than William Shatner and that travel gnome had let on. I could get to Chicago pretty easily, but I'd been there on school trips and such, and it never captured my imagination. And it was cold. I didn't need a plane ticket to get to New York, but five hundred bucks wouldn't last me a week down there, even if I took the cheapo Chinatown bus, even if I got a room at the Chelsea Hotel like every other booze-pickled cliché from the hinterlands. Then I realized that any trip I'd take would be one way. I wouldn't be flying back to Boston, or visiting home in Youngstown any time soon. Five hundred bucks was just enough to not be enough. I made myself a pair of Hawaiian Screws with the pineapple juice and vodka and went to bed, but I could not sleep.

Did Colin do this on purpose? Implant the notion of leaving town in my mind, and then offer me just enough money for it to be torture? Then he could have Yvette all to himself—and where was she anyway? Hiding from me purposefully? I was growing paranoid, hysterical. I was so tempted to simply delete the story, rip up the print-out, but I hated the idea of wasting so much time and effort. I finally settled on a concept that would keep my hatred at a slow simmer and allow me to keep the money and hand over the story with my integrity intact. Clearly, Colin was oblivious, not malevolent, and probably thought he was really helping me out. And I did have to get out of Boston. There was nothing here for me anymore.

I took a couple of days to proofread and edit the story. I rode the T, but didn't spend much time ogling women and sexually humiliating them in my mind. Donuts yes, booze yes. Had to keep warm. By midweek, the print-out looked like a CIA-redacted document, covered in black and scratch-outs. The second draft was a bit more leisurely. I typed till I got bored, then took a nap, or drank a bit more, or just watched the snow fall and fill up the tire tread marks on the driveway below. I needed to find some little kernel inside myself, some remnant of self-control that I could cultivate. Five hundred extra dollars, if it couldn't free me, could kill me. Liquor, hard drugs, the wrong sort of whore with a straight razor hidden in her bra and murder on her mind. Not that I ever paid for sex. It seemed like a common enough activity, if novels from a certain type of writer—confessional, boozed-up, masculinist—were to be believed, but I had no idea how to even behave on a phone to an escort service.

I was sure the girl on the other end of the line would say, "So you'd like an escort, Mister Kostopolos? And what event is it you'll be attending?" despite all logic and reason. A call girl would laugh at my little room, the pile of clothes on the floor, the yellowed and flaking paperbacks bought from street peddlers. And if I paid for a night in a hotel, well there would go half the five hundred bucks before I even earned it. Streetwalkers were beyond imagining. I was sure they all had AIDS and crabs. Every thought I had ended in disaster. Money would just empower those fantasies, and bring them into reality.

Colin liked the story. Of course he did; he had good taste. His parents had made sure of that. His parents also taught him to closely inspect the work he paid for in front of the artisan, and to *hmm* and *hrrm* and snort and tap his finger against the page when confused or intrigued as well, I'm sure. He did that plenty. Only after he read the story and pointed out three typos that I'd missed—homophonic errors are the death of me—did he hand over five one-hundred dollar bills. We were in an Au Bon Pain again. Another one, on the other side of Harvard Square. It was small, not bright and with a wall full of windows like the one we'd met in a week ago.

"A bonus?" I said, pocketing the bills.

"What…oh, wait. No. You can't change a hundred?"

"No," I said. My cheeks burned for a moment. "You can't change a hundred either, obviously. Or you would have."

Colin grew impatient via quantum mechanics. He went from calm to pissy in an instant without passing through any intermediate stages. "Give me one of those back," he snapped. "I'll get change."

I slipped a bill out of my pocket. "Don't think you can go up to the counter and break a C-note."

He rolled his eyes at me and tried just that. It was a small store, but sufficiently crowded that I could hear what he was telling the cashier. He pointed at some muffins, and at the menu board. Then he came back, his eyes wild, and asked me if I could believe that they wouldn't break a hundred-dollar bill.

"I believe it."

"They won't even accept them as currency. How is that even legal?" He turned back toward the row of cash registers, and raised his voice to say, "Is this legal?!" but the workers ignored him. They were good at that. I supposed they'd have to be to keep from pouring broken glass into the oatmeal.

"You stay here!" he told me. "I'll be right back." I watched him rush across the street and nearly get hit by a car as he crossed against the light. Had Colin changed since that day he got me back to my house, or was this the genuine article—the minor conniver unused to inconvenience or being told no, and uninterested in kicking a friend an extra ten percent for a job well done? If he trusted me enough to be a rich little snot in my presence, that was just one more reason to leave town. Finally, he came back and handed me five ten-dollar bills.

"My bank," he said, by way of explanation. Then he patted the story. "Yvette's going to love this."

"I bet she will," I said. Whenever Colin mentioned Yvette, a fist closed around my heart, but this time the spasm was weaker. I liked the idea of Colin passing off my first meeting with Yvette as his own work.

Then it redoubled in strength when Colin explained, "She told me all about your weird typewriter scheme. This is perfect."

"I thought you were going to…" I didn't bother finishing the sentence. Colin bought the story for Yvette to publish as her own work, not his. He'd probably have his father's secretary take care of the submissions too; what if Yvette didn't like the way the glue on stamp backs tasted? We couldn't have that. "Does she know you hired me?"

"It was her idea!" Colin said. "Listen, she knows you're not over her. She was worried you'd just volunteer to write the story without taking any money if she asked, or that you'd do something stupid like write it, then tear it up, or write about one of your, you know, intimate moments and try to embarrass her."

"Why can't she do her own work? Has she been too busy sucking your cock to get any typing done?"

Colin held up his hands. "Not cool, friend. She cares about you. Really, she's worried about you. We both are. She needs this because, to be honest, she isn't doing very well. And we wanted to help you out somehow. Plus," he said, "you took the money. A contract is a contract is a contract, even when it's a verbal one."

"Why isn't she doing well? Too much cock?" I said. "Is all the semen upsetting her tummy? Did you spooge in her eye and accidentally blind her?"

"You're highly interested in my cock today, Bill," Colin said. "You need to restrain yourself before you say something you regret." He folded the manuscript in half and slipped it into the interior breast pocket of his suit jacket. How could he dress like that in the middle of a New England winter? Blue blood runs cold. "Let's just call it a deal, and call it a day. All right? Spend the money however you wish, on anything you want."

"You said Yvette isn't doing well. What happened? I have a right to know!"

"No, you don't have a right to any such thing. But I'll tell you," he said. Then, *sotto voce*, "She was pregnant. One of those things. It happens." I was about to bring up his cock again when I caught the word *was*. Colin thought faster than I did. "She lost the fetus. It was the first trimester, it happens a lot. She didn't even tell her parents. Honestly, we had a few arguments about her aborting it, but she wasn't even sure whose it was, so she claimed I didn't have any say in the issue." He shrugged. "We have an open relationship. Anyway, the abortion topic is no longer relevant. Nor is this conversation. She's fine, physically, just very upset. She needs a break."

"Open…"

"It was my idea. She needs to have more experiences. You know, writers need experiences."

"We do," I said. "We do. Can't have Yvette running around with inadequate sexual experiences. And now a miscarriage. She'll clearly be an award-winning writer one day. If only she'll have an affair with a professor next, she'll be golden." I felt terrible the moment that bile left my mouth. "Oh God, I'm sorry. I'm so fucking terrible." I looked out the window, at the traffic. "I should just throw myself in front of a bus. A poor fucking baby died in a woman's womb and my first impulse was to score some asinine rhetorical point with it. God, why am I such a miserable shit?"

Colin wasn't God, so he didn't have an answer for me. He wasn't wearing a sneer; instead he looked like he was about to cry as well. Like I was an angry puppy about to be put to sleep for my own good. Colin was a compassionate guy, but he only had one way of expressing himself—throwing cash around. It's a blunt instrument, one that drives people mad. Yvette and I both did whatever Colin said, just because he was rich and nice about it. Write a story, fuck a ton of extraneous guys. We were born into it, trained since infancy to obey people with money. Colin didn't even realize what he represented to us, to me. He was the velvet glove, the mythical nice guy; Santa Claus and a generous uncle, and a surprisingly large tax refund and a five-dollar bill found on the street with nobody else to claim it for miles around. No menace, no rage, and so giving. All you had to do was be entirely obedient. Colin had always gotten what he'd wanted, since the time he was a toddler, so he grew up with magical beliefs—desire and fulfillment were one and the same. For me, to desire was to fail. And that was why I was such a miserable shit. Colin explained that to me with a look, like a statue of the Buddha or a long evening watching the sun set into the sea.

Instantly, a second epiphany. "Where does the sun set into the sea?" I said to myself, but loud enough to make Colin frown. "That's where I need to be, to watch the day consume itself. That way I can leave behind the past, all the little humiliations and bullshit I keep stewing in. I'm so sorry to hear about Yvette. I won't bother her anymore."

"You've not been bothering her. I think she might even want to hear from you more often. That's part of why I asked you to write the story. I mean . . ." Colin said, but then he stopped.

"No, no, I'm just living two lives. One full of daydreams and stupid fantasies and one where what . . . what do I do all day? I'll tell you what I did earlier today. I sat in a computer lab and tried to figure out how to get a salesman to visit ten different houses in the fewest steps possible. There were a bunch of us trying, and our answers were averaged together to see if 'parallel processing' was smarter than individual thinking. I barely know what parallel processing means, but it seems to be a big deal. Everyone thinking the same thing all the time. I got twenty-five bucks for it. And that's my day." I took to my feet and wrestled my coat back on. "I shop at the gas station because I'm embarrassed to be seen leaving Family Dollar. It's not like I'm fooling anyone. I don't have a car, Colin!"

"Maybe you should sit back down, take it easy. Let's talk about this story a bit more," Colin said. "Or we can go somewhere else?" I could see it on his lips. He was going to offer to take me to a bar, get me a drink, maybe some lunch. He liked bar and grill–type places that served quesadillas and spinach dip, and fish and chips and clam chowder along with great steins of beer. Colin drank while he ate to keep from getting tipsy, to keep from losing control. He had to practice self-control in order to successfully manipulate the rest of us.

"No, I'm going home. I have to get this down. The sun eaten by the sea! There has to be a Greek myth about it. I should know these things, I'm Greek after all." I headed out to the door and patted my pocket. "Thanks for the dough. Tell Yvette I . . . tell her to feel better, to stay strong."

I lasted about half a block before I vomited into a garbage can. The smell of the trash didn't help me keep anything down, either. I crossed the street and puked again. Yvette, pregnant. The story—a story of us, really—for her, midwived by Colin. Boston's a big city, but it's a small town. Like San Francisco. Hell, probably like New York and Athens and Cairo, too. We can't be anonymous, we can't lose ourselves in even the largest metropolis, or only deal with people on our own terms. We get caught in social webs from which there is no escape. The same eighty-five people, over and over, thanks to accidents of geography, demography, and psychography. No wonder writers and artists decamp for Majorca, Morocco, Paris. Places where they can't be ensnared by the language of others.

How great it must be to live in invincible ignorance of the world around you. To just tromp down the streets, consuming blindly and shitting just as blindly, not caring about a thing.

Not that I could afford to go anywhere like that, save Mexico. In the end, I was a coward. Chester Himes and Dennis Cooper were both expatriates in Paris, but I wasn't as slick as either of those writers, not in any way. I was gangly, bad with both women and men, a dumb shy hick. My parents had been brave enough to come to America, but I was too frightened to leave it. California was close enough. It was a different America. A newer, fresher America.

Alexa found me in Sweetie's up by Telegraph Hill. I took another drill gig, and it had actually been uneventful. Some kids—Chinese versus Italians, the same old story—shot each other up over some bullshit, and I came in to give them each a silver dollar–sized hole in their foreheads so they wouldn't wake up and go after one another all over again. Maybe before the collapse they would have survived their wounds with treatment, gone to prison, and carried on their feuds for another generation. I didn't even feel sorry for them for throwing their lives away.

I was writing on a legal pad when Alexa walked in. Sweetie's was always a quiet place, even before the rise of the dead. Every head turned, and she spotted me immediately and sat down across from me. I said hello, and worked on my sentence. She said hello and when I didn't look back up, she picked up my pad and then smacked it against the tabletop. Her hair was in a severe bun, her face a little dirty.

(12)

"I'm working on a new chapter," I said.

"Billy, why would a book told in the first person even have chapters?" She tapped the pad with her fingernails, all chewed and ragged. "Why would it stop and start again? Whenever he goes to sleep and wakes up?"

I shrugged. "The narrator's read a lot of novels, and decided he liked the format maybe?"

That satisfied her. "Sorry about the other day," she said.

"Sorry for pitching a fit, or killing someone?"

"I'm sorry for both…but, really, why on Earth would someone jump out at an armed—" She caught herself. "Never mind. I've not been sleeping well. How have you been?"

I was tempted to tell her about Thunder. How she was in bed, how she had the same taste for violence that Alexa had, and about Thunder's theory of postapocalyptic women. I told her instead about the dead teens I'd been called upon to drill, how I took the gig because I knew it was close to Sweetie's, how one of the cops had laughed at the bodies as they laid them out for me and said aloud, "What a waste of cock."

"I knew you'd be here," Alexa said. Then she held up a clunky old cell phone. She was on the job.

"Lady driller, eh?"

"Amusingly, the city is actually running low on drills. They gave me the phone and pager, but no other equipment yet. That's government work for you, I suppose."

"I suppose…" I glanced around the room. As is typical when I'm drinking with a notepad and a power drill on the table, all eyes were on me. "Do you think you're up for it?"

"After the Berkeley thing, yes. Seeing that kid, just dead meat, literally, finally jerk off the ground like a marionette being yanked by a string. I mean, I'd seen it before, but only for a moment. Usually I'm running, like everyone else."

"It's true. I'll never get over it," I said. I picked up my pen. "Every time is different—the reanimate dead are like snowflakes, no two are the same." It was difficult to say one thing while writing something else entirely, but I impressed myself with my ability to do it. On the pad, I wrote *is this about city hall??*

"Oh yes," Alexa said. "Definitely."

"I can't help but remember what the priest told me when my papou died. At the wake I said, 'He's dead, he's dead—I don't want to see a dead person,' and started crying and wailing, just like my mother was. And the priest looked at me and said, 'There are no dead people. Not anymore. They're only sleeping.' Not that I ever understood Greek Orthodox theology that well, but it always seemed weird and heavy to me." And I wrote *if you still want me, I'm in.*

"Yes, obviously," Alexa said. "Growing up Greek was so strange, but I guess you can say it prepared you for your job— as a driller—just as it did me, right? Right?" She was emoting like a girl playing a sunflower in the third-grade play. Then her cell phone beeper went off and she looked at it.

"They found you a drill?"

"No, a . . . sleeper." She grinned. "I'll borrow yours, okay?" Without waiting for an answer—which would have been no— she grabbed the drill box by the handle and hefted it. "I had a feeling there'd be some hazing involved in this gig."

"Well, it might just have been bureaucratic incompetence," I said. "Or supercompetence! Maybe they can track us with the phones, or have a chip in the drill, and realized you could just use mine." Even dumb jokes began to feel strangely likely. I reached for my beer.

"I'll bring this back to your apartment later," Alexa said, of the drill.

"I'll be here all night. Just return it here."

"The apartment it is."

"I won't be at the apartment," I said. "Bring the drill here when you're done."

"You have to be at the apartment to collect your drill. It's city property—you're responsible for it. I'll be by later. Wait for me," Alexa said.

"Come back here with it," I said, annoyed.

"The apartment it is!" And with that she left. The second she turned the corner, I was worried she would die. Alexa was too cocky, too eager for some dramatic bloodspray. Was I supposed to follow her? Is that why she made a big deal about meeting me at the apartment later? Was she just waiting for me around the corner, maybe stewing as I dawdled, maybe ready to take off on her own anyway—or was she already gone?

An old guy sitting at the bar, half-turned in his seat, sneered at me and said, "*Maricon!*" I blinked at him stupidly. "Faggot!"

"I know what *maricon* means, *poustis!*" I said. I snatched up my pen and pad, threw some shiny change made out of an old watch at the bar and ran out the door. On the corner, in a bicycle rickshaw, Alexa was waiting for me, my drill on her lap.

The gig, in SoMa in one of the ramshackle rowhouses, was another easy one. A man had called in to say that his partner was dying, and that it wouldn't be much longer now. Then he tied the dying man to his bed, rather expertly, with the bondage gear he had lying around. The man passed before we arrived, but the caller had opened his mouth and put in a ball gag for safety's sake.

"It wasn't AIDS," he greeted us with. He was an older guy, of the right stratum to still be as horrified by AIDS as we all were with what was going on in the US now, so he had to be sure to warn us. "I have some fabric, if you want it?" he said. And he did have a long bolt of some stretchy Spandex or other synthetic, that he seemed too eager to wrap us in.

Alexa mumbled something about official business and safety. I just shrugged.

"Her first day, you know. I've been working for the city . . ." I said, as one should never say "driller" in front of a client, "for a while now. You're very conscientious. Thank you so much for all your preparations." Teary, he explained that cancer had taken his lover, and reiterated that it wasn't AIDS. And then I decided that it probably was AIDS, which roared back to life here after the collapse of the pharmaceutical trade domestically and its relocation to Africa. Now we were paying for AIDS drugs with gold, gram for gram.

Alexa had the drill bit on the dead man's forehead when I walked in. I closed the door behind me.

"Do not wait. Do it now. There's actually more splatter when it's slow. But don't go too fast either! And keep your mouth closed, but your eyes open!" I tried to keep it as quiet as possible, but somehow my lungs made my voice too loud.

Alexa had on gloves and a surgical mask. She shuddered, winced, inhaled sharply, and started the drill. "Shit!" she said, through teeth I presumed were clenched. It was a sharp bit— I'd put a new one on after the morning's drilling—and it bit right into the poor sap's head. It only took a few seconds to reach the brain, then tear into it. Some blood sluiced through the spiral of the bit, but didn't spray the room. Behind me, the client started banging on the door, weeping and crying for his Jerome, for his poor poor Jerome.

Alexa said, "Lock the door and help me clean him up. This guy doesn't need any more grief." The bottom of the drill box had some gauze and wipes and antiseptic sprays—all stuff like the gloves and masks I had never bothered to use, given how I live. I figured it was like letting a little kid get dirty to make him stronger. Overprotect him and he grows up to be a wheezing, allergic asthmatic. Not that I'm a doctor or anything.

Looking at Alexa deftly clean up the blood, then lift the head of the deceased to flip his pillow over to hide the streak of spray on the pillowcase, reminded me of how little I did for my clients. Was letting the blood splatter where it will just another low-key suicide attempt on my part? I looked down at my shirt. Dried blood from this morning. I hadn't even considered it when I went to the bar right afterward to start drinking. Did I always look like a bloodsoaked wreck, like Death himself wandering in to check out the scene? The client started jiggling the doorknob and calling for us to open the door.

"Is everything all right!"

Of course not. Nothing is all right, and nothing would ever be all right again. I thought that. I said, "Just freshening up!" and immediately smacked myself in the face with a meaty palm. Alexa glared at me. I supposed at that moment I had just been relegated to the role of patsy in her plan to infiltrate City Hall, as if that hadn't been my part to play since the very first day we met, since she started trawling San Francisco for allies.

We stayed for a while, taking turns patting the guy's back as he cried over Jerome, hugging the body as best he could given the straps and spread-eagled posture of the deceased. He offered us drinks from his little dry bar.

"Mix your own, help yourself." So I did. Vodka and some grenadine, so it wouldn't look like I was drinking vodka straight. It was good stuff, pre-collapse, smooth. Hangar 1. Most current vodka we're able to get is either homemade stuff that may as well have chunks of potato floating in it, or is outrageously expensive and floated to shore by passing Russian pirates. With Jerome gone, I'm sure the guy wouldn't miss it too much, plus Alexa didn't want anything, so I was basically just consuming a double largely on her behalf.

He finally introduced himself—his name was Terry. He had been in the Navy. He had a wife at one point, in Vallejo, but left her to come down here and be with Jerome. They'd gotten a domestic partnership the moment they could, got married in the San Francisco County courthouse the moment they could, got married again in Alameda when it was actually legal before Prop 8, and then had a Unitarian wedding with a Buddhist priest and an "ultra-reform transman rabbi" when gay marriage was "re-reinstituted." That's what Terry called it. He took a few minutes to carefully wrap the body of his lover in the tarp he had offered us. We looked at pictures on his laptop.

"I love your country," he told us both when we got to the Greek islands part of the extensive slideshow. That's where I should have gone, when I had the chance. Greece, where the living start fires and cause panics, not the dead. Greece, where cousin Taki would hook me up with a scooter and a girlfriend and I could lay on the beach and make my own wine with the grapevines of my grandfather. The news from America would have been greeted with grim smiles from the older generation who remembered the junta, with war-whoops and dancing from the younger generation who remembered Serbia and Iraq and everything else. It would be sunny, not foggy, and if Greek girls are uptight when they're home, German tourist girls never are. The war with the dead would be far away, a priest could say, "There are no dead people" and really mean it. "Everyone you know who died is just sleeping. One day they'll wake up, for better or for worse."

It was dark when we went home to my apartment, which still smelled a bit like Thunder—sweet and rank at the same time. Alexa noticed immediately, of course.

"It smells like fucking in here, and homeless guys." I opened a window.

"Everything smells like that everywhere now," I said. She found a lemon and tore it open just to get a different scent into the air. "Now it smells like soup," I said.

Alexa, on the couch, her nose still wrinkled, asked me, "Is it always like that?"

"No, that was probably the smoothest, nicest drill gig I've ever experienced, or heard about. If you had an ER shift the physicians wouldn't be so kind as poor old Terry and Jerome were. They might strap someone down, or just lock the door behind you and hope for the best."

"Really…?"

"Well, I'm just guessing they hope for the best. Maybe they're like the Bowies of Berkeley, hoping for a decent experimental subject."

"You thought they looked like David Bowie?" Alexa said. "They reminded me more of Devo. With the orange jumpsuits and whatnot."

I sat down next to her, letting our knees touch. She didn't mind blood. How could she, anymore?

"Why are we even talking about them? That was a crazy night, in a long line of crazy nights." The vodka had made me warm. I decided that I wouldn't fuck Alexa that night, not even if she initiated it. Not that I suspected she would initiate anything, except a discussion about her plans.

"Give me your laptop," she said. "Not for keeps; I just want to show you something, if you have any net." I did, and she did. Building plans, BART and MUNI tunnels, hand-drawn sketches on cocktail napkins scanned and uploaded along with every splotch and wrinkle, PDFs of rants and speculations. All publicly available on a freebie website.

"If it were secret," Alexa explained, "the surveillance state might take it seriously. Out in the open, it looks like a prank or a hoax, so we can operate with impunity."

"You hope."

"I *think*," she acknowledged. "But it's not like life is so great now, is it? What do we have to lose?" Another person with a suicide installment plan. My mind always drifted there; I couldn't help but encounter people like me, as my daily life and habits kept the people who passed for normal away from me. Alexa's enthusiasm and belligerence did have another possible origin—she was a cop. Back in the war on terror days, plenty of FBI agents made their careers by finding some mental defective immigrant from a Middle Eastern country, cultivating his crazy ideas to blow up the Pentagon with a remote-controlled airplane from Radio Shack, then arrested his ass just in time for a slow news day, or the kickoff of a re-election campaign. This could all be a set-up, Alexa could just be a city government honeypot. No wonder she got a driller gig so easily, no surprise that she was able to shoot Magpie down in cold blood and be ready for more, ready for gore, just a few days later.

Greek kids in America are all paranoid. Comes from our parents—they were either running from the junta or, later, running from democracy when the junta was overthrown. Alcoholics also have a bit of a problem with paranoia. Then there's simply the conditions of existence—the way we live now. *I should bring showers instead of sunshine, melancholy in lieu of mirth.* It's a cliché to say that it's not paranoia when they're really out to get you, and wrong besides. It remains paranoia, and paranoia is terrifying, crippling. I needed another drink already. I wanted to run screaming out of my own apartment, find a revenant, drink its black blood, just to end the gnawing sensation in my head, the constant twisting of my stomach. I got a drink. Alexa frowned at me. I took her lemon and squirted a twist into the little bottle of Jack just to double down on how annoying I was being to her.

"What's your problem?" she demanded, and I giggled at her. I sounded like a fat retard in the mental hospital. I could imagine another me, from another world, sitting in some well-lit room with steel meshing securing the windows, wearing a hospital gown and drooling onto my chin. Institutional pudding and Xanax would have made me obese. My pants fit like a child's hand-me-down shorts.

I caught my breath and said, "What *isn't* my problem?" I finished the bottle. "Let's say we find out the unbelievable truth—even if there is some remarkable clue in City Hall, and not buried under a ton of bodies in the Empire State Building, or hidden behind a panel on the International Space Station, or encoded onto the bicep tattoo of some Navy SEAL in a cave in Afghanistan. Then what? Speak truth to power? There isn't even a significant platform to get anyone's attention anymore. And if we do figure it all out, and do everything right, and manage to tell everyone in a straightforward and comprehensible way that will leave no room for doubt, and then if we don't get shot for doing it, then what?"

"Then we'll know. I don't even care to tell anyone about what we find. I just want the world to make a little bit more sense, and . . ." Alexa hesitated for a moment to twitch an eye and take a thoughtful chew of her lower lip. "And maybe reverse everything? That sounds like a comic book daydream, doesn't it? Fix the dead, get them back to their families, their work. Get some help to repair the country. But I don't even mean it on that level—I mean I want the information so we can show it to someone, somewhere outside of the US and maybe get a little help."

Back when the crisis first began, the President and Congress were very clear that they were going to handle the "outbreak" as we called it for lack of a better term—the joke was that grandmas nationwide were breaking out of their coffins—without international assistance. A week later, the President was gunned down by the remnant of his own Secret Service detail after his daughter had fallen down a flight of steps and died in his arms, only to awaken and infect him with her teeth in his neck. Then the joke was that the Vice President had messed with the runners on the stairs in the hope of precipitating some event. Whoever the President is now—I think we're down to the President pro tempore of the Senate—he or she is hiding in a bunker somewhere, and her phone doesn't have international dialing. The City is on its own for the most part, and San Franciscans like that just fine. We'll make our own deals with Asia and Latin America and through Russia, the rest of Europe. The joke is that all we have to trade is cockrings.

"So, you're a real hero type after all, hmm?" I said.

"I have a theory. We could all be heroes, except that everyday life gets in the way. If you have to work all day, feed your family, have your teeth cleaned every six months, keep income tax forms for seven years, when do you have time to do something important or meaningful in one go? Volunteering at a soup kitchen or with the *philoptochos* like some old lady is one thing, but . . ."

"But it's not flashy, not the spectacle. But remember, 'In a world which really is topsy-turvy, the true is a moment of the false.'"

"Wait . . . what?" she said.

"*Society of the Spectacle?* You know, it's—"

"Billy, quoting books randomly doesn't make you seem smart or cultured. It makes you seem like a nervous, insecure douchebag."

When a woman says something like that, and you're not a Neanderthal who thinks smacking one in the face is acceptable, the only alternative to a fierce objection followed immediately by an all-night screaming match and a ritual reading from the Book of Flaws which all women have memorized is to play it as it lays.

"I am a nervous, insecure douchebag, Alexa. I don't think either of us are surprised by that. '*Γνῶθισεαυτόν*—'" I laughed because I knew she couldn't object to that quotation. "And I do know myself." I glanced over at my collection of legal pads, all covered in scribbles and scratch-outs. "I don't know much else, I suppose. That's why I'm an unskilled laborer. As are you, as of tonight."

"If you don't want to help, Billy, that's fine. You can sit here and drink yourself to death. Or you can come with me, and then after we see what there is to see, you can come home, sit here, and drink yourself to death. Or if they catch us and float us out on a prison barge, you can sit out in the bay and drink yourself to death. You'll find a way, I'm sure."

"Half the booze in town is prison-grade homebrew anyway," I said. "Fine. My book needs an ending of some sort. I'm in." Then I added, "Is anyone else in? Do you have a bunch of other guys you visit occasionally?"

"Yes, I do have a bunch of other guys I visit occasionally. And I'm sure you stick your penis into anything that isn't trying to kill you. But no, don't worry, you won't have to meet them and then mutter dumb insults to yourself between the beers they'd buy for you because you look just that sad and pathetic." For a moment, I wondered if she had somehow managed to read some of my work on the legal pads.

"You could be nice to me, occasionally," I said. "I . . ." I was going to say that I was nice to her, but that wasn't quite true. "I'll do my best to try to be nice to you." In return, Alexa took off her top. Then both our cell phone pagers went off. We were asked to report to the same place. Something big must have happened. Another earthquake—not likely. I rarely felt the small tremblors, but one big enough to kill a lot of people even I'd notice. A mass shooting or murder or bus accident more likely, or a new contagion ribbing through an apartment block or hospital ward. In some dim corner of my brain, I wondered if this was all just another layer of conspiracy, the final set-up. I agree to aid and abet, Alexa takes off her top, and we get called to duty.

The call was in Japantown, pretty close to the Civic Center and City Hall. It would take us awhile to get there. Even before the reanimations, Japantown was a geographical oddity—almost impossible to get to without seriously meaning it. It's not much of a neighborhood either, dominated by a theme mall and a few concrete slab buildings supposedly reminiscent of Tokyo's industrial housing blocks. With the buses mercurial and the unofficial transports worse, it might take an hour. But Alexa was curious and I was resigned.

"Is it a trap?"

"Maybe," she said, her voice muffled through her sweater, which she was snaking back into.

"Is it a trap you set?"

Her head popped out of the neck-hole just in time for her to peer at me, eyes wide. "You're not that important, friend," she said.

"I can tell you're serious. You're talking like a movie cowboy all of a sudden. Anyway, two drillers, one drill. You want it?"

"Oh yeah, I fucking want it." She went to the sink where she'd wiped down the equipment and quickly put everything back in the box. I grabbed a baseball bat, not so I'd go down swinging if I had to, but to have something to do with my hands. My fingers clenched the aluminum compulsively. This was strange and stupid, a new kind of oppression that people trained to obey the dictates of everyday life could never understand, never see as anything other than the freedom of anarchy, the audacity of will and desire. But I'd spent my adult life trying to avoid adult life, living a simplified version of it without dreams of a family or concern for the polity, so I had a special sensitivity to the traps laid by the world. The most obvious and straightforward of social demands—wear a seatbelt, don't spit, drink only in the evenings, save money, don't vanish in the middle of the night, defend yourself when punched in the face by an angry husband instead of just laughing at him because no matter how hard he hits, you still fucked his wife—all were inhabited by the spirit of tyranny. City work, the war against the demon futility, was just another aspect of mental indenture. But I was going, because Alexa had just shown me her tits again, and because I said I would, and because I didn't want to be alone.

The Japan Center was ringed with police wagons and fire trucks. They hadn't aged well. Several had unrepaired crumples or obvious DIY fix-ups—duct tape and plastic sheeting for a side window, a ruined ladder twisted like a bow atop a wrapped gift, scratches and innumerable small dents. Ditto the personnel in mix 'n' match uniforms, scars and bruises, even a few fingers missing to the second knuckle on the right hand of the cop who waved us behind a cordon, where several other drillers waited along with a few medics by a tent.

We were briefed via gossip. A revolutionary, or religious, or just plain suicidal sect had barricaded themselves in the mall as best they could. There were hostages, or at least suspected hostages. It wasn't a Japanese American or local action—virtually everyone inside appeared to be white, which further fueled the suspicion that the hostages were just sect members ready to be rescued in order to explode their dynamite belts in the midst of us. Or the whole thing was just a distraction, or the prelude to the Canadian invasion. Or the hostages were going to be killed, and the cultists would kill themselves or just wait for the reanimates to do it, then they'd storm out of all entrances, take out the police, and the plague would finally spread uniformly across the city. The end of the world between two rows of spittle-slick teeth, finally. Then, a hand was on my chest. The guy from the other night stood before me, smiling.

"You a driller?"

I shrugged. "Sure."

"I could tell, I could tell with you," he said. "You was calm, man." Then his hand slipped from my chest to my hand and he shook it. "Cornelius. Call me Junior." To Alexa he said, "This your man? He a rock."

"A rock!" I said to Alexa. "What's news, Junior? Why are we here?"

He shrugged. "Where there be bodies, there be drillers."

"They don't expect us to go into the mall after a big firefight and poke around in the dark, do they?" Alexa was staring past at the Japan Center itself. As malls go, it was a fairly small one, split into two buildings, and only a few stories high. Lots of entrances and exits, but not so many that the cultists were going to be able to slink away. Ten seconds around the police, and I was already thinking like a cop. Secure the perimeter! Don't let the criminals escape! Standing by to crack heads open, sir yes sir!

"We're not here for them," Alexa said, still looking past us and across the street. "We're here for the cops. When the cultists start shooting and killing us, we're here to drill their heads open." She had spotted something up on the roof, and she wasn't the only one. Shouts, hands in the air, then a spotlight filling the night. There was a gun, a big one on a tripod, and it roared to life. Junior tackled us both as bullets streaked over our heads in a wide arc, sweeping through the cordon. Legs were everywhere, knees too, and flailing. I grabbed Alexa and Junior and got up. They had their drill boxes held over their heads. Junior took us down again. The rhythm—I'm up, he sees me, I'm down. Junior, a soldier, chanted that. Long strides with my long legs, a wide wingspan; I knocked us a hole in the crowd and we swam through it like dolphins breaking the waves.

An explosion somewhere behind us felt like the earthquake, but the sky shone red, a tiny sun rising. The Japan Center was on fire. Then a parked car across the street on Laguna went up, as did the one next to it. I caught a glimpse of the third car—an obvious wreck, but the city is full of them—and thought I saw a small spark reflected in the spidery remains of the windshield before it exploded too.

"Run!" I said, but Junior grabbed me.

"They want us to run," he said. "We move, but we stay."

I looked to Alexa, waiting for a scream or tears, but she was stone except for her wild eyes, ready to fight. The police were returning fire now, from behind their cars, but it was pistols versus military stuff. We made way for firefighters running with hoses. The scene was the opposite of anarchy— suddenly everyone was in charge, full of authority, shouting orders and then instantly carrying them out. A stolen city bus rolled down the cross street and machine gun fire poured from two of its windows. Another faceful of asphalt, another quick stagger back to my knees, my feet.

"What is this, a coup?" I shouted. My baseball bat was long gone. Useless, but I would have felt better with something to swing.

"They're killing the whole city, they want to take over! Don't you see?" Alexa grabbed my arm and pulled me toward the remains of a hardware store. Junior sprinted ahead of us and made the door first.

The store was wall-to-wall bare. Not even shelves, not a single screw was on the floor. Tools and materials went quickly when the dead arose. We could hide, barely, in the shadows. Junior took out his drill and handed me a spare bit; I clutched it in my hand like a knife. The police had rallied somehow, and charged the mall entrance where the gunfire from the roof couldn't reach them. One of the paddy wagons rammed the bus as it turned the corner for a second sortie, and there was some hand-to-hand fighting amidst the wreckage of the vehicles. Nothing exploded. Few things do.

We watched for a little while.

Junior was muttering a play by play: "Watch it, that hose is crushed. Oh, they're going up the side steps now. That'll be a shooting gallery. Is that a helicopter, can you hear that? No, it ain't a helicopter . . ."

Alexa drifted deeper into the store, and rushed back to tell us that she had found a door to the basement. I moved to go, but Junior grabbed my arm.

"Dawg, we got a job."

I handed him his drill bit back. "You're going to get yourself killed, and there won't be anyone to cave your head in afterwards. Come with us. Whatever's going on, we won't know who won till the morning, and we won't ever know what it means, probably. 'What do you think of the French Revolution? It's too soon to tell . . .' Know what I mean?"

Junior nodded. "Go with your woman, it's cool. I'm waitin' on this out here," he said. He was as crazy as anyone else, so I had no problem leaving him to try to do whatever mad thing he wanted to accomplish. Drill everyone and stack them up like cordwood probably, but there would be no applause for him. Alexa and I got the basement door open pretty easily thanks to my drill. It was more than ten feet down, unusual for San Francisco construction. We had only the light from our small cell phone screens to guide us around the room, which was as bare as the upstairs, but at least not so exposed. To save batteries, we clapped our phones shut and huddled in the dark, in the cold. There was no reason to even think of going back upstairs.

"Junior was a good guy, but other than that, how are we supposed to even know which side to take?" I said, mostly to myself.

But Alexa answered. "Not the side starring the people who laid the trap and tried to kill us, obviously."

"Why not? Don't you believe that the city government is up to no good? It's not like we elected them anyway. They're just old bureuacrats who didn't die and wouldn't go home."

"I'm constitutionally incapable of signing up with someone trying to kill me. That's why I never voted for an anti-abortion candidate, even if I liked all his other positions. No matter how good he was on other issues, if he wanted me bleeding to death in a back alley, with a wire hanger sticking out of my cunt, I voted for the other guy."

"And if they were both like that?"

"Wrote myself in," Alexa said. "I wrote myself in a lot, actually."

"You sound like my father," I said.

She didn't say anything. I couldn't see her face, or even much of an outline in the dark, so I just spoke some more. "He'd blame the CIA on both sides of the conflict. He'd see strategic calculations in all the chaos upstairs, like it was all part of a conspiracy."

"Conspiracy to . . ."

"I don't know. But he'd think that we were the targets of it."

"Because we're Greek?" She laughed.

"Nah, because he doesn't actually know anyone outside, and he's a warm, compassionate person toward people he knows. He was, I mean. He knew, I mean."

She didn't say anything to that, but did reach out and after some preliminary scrambling around my shin, managed to give my knee a supportive squeeze. Not that there wasn't a small hill of bodies being piled up above our heads somewhere, not that virtually everyone that everyone knew is already dead—there are dead people, regardless of what the priest says—but there are some that always hurt. I burst into tears and wailed. It didn't matter who heard me anyway. After awhile, we slept, all tangled up in one another, arms for pillows.

I'm tempted to start this page with the sentence, "Greeks are Greeks only when Greeks are around Greeks," but that's a darling born to be murdered.

By Greeks, I mean Greek Americans anyway, and even with that qualifier I'm deeply suspicious of the claim. What I mean to communicate is that Greek Americans often try to show how Greek they are to other Greek Americans. Except for my family, it seems, they all head back to Greece annually if they can. They celebrate Easter on the "correct" date and crow about inexpensive chocolate rabbits when the feast is a week after everyone else's. We show off the language, call black people *mavri* and other white people "whites," as though we're not.

My Somerville landlord liked to do this. His name was Kyriakos, but he called himself Charlie, which sounds about as much like Kyriakos as René does. But I called him Mister Papatheofanis. He called me *reh*—one of the non-word words Greeks use. It's like "Hey you," except it really means, "I'm in charge; you're some schmuck."

(13)

"*Ella*, reh," he called to me as I tried to quietly walk up the steps to my room. It was cold enough that steam poured from my mouth, even inside. "I hear you out there, I have message. From some white girl. She came here."

Papatheofanis didn't keep his apartment any warmer than mine, I had to give him that.

"*Yasas*," he said when I walked in. He was sporting a sleeveless undershirt of the sort middle-class snobs used to call "wifebeaters" because only working class ethnics engage in spousal abuse, don't you know. He stood up to shake my hand and pat me on the shoulder. Boxer shorts, black dress socks, and well-worn beach sandals that probably rocked the beaches of Chios back in the 1960s. "She still here. Sleeping in the *sala*."

"Who is it?"

"Betty," he said, his b a soft *beta*. "Your girlfriend, eh?" he asked. I had no idea what he was talking about until I slipped into his tiny living room. Papatheofanis was a widow, so the room was feminine, with a chaise lounge and a worn couch, an enormous television from another era, a large round coffee table swimming with photos in black and white and color of old dead Greeks next to donkeys, Theofanis as a young man in a kitchen, and gap-toothed grandkids with thick eyebrows and heavy bangs standing in front of ridiculous backdrops. A dude ranch. A waterfall shooting rainbows. The room was dark and there were no wall switches. I walked in and switched on a lamp. On the lounge, looking like a pile of laundry, slept Yvette, her back to me, her face buried in her hands.

"Is she all right?" I asked.

"Is she?" Papatheofanis asked me in return. "I have message." He pulled a crumpled piece of paper out of his boxer shorts and handed it to me.

"You answered the door dressed like this, Mister Papatheofanis?" He just looked at me. "I mean, isn't it cold?"

He shrugged and patted his pot belly. "I got a fire in me, eh?" He hiked his chin, then bowed his forehead and clicked his tongue toward Yvette, like he was saying *No!* to her. A Greek no looks a bit like an American yes—it's a nod. "Anyway, take care of this *malakies*, okay?" To hammer home his lovely point, he made a fist and jerked off an imaginary three foot long phallus, then went back to the kitchen. I heard a fridge opening, the wet pop of a stopper, and then the sink going. An ouzo, with water, surely.

I shook Yvette's shoulder, but she didn't awaken immediately. I kissed her on the cheek, then the lips, then was weirded out by my own behavior and by her torpor. I patted her cheek, just short of a slap, and then she shifted her weight on the little couch and opened her eyes till they were slits.

"Hey," she said, dreamy. "Wanted to see you. Colin tol' me you lived here." She was close enough that I could smell her breath. Not a trace of alcohol, so I instantly decided that she had taken sleeping pills and had come here as part of a very intimate see-what-you-made-me-do suicide.

For a moment, I was giddy—she liked me! Saner, less booze-soaked parts of my brain prevailed. I shook her roughly. "Yvette! Wake up! This very moment, you hear me!" From behind me I heard my landlord's voice.

"Slap her," he said. "Slap Betty awake."

"Yvette!" I said, to him and her both. "Wake up."

Yvette stirred in my grip. "I'm fine, I'm fine," she said.

"You're not fine," I said, and I was right as her head began to droop again. I teared up; this was insane.

"That your woman?" Papatheofanis asked. He clinked the ice in his glass, just in case he wasn't heard from seven feet away. "What you crying for, eh?"

"Mister Papatheofanis, what was she like when she got here?"

He shrugged. "Like that. Sick, eh?"

I remembered the note and read it—it was the first page of the story I wrote for Colin, marked up with notes for revision. Harsh professor, it seemed like. "Yvette, you did not swallow a bunch of sleeping pills *over this*, did you?"

"No, no," she said. "Had big fight with Colin. Over him."

Papatheofanis walked over. "C'mon, get her up."

"No, she needs a doctor!" I said. "She needs her stomach pumped."

Papatheofanis snorted. "Doctors, bah!" he said with a wave of his drink. I pictured him spilling some, it landing on my outstretched tongue. "You got money for a doctor? She got money for one? You go to ER, you get a bill for twenty thousand dollars! Get her up, we work it out of her." He finished off his ouzo, dropped the glass onto the thick carpet, and grabbed one of Yvette's mostly limp arms. "Come, we do the *kalamatianos!*"

Papatheofanis was the world's fattest hobbit, and his shoulders were as hairy as the tops of his feet. Yvette was short, like most girls, and the top of my forehead could touch the low ceiling if I stood on the top of my toes. We made a ridiculous trio, arms thrown over shoulders, stomping ten steps to the front, then two back, as Papatheofanis scatted and teetitteetitteetitili'd out a song. Yvette's eyes were open now, half-amused, half-shocked to see who she was with, how she was marching back and forth in front of the bay window to an audience of snowdrifts and cats.

"Opa!" Papatheofanis shouted, then he bent his knees hard, squatted, twirled, and performed an odd kick to his own palm. Yvette blinked rapidly, her ankles folding under her. Only we were keeping her up at first. Then she made a face and vomited across her front.

"Keep dancing!" Papatheofanis ordered, drunk and manic. I was just glad to be next to Yvette again, to smell her shampoo and, yes, even her puke. I counted the remnants of only five pills. Though a skinny girl, she would have been fine, I guessed.

Finally Yvette demanded water. We sat her down on the larger couch.

Papatheofanis told me, "Keep Betty upright! I get the water!" and he came back with another glass, with sparking water and a lime in it. Yvette sipped it slowly. She didn't ask for paper towels or a rag with which to clean herself, and neither of us thought to offer her one.

"Oh, if Mrs. Papatheofanis was alive, she'd be dead," my landlord said. He had a second glass of ouzo and water for himself, and he held it against his forehead as though it wasn't the dead of winter, as if he'd bothered to turn the furnace on at all today. Yvette's fingers were blue. I wondered if I could get her into the shower, clean her up, innocently see her body one more time. Even that fantasy was ruined by a sudden ridiculous fear that the pipes were frozen and would burst. Why did I care? I was leaving town, going somewhere else.

"So you had dinner with Colin, you had a fight over the story, and he dumped you."

"How do you know I had dinner with Colin?" Yvette said slowly, her voice rumbling with suspicion.

"Pad thai, it's all over your shirt. That's a Colin meal. A Boston meal. You didn't even know what pad thai was before you moved here."

"Yeah, well, you followed me . . ."

Papatheofanis's mood turned. He had his arms crossed over his chest now, and stood as upright as he could at five foot two. "She get rid of everything, eh? She can go now. You go now, eh Betty?"

"Yvette!" I said to him.

"What am I saying? Veh-tee."

"That's the opposite; Veh-tee. Eee-vhet."

"I don't know these *xeni* names," he said. Yvette tugged on my sleeve.

"I wanted to say . . ." she started. "I wanted to say goodbye. I'm sorry Colin made you write a story . . . he was being a prick."

I felt the eyes of Papatheofanis upon me. He switched to Greek, which I only barely understood. *How many cocks is this woman sucking?* was the gist of his remark. And then he said another sentence, and all I knew of it was the word *keratas*—cuckold—and that he was discussing, between his drunken self and his more reasonable sober self, why on Earth he would rent to a man who was not a man. His mood had soured, likely because of the stain on his carpet, which he would certainly not clean himself. That's what he had a wife for, and so what if she had been dead for five years and he was all alone, as his daughter and only child had met a college boy and moved out to Colorado to have babies named Blaine and Carter. For Papatheofanis, the universe had turned upside-down. I was downstairs in his apartment instead of upstairs in my little garret. A woman had dirtied his room instead of cleaning it up. A woman was crying because of her affairs, rather than weeping over the affairs of her man.

So I exploded. "Oh, he was being a prick! You know a lot about him and his prick, I'm sure! And now you come crawling back to me, eh? Eh?" I shook her by the shoulders, not too roughly. I would have been pleased if her head popped right off and rolled across the carpet like she was a broken doll, but I had her in my arms again and I knew my anger was just a performance. I wished I could take Yvette upstairs, let her sleep it off on my couch while I kneeled on the floor before her and just *watched*, but I couldn't. For a moment, I was seething—she ruined my life. But no. My life wasn't even that bad. I was a lucky guy. I didn't have to go to some stupid job every day. I was a writer, albeit in some vanishingly small way. But nobody could take that from me. I started mentally listing good things about my life: I didn't have cancer; it was snowing outside, but I was standing inside; I wasn't overly anguished about Yvette now that she was right in front of me, sad and pathetic; Papatheofanis would probably fall asleep soon and forget all of this in the morning; even if he woke up in a rage, I had five hundred dollars and could go anywhere I liked, and could afford, for five hundred dollars.

"Get this girl out of here," Papatheofanis bellowed. Then he left, muttering, to his room. Whether he was just drunk or actually trustworthy was beyond me, but I had Yvette, and I bet I had that bottle of ouzo Papatheofanis had been working on in the kitchen.

Yvette looked up at me, her eyes teary. "Don't call Colin, okay?"

"Of course not," I said. I called a cab instead, and put Yvette in the vestibule atop the porch to wait for it with a handful of crumpled dollar bills. It had windows, and some insulation, so she wouldn't freeze. That's how she'd made me feel for months. Isolated, in a little box, just on the wrong side of chilly, and waiting in the dark for a dubious rescue. When I led her out there, she had opened her mouth as if to say something—probably not "Thanks," or "Take me upstairs; you can have me." She looked as relieved as I did. We'd managed, together, to mess up so completely that we didn't have to talk to one another anymore, or even think about one another anymore.

What would have Yvette said, had she been just a bit more sober, slightly less sobby? "*Malaka*," maybe. That was a Greek word I'd taught her—it means effeminate asshole, or wanker, or someone who jerked off so much he's become some sort of halfwit. She had often misremembered it as "makala" and "kamala," but always liked the idea of a retarded masturbator. Or maybe she just wanted to say "I'm cold" but knew I only had one coat and thus none to lend her, since we certainly weren't going to encounter one another again, and Colin wasn't going to be a good go-between to get my coat back to me.

I certainly knew she wasn't going to say, "I'm sorry." She had nothing to be sorry for. I followed her to Boston like a fool, acted the fool every moment we were together, tried to fool her by inserting myself into every aspect of her life out here in this great and undiscovered country of New England, and when she finally turned to me I treated her poorly to impress an idiot boozebag stranger whose only tie to me was ethnicity. Ethnicity, the great lie of the world. America's great success showed that to be true, and its great failure was further evidence. There was a new race now, built upon the nonsense of the old. Reanimates had conquered America, *sans* plan or ideology. There was no community among them, just a deadly sameness. Anyway, they're all dead now. Yvette, Colin, Papatheofanis, the various boobs in the workshop, all those women I abused in my mind while riding the T, even confident Aishwarya.

In the early days of the crisis, Google and Facebook and Twitter and a few irony-limned startups like IT'S ALIVE!! (always all caps, always two exclaims) were busy as could be with people updating their locations and circumstances. SEND HELP was trending for weeks, but no counteroffensive could be made against an enemy whose numbers replenished after every skirmish, and the government made matters worse by doing their best to seal the borders to keep help from coming overseas. Not that the rest of the world was all that eager to do anything but make popcorn and set up a new United Nations in Lisbon of all places. I never saw Yvette's name on any site. Colin had made it to Cape Cod and was part of some scheme to just shoot up to Canada and beg for asylum. I imagined steamer trunks stuffed with gold ingots and useless dollars filling the hulls of pleasurecraft, crew members pushed overboard to make room, ships running in frantic and futile circles, then finally them all sinking. Colin's went down, at least.

"I can't believe this is it," was his last message to the Internet.

Maybe Aishwarya is alive. I used to daydream about that occasionally. About coming across her out here. Maybe she'd even remember my face, and tell me the miraculous story of a forty-person troupe comprised of her extended family slashing their way across country to San Francisco, like the pioneers of old. But no, she's dead, I know it. The Boston metroplex went especially quickly, as all the resources up and down the Northeast Corridor were mustered in an attempt to save New York City. I hope she had a quick death—all teeth and bloodspray. Better than a slow decline amidst the ruins, or a terrifying inevitable checkmate from the resource microwars on the block, I think. I'm living the latter two, and certainly would have preferred the former. Apocalypse is a Greek word. It means lifting the veil. That's why the last book of the Bible is also called Revelation. You can't lower the veil afterwards and pretend to unsee all that has been seen. Even moonshine potent enough to make a man blind won't help.

San Francisco is . . . okay. We're all crazy here, just like we were before. We're ruled by men with guns who kill us for our own safety, just like we were before. There are fewer distractions now, except for one another. The façades have all been torn down, the glaze rubbed off with steel wool. It's hard to live after revelation. Better to wander the world in a daze, in doubt, sure that there's some good life story out there to live. Go to school, get married, have a baby, die painlessly in your sleep if you can, with smiling relatives around the hospital bed if you can't. They won't start screaming and fighting till after you close your eyes for the final time that way. That's the life my parents wanted, and they sure as hell didn't get it, but at least they didn't live to see me now.

After I saw Yvette out, I went to bed and dreamed of us dancing in a black and white field taken straight from the few photos my parents had of their early lives in Greece. Papa smiling at the camera, two goats on either side of him staring dumbly forward. My mother in a long skirt, leaning against a motorcycle that is leaning against a fence, squinting up at the sky, gray grass all around her. We all danced arm in arm, and we all fell down when the world rolled out from under us. In the morning, I called my parents and told them that I wouldn't be coming home for Christmas, because I had gotten a job in California and had to start right away. At a magazine, for the shipping industry. Shipping is lousy with Greeks.

Papatheofanis had introduced me to an old friend, see, who set up a phone interview, and I did really well. Not much money to start, but enough to make moving worthwhile. And in San Francisco, all the backyards have orange trees too. They pretended to be excited for me, and I pretended to believe that they believed me. So we were all happy.

Junior woke us up in the morning. He looked like a cartoon character that had been in an explosion—clothing torn, a black eye, soot and ash everywhere. He was upset with our desertion and showed it with a kick to my shoulder, then a stomp on my forearm when I didn't immediately spring to my feet.

"Yo!" he said. "Wake the fuck up. We won. And I got something for you." I extricated myself from Alexa's limbs and dragged to my feet. Alexa stayed on the floor, but she was awake now, dazed as if emerging from an incomplete afternoon nap and confused to find that it was dark outside.

"Bring her down!" Junior called up the stairs, and down came a well-beaten police officer. He dragged Thunder down the steps by her wrist. Her face was smeared with greasy stripes of eye make-up and dust.

"We found this bitch inside. You want her free, or fuck her?" Junior said.

Alexa scrambled to her feet, one bitch smelling another.

(**14**)

"Normally, we'd just punch her ticket," the cop said. "But Junior says you know this girl." He shoved Thunder and she took half a step in front of me.

"What the hell's going on?" I said. "Thunder, what were you doing in the Japanese mall?"

"We wanted in. You know, City Hall? It was the only way."

"Clearly not," Alexa said.

"What do you think is in City Hall that's so important?" I said.

Thunder shrugged. "I don't know. But if it were nothing, they wouldn't be keeping it a secret, would they?" Behind her, the cop and Junior exchanged looks, then looked at me expectantly.

"Okay, I'll—"

"Don't…" Alexa hissed.

"—take—"

"…fucking do…"

"—responsibility—"

Alexa howled at that. "You? Take responsibility? Fucking right."

"Do I need to sign her out or anything?" I asked the cop, who shrugged. Thunder moved to my left side, keeping me between her and Alexa.

The cop said, "There are two reasons, potentially, to keep people from a place. To keep something in, or to keep something out. Think about that, okay?"

"That's cryptic," Alexa said to the cop.

"Almost a Zen koan," I said to Alexa.

Junior's phone beeped. He looked at the text and nodded toward the steps. "Let's go. All y'all." Even the cop obeyed without hesitation.

The street had been torn from the ground, given a good shake, and then plopped back down. The mall's exterior was scorched and black—now it matched most of the rest of the block, most of the rest of the city. Bodies, both uniformed and civilian, were stacked neatly in one corner, a precise hole in every forehead, open and expectant like a mouth expressing surprise. Junior guided us to a large bus of the sort that used to take old people to Reno for unfun vacations and we all walked up the steps. Most of the seats had been torn out, and replaced with long, slim desks on either side. A few people manned laptops and in the back, toward the restroom, sat the social worker. She smiled and waved when she saw us; when she saw me, anyway.

"Hello!" she said. "So we meet again." She laughed aloud.

"The mad scene: enter Ophelia," I said. She laughed at that as well. She did look mad. Though the bus, some sort of mobile command center, was slick and appeared new, the social worker's own dress betrayed reduced circumstances. Her suit jacket had a mismatched button, and she had to settle for "nude" stockings—the pinkish-beige of Caucasian nylon looked fairly awkward on an older black woman. Men's boots too. A sidearm in a holster strapped to a large leather belt, like a movie cowboy.

The social worker looked at Thunder and introduced herself as Dr. Jaffe. Thunder decided that her name was Ashley, or perhaps it truly was. Then the doors closed behind us.

"Yo!" Junior said, to nobody in particular.

"Relax, it's just a precaution. We're not driving off anywhere," Jaffe said. "Someone probably spotted a reanimate outside, or an undrilled corpse. We're actually waiting for a mechanic and a tow truck. It was a pitched battle last night, I tell you. For the future of the city." She looked at Thunder. "So, tell me dear, what would you like to know?"

"What's so special about this city?" Thunder said. "Everywhere else I've been, all around the Bay, is an utter wreck. You have electricity most days, wireless. The friggin' traffic lights still work. I met someone who received a letter from a friend in France."

Jaffe shrugged. "Mostly, it's just a quirk of geography. We're a port city. Hilly. Temperate climate. Before the chaos of the reanimate uprising, we had a highly educated and technically astute population base. We still do, though the base is much smaller now, of course. You may as well ask the Arabs why they have all the oil—does Allah like them best?"

"Luck's a relative thing," the cop said. "San Francisco isn't lucky, it's a shithole overrun with zombies and heavily armed assholes who are trying to destroy what's left of civilization. Siberia is lucky, compared to us. The people in the slums of Tijuana are lucky, compared to us."

"That's not everything though—no graveyards. No cemeteries. Even long before the reanimations, the city would ship bodies to Colma. Is that a coincidence too, a lucky happenstance?" Alexa demanded to know.

Jaffe shrugged. "If I said yes, you wouldn't believe me. If I said no, you wouldn't be any less angry about it. Tell me what I should say, young woman, to make you happy and I'll do my best to say it convincingly."

"'Neither confirm nor deny' is the same as a confirmation!" Alexa said.

"Or a denial!" I said. Only Junior laughed at that, and just barely. "I mean, why not ask why Colma accepted all those bodies, hmm?"

"Are you saying that this was some sort of experimental virus gone out of control, and that there's a secret lab in Colma that had spent decades experimenting on dead bodies in order to reanimate them?" Thunder said.

"Hmm, that's a new one to me . . ." I glanced around the bus. Nobody seemed to be taking Thunder's new notion seriously. Then I asked Jaffe. "What is any of this to do with you? I mean, who are you? Why do you get a bus, why do you know what's going on, or get to pretend to?"

Jaffe said plainly, "I'm the mayor. After a fashion. You're a Greek boy, yes? Ever read deeply into the notions of the Greek Orthodox church?"

"Nope," I said. I looked at Alexa.

"You're an . . . ethnarch?" she said to Jaffe.

"More or less. We're in the kingdom of the death, an oppressed minority. The actual ruling elite of San Francisco died early on, mostly thanks to stupid stunts for the news cameras. Someone had to step up to take charge and administrate the city government for the living, and that was me," she said. "Really, William, it was all over the Internet. I'm happy to step down if the citizens can get it together to elect a replacement. Heck, I'll step down right now and let one of you take over. Or all three of you. You can be a troika."

"You're the mayor of the city, but you go on door-to-door missions finding people in case they're not dead yet?"

"I haven't had to do that in some months, sadly . . . You were actually the only one we ever found. I suppose we can say that you were well-preserved," Jaffe said. She made a drinky-drinky gesture with her hand. It was clear to me then that every last human being in the city was insane. Alexa and Thunder were rampaging maniacs, getting out all their aggressions on the ruins of the world. Most of the clients I'd met while drilling were hanging on to a dead past, blind to the world around them. Even Junior was some sort of weirdo. It would take a crazier person than all the rest to climb to the top of this shitheap and declare herself Queen and Protector. And here she was. There could be no secrets here, just dumb accidents and ridiculous fate. No conspiracies, just the futile graspings of deranged minds for some narrative that could make sense of their lives.

"I'm not the only well-preserved one around here," I said. "You're the witch of the place."

"I love this city, friend—"

"'I'll tell you what real love is," I said. "It is blind devotion, unquestioning self-humiliation, utter submission, trust and belief against yourself and against the whole world, giving up your whole heart and soul to the smiter—as I did.'"

I heard Thunder whisper to the cop, *"That's from Charles Dickens."*

"I've done all that," Jaffe said. "I do that every morning before breakfast. We have some chickens in a coop in a courtyard. When did you last have fresh scrambled eggs, English muffins, orange juice? I have that every morning, you know. So too do the full-time city workers." She nodded toward the policeman, and then to Junior.

"You see, I'm all carrot, no stick. There's no use in killing anyone, and it's expensive—and superfluous—to imprison them. So all I am going to do is let the three of you off the bus now. Cornelius here can protect you from any remnant reanimates while in Japantown, I'm sure, and Officer Grady will also accompany you so long as you like. Then tomorrow, I'll give you a call. What I'd like to know is what young Ashley here was up to, and who her confederates might be. Talk to her about it," Jaffe said. As an aside, she said, "And I apologize for speaking of you as though you're not standing right here in the room with us, Ashley, but you've been a bit rude to me." The bus door opened again, and the cop made a sweeping gesture with his arms to usher us all out. "I'll call you tomorrow," Jaffe said to us.

Outside, we let the cop and Junior go immediately. The cop was happy to get right back on the bus, but Junior had words for us.

"You know, I would of plugged this girl, bam, like that!" He snapped his fingers. "But I seen you two together. You a driller, man, and we gotta hella watch our backs. So do right by the city, you feel me?"

"Uh…all right," I said. That seemed to satisfy him.

We walked down to the Civic Center and found a place to sit in the old Asian art museum. I'd decided that I was just going to sit down and stare at Thunder until she decided to say something, but Alexa started arguing with her immediately.

"You were an armed group with no goals, no plans, no strategy—you expect us to believe that?"

"Why not? You shot the shit out of my friend with no goal, plan, or strategy! You're a fucking murderer; you don't get to lecture me on moral issues," Thunder said. A powerful rhetorical ploy, but Alexa didn't fall for it.

"He jumped out at us. Actually, your little stunt with your 'new' friends—if they were really new at all—is just like what you tried to pull on us in Berkeley. Lure us in, then attack."

I was struck by an epiphany at that very moment. I needed a drink. I could get one too, if I wanted to. I was entirely, utterly free. "'Anything, anything would be better than this agony of mind, this creeping pain that gnaws and fumbles and caresses one and never hurts quite enough,'" I said, straight out of Sartre, but the girls ignored me. I wandered away and out of the great hall of the museum.

The public common was busy, as always. Tents in bunches, vans from out of which spilled whole desperate families, the smell of street meats, tiny pawnshops one card table wide—it would be easy to find a drink. I could trade my cell phone for one. Let Mayor Jaffe call someone else first thing tomorrow, offer him eggs in exchange for information. She'd get a better deal from whatever random boob took her call anyway.

I found myself chanting, "Drink, drink, drink," as I wandered through the agora, and though I was the only one singing about booze to himself, I didn't garner any attention, wanted or unwanted. We were all muttering freaks now.

I found a stone soup bar operating out of the back of a repurposed hot dog cart. Stone soup is essentially a randomly generated highball of haphazard proportions. If you brought something to pour into the bucket—booze of any type, or fruit juice, or soda—you could drink a double for the price of a single. The rest of us had to pay, which funded the base broth of the soup. I got a cupful for some change and my shoelaces. The soup du jour was a brown and orange swirl, typical of a town with a fair number of orange trees in vacant lots and in hidden backyards. Tasted like feet, but one gets what one pays for, especially after total economic collapse. My body was hungry for the sugars and the vitamins, and straighted right out. I could picture every little cell in my body, little cartoon blobs with gaping toothless mouths, opening wide to take a dose of the medicine.

Only after my first swallow did I bother looking at my fellow patrons. A fat fag on my right—not a slur, he wore a black T-shirt with the words FAT FAG spelled out in glued-on acrylic diamonds; huge arms covered in pre-collapse sleeves. On my left, a painfully thin woman; she looked like a collection of chicken bones wrapped in soiled paper. I've seen a lot of ugly people in my time, but this woman was in the top 99 percent. More wrinkles than features, a jaw shaped like an iron, eyes nearly sunk together in the middle of her face. She drank slowly, tilted her cup past a lipless fringe. Her teeth were crooked, like tombstones after an earthquake, which is how she managed to get any stone soup down her throat. Her jaw was clenched.

I turned to the bartender, a young Mexican guy with a decent mustache who sat behind his vat of grog in a full lotus position, and asked, "This woman is dead, isn't she?"

"I think so," he said slowly, like a Berkeleyan. Maybe he drove out here on the weekends to make some extra money, or to poison San Franciscans. "What should we do?"

The fat guy said, "Oh, just leave her be. Maybe you should mass produce this stuff and hand it out to the dead when they come waltzing down the street. Then all our problems will be solved!" He giggled.

"How long has she been this way?" I asked.

The bartender shrugged.

"Jesus Christ, did she pay with soup or cash?"

He shrugged at that too.

"Well, how long has she been here—and think before you fail to answer, okay?"

The guy shrugged anyway, but then he said something. "She was waiting for me. She even slapped the side of the car to try to get me to hurry up." Both Fat Fag and I laughed at that one, and exchanged looks. "Oh wait, I remember, she did pay with something. Something . . . something . . ." he looked around his legs for a moment. "This," he said finally as he held up a keychain with both standard keys, the old-fashioned skeleton key with long shafts, and some plastic fobs. He jingled the keychain at her. She glanced up at it and growled like a dog, then went back to dribbling her drink on her chin and blouse. She had flat fried-egg tits.

"And you accepted mysterious keys as a payment because . . ." my new fat friend asked before I had a chance to. He patted me on the arm. "This should be good," he stage-whispered. He had wisely determined that the bartender wouldn't even realize that we were just mocking him now.

"She said they were important," the bartender said. "That they'll open all doors, reveal all truths, expose all secrets." He didn't seem capable of lying, or joking. I looked over at the woman again. That old urban legend was true—a juicer of sufficient enthusiasm would continue drinking posthumously, thanks to whatever force animated the reanimates. In an instant I experienced a very complete daydream. Myself, a few years from now or maybe even a few days. My drill soaked in blood at my feet, a wound that would not heal soaking my pants. But my arms were good, still strong. And with my right I'd scrawl on my legal pads furiously, recording every sensation and cogitation, with my left I'd drink from an aluminum water bottle; a big one, like hikers used to use. My blood would turn thick like molasses and slow down my heart, and I'd still write, and still drink. Like this woman next to me, but still scratching with my pen against the page. Maybe writing the same last words over and over, posthumously performing one final fiction—*and then and then and then* till the page fills up and the ink runs dry.

What could the corpse tell me? She was dressed casually, and rattily, but not like a typical wino lady. She had had a job of some sort, and a wardrobe for it. Khakis and a blouse. She wore sneakers that were still white, like someone who only wore them occasionally. Maybe she had sneakers while commuting and then switched to dress heels right outside her job. Her hands were gnarled and fingers twisted, but not too outrageously. So some sort of office gig. There weren't many office gigs left for older women—except for City Hall itself. Where we were. I needed those keys.

"How much were those keys worth to you?" I asked.

"I told her she could drink as much as she wanted," the bartender said. "And she is, I guess."

"What do you want for them?"

"Yes, what do you want for them?" Fat Fag said. "Whatever he offers, I'll double it!"

I didn't know whether he was kidding, suddenly serious, or simply asking for me to take off my belt, wrap it around my fist, and beat his face into a puddle of meat sauce, but I knew better than to react. I kept my eyes focused on the bartender, trying to drag him out of whatever half-booze half-pot haze he had put himself into with sheer force of will. I needed another drink myself, but needed every trade good I had access to for those keys.

"Uh . . . make me an offer?" the bartender finally said.

"How about a laptop? Works, wireless, the whole bit. I've kept it in good shape since the reanimations. Even got some cracked Chinese software on it, so it's almost up to date." I regretted that even as I said it. I couldn't dare give away my computer, not for anything. I also had nothing else to bargain with—the stupid laptop was the only thing of value I owned. If Fats was serious about outbidding me simply for the sake of pique, I was already done.

"A laptop, eh?" Fat Fag bent over, seamlessly really, without a huff or a grunt of exertion and pulled a smartphone from a brown leather satchel at his feet. He put it on the bartop—the open hatch of the vehicle—we were sitting before and proffered it with a wave of his hands. "All yours, for the keys!" Then to me he said, "If you have your laptop with you, I might give you a single key from the chain for it."

"Why are you doing this?"

"Why are *you* doing this?" he asked. "You must have a reason, and it's probably one you don't want to share. So let's just say that I might have a similar reason . . . or perhaps I don't. But I definitely don't share."

Thunder and Alexa appeared behind me. "C'mon," Alexa said. "We have to go."

"No, not yet," I said.

"You may as well," the bartender said. "I'm closing up shop." He held the keys out. The woman near me growled, her throat dead and dry. Everyone was stock still for a second, but then the woman took up her cup again and tried to pour more of the stone soup past her lips. The bartender and Fat Fag made their exchange, and the keychain caught Alexa's eye. She knocked the cup from the dead woman's hand. The woman howled in the way that only a reanimate can, and panic spread in a wave. I jumped back, both phone and keychain hit the floor, and the woman went for the closest target—the bartender.

"You shits are crazy!" the Fag howled. "She's gonna kill us all!" That didn't help the panic. People started surging away. Someone hit the public sirens.

"No she ain't," Thunder said. She kicked the woman square in the ass, and she tumbled into the car, atop the thrashing, shouting bartender. Then she kicked the hatch up, and slammed down the back windshield. Alexa had already grabbed the keychain and kicked the guy in the balls.

She had her own cell phone out and shouted, "Stand back, we're drillers, we're handling this!" A few people turned and looked at us expectantly, then to the rocking car. The windows were streaked with red and black. We ran, blended into the crowd. Out of the corner of my eye, I caught Dr. Jaffe's bus rolling out of the City Hall parking lot—if she was evacuating or coming to the rescue, I didn't know.

"Should we try it now, before they change the locks?" I said. It was hard to run. The soup was powerful stuff, even for a heavyweight like me.

"Way ahead of you," Thunder said. We ran a long circle up to Market Street, then to Gough, and back around. City Hall and the environs seemed clear. After the battle in Japantown, there probably weren't too many city employees left anyway, and a general evacuation made sense given the amount of traffic and trade in the shadow of the building. The steps were clear. Then Alexa's phone rang, as did mine.

"It's Jaffe," I said. Thunder grabbed the keys from Alexa and turned to run back down the block, but Jaffe's bus turned the corner. She was literally waving at us from an open window, her phone to her ear. So I picked up and said, "Hello." She said something, but I couldn't hear it over the braking of the bus. Alexa trotted up to Thunder and grabbed her arms, like she was performing some sort of ridiculous citizen's arrest. I lost track of the keys in their tussle, but then Jaffe stepped off the bus, so it didn't matter.

"Well," she said, both into the phone to me and to the girls, "What's the story, my morning glories?"

I hung up and jogged down to meet with Jaffe. "Have you heard about the reanimate, the evacuation?" We were on the opposite side of City Hall, so the locked-up woman and her new Berkeleyan comrade were probably still tearing one another apart, but only just out of earshot.

"Yes, yes, we have a tow truck coming out," Jaffe said. To Thunder, she said, "Good work, by the way. I hope this means that you've decided to come around to the side of the angels." She smiled at all of us and said, "Let's go inside and talk about it." Alexa and I tried very hard not to look at one another, not to give anything away, and we almost succeeded.

Jaffe's office wasn't a large one, and at one point it was shared. I presumed it was the same one she had back before the reanimate apocalypse. Two desks, four chairs, some bookshelves with no books of interest—textbooks, policy guides, binders—but a whole raft of cell phones and cell phone chargers of different vintages. Laptops and towers and hard drives too, all the way up to the high ceiling. The unused desk was covered in dust, its computer covered in a plastic sheet. I pulled a chair over from that side of the room and squeezed in next to Alexa. Still wasn't sure who had the keys when Jaffe began to speak in measured tones, as if she had been practicing.

"We, as a city, are suffering greatly. Not only do the dead continue to menace us internally, thanks partially to the turnover in drillers . . ." I squirmed when she looked at me, ". . . and externally. Our borders are porous, despite the Bay, despite the guarded bridges, despite the ever-burning fires of Colma. And then we come to the living.

"San Francisco is no longer a democracy. How could it be? We live in a large city, seven miles by seven miles, surrounded by the remnants of immense wealth, and perhaps there are forty thousand people left alive. We're all squatters, all criminals. Most of us are just trying to stay alive one more day, the rest seem almost eager to die. What's left is the permanent government—the bureaucracy, if you will." Jaffe remembered something, and reached into her desk drawer. For a moment, I thought she'd produce a gun, but she actually withdrew a small white box. "See's Candies?" she offered.

The girls ignored it, but I opened the box. The little chocolates didn't look bad, though there was a bit of bloom on them. I put one in my mouth and sucked on it, betting it would be too hard to simply bite.

It wasn't bad, and I said "Thanks" with my mouth full.

"'Bureaucracy' used to be a dirty word. Something people complained about. But like the song says, 'you don't miss it till it's gone,'" Jaffe went on.

Alexa and I exchanged another look and silently decided not to correct her on the lyric. Thunder, too young for the reference, just slumped and stared ahead, looking past Jaffe the way a Zen archer looks past the target. She was a sullen child sitting between a raging mother and a dubious, half-buzzed father.

"But we're not gone!" Jaffe said, suddenly emphatic. "While the elected officials were killed doing their media stunts, or went to ground and never ever came back up, we were still here, silently doing the work we had been trained for, the work necessary to a keep a semblance of civilization alive, even as the typical citizen turned to . . ." She frowned for a moment, then decided on a term. "Primitive accumulation." Ah, so Jaffe was a college Marxist of some sort, clearly. I sniggered and almost choked on my candy.

"When I find people who are capable of accomplishing something, I try to reach an accord. To bring them in. William," she said to me, "did you know that you are our longest-serving driller? It's only been a month, true, but most people don't last more than a week before either quitting, vanishing, or . . . succumbing.

"And you . . ." she looked at her notes. "Ashley. You were part of something significant. But I think you'll agree now that you were on the wrong side, if only because your side no longer exists. Do you think we're keeping secrets here? I'll tell you now that we're not—you can have access to whatever information you need as part of your job description."

Then Jaffe shifted in her seat and looked at Alexa, whose face betrayed some curiosity as to what Jaffe could possibly say about her.

But Thunder interrupted. "But, Dr. Jaffe, you see, the thing of it is—" Then she grabbed Jaffe by the lapels, and threw all her weight into slamming the older woman's head down against the desk. One, two, three times! Jaffe's skull dented. Thunder hit it again, and again. It looked like Jaffe's features had slid off her head. She didn't have time to scream; Thunder had caught her mid-inhalation.

"Let's go!" Thunder shouted. "I have the keys!" She ran out of the room. Alexa and I tore after her, though I wasn't sure if we were going to search City Hall or just try to kill Thunder for what she had just done.

"Bureaucracy!" Thunder said to us before a set of locked doors. "Everything's labeled!" And she waved a transponder at a little pad on the side, and the doors unlocked, and buzzed loudly.

"Well, everyone heard that," Alexa said. She took off doubletime, and I followed.

"Where are you going!" I called out to Thunder.

But Alexa answered first. "After her!"

Then Thunder said, "The basement!" She was slow enough that we caught up with her right away, at an elevator bank. She had a key for it, and the car came right away.

"Well, since you're both here, this is the story," Thunder said. "We did the whole Japan Center thing so that one or more of us would get captured or brought here somehow. It's been known to happen. City Hall is great at co-opting movements. The woman at the bar, the reanimate, she was a mole ready to pass her keys off to us. She just died, somehow, beforehand."

"Wait, if you had a mole with the keys, why would you need to infiltrate this place?" I said.

"Obviously," Alexa said. "She wasn't a willing mole. What do you do, poison her slowly or something? Trade keys for antidote? Those Berkeley scientists seemed capable of that level of chemistry. Or was she just a boozer you caught in a compromising position?" Alexa looked over Thunder's head to glare at me. We were headed down, not to the basement, but to a sub-basement. Not the kind of structure most buildings in an earthquake-prone city would have.

Thunder didn't answer Alexa's question; she just said, "Some things it's important to see for yourself."

I said, "Well, that's a non-answer," but Thunder didn't rise to that bait either.

The elevator opened into a short hallway with thick double doors right across, and those in turn opened up into a surprisingly well-lit, half-done classroom of sorts. Spackle was still visibly sealing the gaps between slabs of drywall. A mismatched collection of desk chairs were scattered around a projection screen. There was no video projector though—just an ornate wooden cabinet with an old-fashioned and frayed electrical cord coming out of it.

"This is the orientation room for city workers," Thunder said. I went to the cabinet and opened it up. It was a film projector of sorts, but old. Film was threaded through the gearwork, and it looked strange, as if manufactured prior to the standardization of film sizes. My brief stay in the high school A/V club was paying off. No audio, or rather the audio was run separately, thanks to an ancient cylinder phonograph.

"There's a breeze down here," Alexa said. "Not musty at all."

"Can you work the video?" Thunder asked.

"It's not a video, but . . . maybe?" I said. I told Alexa to kill the lights, which had snapped on automatically when we entered. She found the switch, and an oversized vent at the top of the wall.

"Check it out," she said, but I don't remember, even now, if she said it immediately before we heard the first thump, or just as it sounded. But another one followed, and another right after, as if something was tumbling down the duct.

"Turn off the light . . ." Thunder said, quietly, but Alexa didn't. Jaffe looked like a bag of laundry splitting open more than anything else as she rolled up to the vent and spilled out as the grating gave way. She hit the ground hard, wetly, but without a grunt or scream. The first thing I realized was that Alexa had left her drill—my drill, actually—up in the office. Not that it mattered, as Jaffe was already a reanimate. She lurched to her feet and through hammered features glared at us, driven by her last conscious thought to bring us on to her team. Now though, her team was the dead.

It is curious to break a first-person narrative into chapters. Suspense of the traditional sort is impossible, and it is not as though human beings normally relay accounts of their lives in chapter form. It's a habit we've picked up from novels, and from memoirs which are simply novel-shaped objects. Novels can be a bit tawdry. Is there a cheaper trick than ending a chapter with the main characters in deadly peril? Probably only one: the secret plan a character has in a crime or mystery novel that will solve all the problems of the book. We get to know all of the protagonist's innermost thoughts, likes and dislikes, childhood encounters with ancient evil, sexual tastes, etcetera, but when it comes time for the story to wrap up, we never get to see the content of the forbidden box, or the text of the hidden letter, or the contents of the protagonist's head.

Clearly, I survived the encounter with Jaffe's reanimated corpse. It involved the usual thrashing about, though I have

trouble even now thinking about it. The desk chairs were nailed to the floor, so I couldn't pick one up and brain her with it. The projection screen wouldn't have killed a baby, and it rolled up into the ceiling, so there was no metal casing to use as a weapon. But we did outnumber her, and we were so close. Jaffe had broken a leg, so she could only limp at us, dragging half her body behind her.

The girls rushed to the projection cabinet, where I stood. We knew without speaking that wrecking the cabinet to manufacture a makeshift weapon would defeat the whole purpose of getting into City Hall in the first place. But the cabinet did have doors, and the doors had hinges. I grabbed the keys from Thunder and found a key with a thick stem, slammed it under one of the hinges, and pried the aging pin free. The three of us together pulled on the door and freed it from the other hinge. Then I raised it over my head, and swung down atop Jaffe's. The wood was light, though, so it just bounced off her skull. We backpedaled a bit, and held the door horizontally as a shield.

"Her head's already half-destroyed, she shouldn't even be walking!" Thunder said.

"Well, it's like the woman who liked to drink—if you have a lot of passion for something, some trace of that can survive," I said. "Some of those perceptions aren't so hysterical after all."

"Shut up and put the door down across two of the chairs, quick!" Alexa said. She tugged on her end and we let go. Then she hopped up onto another desk chair, and wobbled. I didn't know what she was planning on doing at that moment, but I held her still. Then she jumped, and landed on the door. It splintered, but didn't break.

"Fuck!" she shouted. Then she just jumped into my arms. I stumbled backwards.

"Good idea, shit execution!" Thunder grabbed the door and swung it against the desk chairs. Four, five times, like Babe

Ruth, all gut and ferocity. I closed my eyes. For the first time, I was afraid to die. Then I heard a sharp crack. The door had split near the edge. Thunder tore and kicked at it, and had a spear.

She howled, "Fucking bourgie bitch!" and drove the point of it into Jaffe's eye. Jaffe swung her arms, and tried to jerk free.

"Grab 'em!" I said and I got a hold of her right hand and elbow. Jaffe got the left. Then Thunder pushed while we pulled. There was a quick slide, then something jammed in Jaffe's skull, then Alexa and I yanked harder and Thunder slammed her shoulder into the wooden plank, and we pushed past it, deep into Jaffe's head. Her neck snapped backwards, and she was done.

"Holy fuck!" Thunder said. Two or three more times. "Holy fuck, we nearly died." My hands were numb. Jaffe's arm was so cold already. I'd seen a lot of death lately, and a fair amount of posthumous bodily destruction as well, but it was different now. Jaffe was an acquaintance. Someone whose face I knew, who I had drank with, albeit briefly, who had been in my home, albeit under armed guard and only for a moment. Outside of Alexa and Thunder, she was pretty much it since the crisis of reanimations had occurred. And Jaffe was—had been—a great deal saner than any of us. Did our curiosity just damn the city, the last city in America? It is a question I still ask myself silently, but then I asked it aloud.

Alexa said, quietly, "Well, she saw whatever is on the film here, and if it made her want to keep the city going, we should watch it too. It's a good thing. We need to spread the word." Thunder yanked the spear plant from Jaffe's eye and ran it through the handles of the double doors to bar them. I went back to the cabinet. The equipment was old, and simple for it. I found the switch for the projector and the cylindrical phonograph. Thunder hit the lights. Some leader film, hand-drawn it seemed, in an archaic hand, ran, and when it hit 2 I put the needle head onto the cylinder.

"Why did they never make copies of this onto a better format?!"

"By the time they knew what they had, they couldn't risk copies getting out . . . now shhh!" Thunder said.

On the screen appeared a title card *living dead man—1917*.

The cylinder crackled and popped, and a distant tiny voice I could just barely hear explained.

"Found in 1906, this man you see before you is not alive. He is dead, yet still ambulatory. He has been preserved through the work of the finest Russian taxidermists and morticians." The screen still showed the title card as the film and cylinder weren't synced up. Then the scene shifted to a plain room, and a man in rags walking toward the camera. He was desiccated, nothing but parchment stretched over bone. The film was full of flakes and hair and quick jittering leaps in the frame. The man walked toward the camera, stopped several feet away, turned, and limped off toward the left to the edge of the screen. It was all in long shot, as was the fashion of early silent film.

Another title card *long years of struggle*, then the shot changed. The man and another fellow, well-dressed this one, with a stiff collar and a three-piece suit, a pencil mustache and a sizeable paunch, made expansive gestures and patted his own diaphragm.

The cylinder, a second or two behind, said, "Aaaaaah!" in a new voice. The reanimate mimicked the man on the screen, and then we heard a higher, more dry, "Aaaaah!"

The narrator explained, "At first, this living dead man knew nothing but rage and anger. He had been embalmed and was being prepared for burial when he sat up from the table on which he was being prepared, and attacked the men who were caring for his final needs. He was beyond communicating with, but psychologist and linguist Doctor Willis Armstrong of the University of California, Berkeley, spent long years of intellectual struggle training the man to speak once more." On screen, the pair were working through some vocal exercises. It was real footage, in a way. Not contemporary, of course, but also not a recording of an actual training session. The reanimate had been sufficiently tamed to play-act for the camera.

"Jesus," Alexa muttered.

"A message to the future!" the narrator said. Then a title card came up, reading the same.

"Beware," said that effete, dry-sounding voice, over the card. Then the card was replaced with another long shot of the dead man. Armstrong, now in a white lab coat, stood on his left, and another man in a lab coat—this one had a thick mustache and sideburns—on the dead man's right.

"There will be more such as I am." The scientists nodded solemnly, as though having just told a patient of a terminal cancer diagnosis.

The narrator explained, "Scientists for years have studied the blood and tissues of this man. What causes him to ambulate and cogitate remains unknown—perhaps the embalming procedures have damaged or occulted the bacterium or fungus that causes this remarkable disorder. We only have this man's testimony, which must be taken with a grain of salt, as so little is known about him. He does not remember his own name, or where he is from. He has mastered language and manners once again, but all he knows from his previous life is that he was once a prospector."

The dead man stepped forward and opened his mouth again. "I came to San Francisco as a young man. I was party to much sin and wickedness, to privation and moments of joy." His voice on the cylinder was slow, like poured syrup. "I awoke an old man, a fire burning in my lungs. A fire I had felt but once before, prospecting on the banks of the Feather River years prior. A foul-smelling fog bank settled upon my camp. I believed I had consumption, but the disease passed and I returned to the city proper to live out my days. Now I am naught but disease."

He stepped backwards into his place. The two scientists also took a step backwards, leaving some space between them and the dead man.

A new title card went up *could it be?* Then a second one. *A disease that affects only the dead?*

"We do not know if this disorder is contagious. The man has been under quarantine for onto two decades. The disease may well lie latent in the tissues of the respiratory system until bodily functions cease, only to emerge and infect the muscles and sinews of the body." We were back to the shot of the dead man and two scientists, but now the fellow with the sideburns had a pistol in his hand. He fired and the film went white. There was more jittering and skipping. Returning to the shot, the reanimate was crumpled into a heap, the top of his head shattered. That was not a pantomime. Having spent years treating the man, teaching him to speak again, and the rudiments of civilization, they snuffed him on film.

"Our brave colleagues have given their lives to investigate this plague. Not only have they spent years working with the subject, they have committed themselves to the care of the city until the end of their natural lives, when they will be immediately dissected for reasons of both medical research and the public safety."

The shot changed again. It was a sunny day, a tombstone on a hill. Above it, a leafy branch swayed in a long-dead breeze. "Any cemetery, any graveyard," the narrator said, breathless now, "can become the site of anarchist insurrection if this disorder spreads, if the mysterious fog returns. A public panic must be avoided. Cemeteries must be reinforced to prevent escape, or eliminated entirely and other forms of disposal encouraged among the religious communities of America."

A new shot, this time Fisherman's Wharf as it used to be— before the reanimates, before the tourism. Working ships and small fishing boats, panning from left to right. In the distance, Alcatraz, but without the famous concrete prison. Homes, it looked like, or a military garrison of some sort, and a dock. Fog began to roll in, though it was so close to the lens it was likely simply some smoke from a fire lit just off-screen and wafted across the camera's field of vision by a man with a fan.

"We do not know when the mysterious fog may return. We do not know if it has returned. We only know that we must take every precaution. The armies of the dead outnumber the armies of the living. The death plague must not be allowed to spread, the public must not be allowed to panic!"

A new title card *confidential! distribution of this film or its contents by any means is strictly forbidden on special order of the city and county of san francisco.*

"From the city fathers, to the people of the future, beware!" There was another, deeper sound after "beware." It sounded like a repetition of the word, actually, but was too muffled to hear properly. There were no credits, no other title cards. The cylinder continued a muffled monologue for a few extra seconds, but there was nothing intelligible. Then the film was over.

"I don't fucking believe it," Thunder said. The blood had left her face. She wasn't raging anymore, just stunned. "That's all? That's all there is?"

"I wonder if that fog had anything to do with the steam vents from the quake the Berkeley people were studying," Alexa offered. She looked at me, I shrugged.

"They found a reanimate a hundred years ago, trained it back up to humanity, then killed it as part of a government scare film that nobody ever saw. That doesn't explain anything really—why hasn't the plague spread to Canada? To Mexico?"

"What makes you think it hasn't by now?" Alexa said.

"I killed people for this . . . to watch this . . ." Thunder said, to herself.

"It's like any sort of infestation, like Africanized honeybees. Starts slow, then roars to life in the right circumstances. What's the etiology of this plague—it actually infects the living, but becomes active after the host dies? Were all the scientists looking in the wrong place somehow? The zombies go on rampages, spread the virus or whatever just by being mobile, and kill people so they get infected too."

"So we're infected now?" I wanted to cough, but held it in. "When my grandmother died, I was terrified. I wasn't even sad for her loss, or sad for my mother—I was just afraid. I knew that one day I'd end up like she was. In a box, in a room somewhere, dressed in clothes I never dressed in normally, people I used to know weeping or standing around with frowns on their faces. I was sad for only one reason—by the time I died, there would be no relatives around who still knew any Greek. All the muttering would be in English . . ."

"This is bullshit, this is a fake movie. Has to be. Right?" Thunder said. She looked at me, as if I'd know.

I shrugged. "Well, we can fake anything with computers, right? But I don't know, the hardware here is actually harder to synthesize than the actual visual and audio stuff. It looked like authentic Thomas Edison stuff. No plastics. Even the film looks as ratty as an old film would. Maybe that's why they didn't make copies on VHS or DVD, or just upload it. Nobody would believe it if they saw it on their computer screens."

"We should still upload it," Alexa said. "We can. It doesn't matter if it isn't believed, right away."

"And tell people what—watch out for evil clouds swooping down on you?" Thunder put her head in her big hands and started sobbing.

"That's even assuming that the reanimate knew what he was talking about. Sounded like a guess, from a certified amnesiac," I said.

"Still, it's something. Do we take it?" Alexa said. "Or just head back upstairs, break back down here, and set up a video camera and run the film again, to tape it?"

"And they shot him . . . he could talk, understand, and they shot him anyway . . ." Thunder was on her own now, as divorced from the world as any reanimate.

"So, the city of San Francisco did know something long before anyone else did. And they didn't tell anyone else because . . ."

"Maybe they did, and nobody believed it," Alexa said. "Or maybe they did, and there were other forces at work—I mean, what if a cop showed up at your grandma's funeral with a power drill and a tarp and told you it had to be done. It would raise a lot of religious questions, biological ones . . . and as long as there was only one reanimate, or a few, it could be kept quiet."

"We should just go for now," I said. "Let's get a drink. Talk about it, sleep on it." Alexa and I were at the door for a long moment, waiting for Thunder to pull herself together. There was a spare set of keys on Jaffe's corpse, so I retrieved them and told Thunder to come upstairs when she was ready. We stepped outside and waited for the elevator. Of course, it was full of what passed for San Francisco police, pistols drawn. I threw my hands up and started talking immediately, about history, and theories of history. Why did the Soviet Union fall? The Cold War? Markets versus command economy? Gorbachev's personality? Are you sure, are you sure your guess is the right one? Does it explain everything, does anything explain anything? If markets are so awesome, why is Cuba stuffed with refugees?

One of the cops called me a Communist and slapped me across the face. Alexa had her hands up as well, but she wasn't talking, so she didn't eat a backhand. They marched us back into the room, where Thunder had managed to rewind the film. Without a word, she started the projector again, and put the needle back on the cylinder. Jaffe's corpse, and the huge gouge that used to be her face, went unremarked upon. The cops had heard rumors of what went on down in the sub-basement, but apparently had never seen the film themselves. One of them even took a seat.

After the film was over, the police moved into action. There was none of our hemming and hawing; of course the film would be copied and uploaded to the Internet. Two

officers were dispatched to get an old camcorder, and a DVD
player, and a laptop, and every cable they could find since some
of them would likely come in handy.

Finally, one leveled a firearm right at Thunder's head
and said, "What happened here?" He shrugged his shoulder
toward Jaffe.

"She was dead when she came down here," she said, and
the blood was black enough that the story stuck.

"How'd you get down here?"

"We found the keys," she said plainly. "From that woman
who worked here. The white woman—she was the one who
died and reanimated out in the agora before. They had fallen
out of her pocket or something, and when we evacuated the
park I saw them and grabbed them."

"So how did Mayor Jaffe die then?"

"I dunno, bad tin of sardines? We were running from chaos
outside, trying to find a safe place, and ended up down here.
She cornered us, so we had to end her. Luckily, both my friends
here are certified drillers."

"I'm actually a record-holder," I explained. "I've drilled
more than anyone. I just don't quit."

In the cop's face, I read Jaffe's story. She wasn't a great
leader, not someone who inspired people. She was just a quiet,
competent person who took responsibility for her own job,
and when another job opened up, she was promoted. Then one
day, after the zombies came, there was nobody left to promote
her, so she promoted herself. She knew to keep a low profile,
and didn't position herself as a warlord and thus a lightning
rod for a world of troubles and conflict. She just did what she
did, using her common sense and taking the conservative path.
She showed the movie to people she knew wouldn't be freaked

out by it, and kept its distribution limited for the simple reason that most people would freak out instantly.

But why share it at all? How did she get to see it herself, the first time? City governments don't have classified files, they just bury things so deeply under paperwork and nonsense that nobody can be bothered to reach them. But Jaffe did—probably after the reanimations began. And she maybe knew the extent of what was coming before others did, and decided to lay low while the mayor and the city supervisors got themselves killed. Then she helped herself to a slightly bigger chair in a slightly bigger office, in the good part of the bad part of town. Clever, useful, even generous after a fashion, but it was still a knife in the belly. Jaffe wasn't how America was supposed to work, even when ruined beyond repair.

The cop nodded. "Makes sense. Lots of expired canned food floating around these days. Even in City Hall, we can't afford the organic stuff all the time."

After that, the cops ignored us except when one asked the room at large if anyone knew what kind of cable was needed for the DV camera she had. I did—Firewire. It took an hour and three failed attempts to get the film recorded right off the projection screen, and the file uploaded. We held our collective breath, waiting for the Internet, or even just the power, to konk out as it often did.

"Look, I need to go," I said, finally. "It's up. People will look at it, or they won't. It'll be on the front pages of the *Taipei Times* tomorrow, or it won't. I don't know what to make of the film, and it didn't help me understand anything, except that I don't want this anymore." I handed my city-issue cell phone to the nearest cop, but he threw up his arms as though the phone were infectious. So I just put it on a desk and made to leave.

"If we need to reach you—?" one of the cops called out.

"You already know where I live!" I took the steps, and stopped by Jaffe's office to liberate a few cell phone chargers and batteries. "But as to myself, my guiding-star always is, 'Get hold of portable property,'" I said aloud to the empty room.

Life had returned to the Civic Center. Tents were being righted, fires lit for the evening. A few percussionists were out, beating on white buckets and scavenged tom-toms. How many of these people even knew that until a few hours ago, San Francisco still had a mayor? Unelected, incognito, the Taoist answer to government.

> The best leaders are those the people hardly know exist.
> The next best is a leader who is loved and praised.
> Next comes the one who is feared.
> The worst one is the leader that is despised.

Jaffe was despised, but only by Thunder and whoever her real friends were. The rest of us, the real San Franciscans, hardly knew she existed. Whoever the next mayor is, he'll probably be despised. Almost certainly be a he as well. The sporadic electricity, the still pretty good plumbing and water, these I suspect we left behind on the floor of the sub-basement of City Hall.

I found a liquor kiosk whose contents hadn't been completely smashed or looted by the afternoon's general evacuation, and made some trades. It was Saturday night, time to party, and my idea of a party was a sponge bath, drinking, and writing. I didn't even want to think of my role in what just happened, in what might be about to happen. Though in the end the film would likely just add to the worldwide confusion over the reanimates when it wasn't being denounced as a hoax and a fraud by debunkers both amateur and professional; things were going to change. What military power wouldn't want to invade a still-functioning port city if they could somehow protect themselves from "the fog," and then get it in a can and sell it? Some tin-plate dictator would at least try now.

I had a two-liter Coke bottle filled with beer, and a few airline bottles of Bacardi. The future was before me like the night, dark and endless. I had a lot of pages to transcribe, but I've always been a fast typist, albeit with only two rapid-fire fingers. Colin called it the "hunt and peck" method, but I always preferred to think of it as "search and destroy," one letter at a time.

This wasn't what California was supposed to be like. An understatement I instantly want to scratch out—let the pen tear the pages. Boston was so cold, and so dark. It was heavy with history, and ridiculous parodies of history. Tour guides in tricorner hats and petticoats. Then there was Harvard in Cambridge, pretty much a great middle finger to me and everyone else like me. And it had been a huge brick Fuck You since before the country had even been founded.

San Francisco seemed like a place of hope. Expensive sure, but the dot.com bubble had already popped, and even the homeless could thrive there thanks to the temperate weather and compassionate, liberal, guilt-riven populace. California was the shelf where America stored its hustlers, a place for reinvention and imagination.

I cried, "Los Angeles, give me some of you!" like Fante's Bandini once did, but I knew I'd need a car to get around. And I'd be one more wannabe writer, just like every broom-pusher and bagboy with a script. The only thing that differentiated me from them was that if I sold a book or another story, I might make a few grand, or another fifty dollars. If one of those assholes sold one of their asinine scripts, they'd make a house. I was too egotistical, too fragile, too incompetent and unsure of myself for LA. And I couldn't afford to relocate and instantly buy a car.

San Francisco, where the Beats drank and fags still hustled on select street corners. San Francisco, which still had Italians in North Beach, and nearby Oakland, which had a real live Greek ghetto. There were still SROs full of shaky-limbed alkies, and overstuffed libraries, and a great big park full of little hidey-holes to sleep in. And maybe some kind of new job for some kind of new person. The Internet was practically hatched in California, and what was the Internet except for a big pile of mostly text? There was something out there—something out *here*—for me, I knew it.

I also needed an entire country between Yvette, with her four little sleeping pills, and me, before I did something extremely stupid. I was never anything but a side character in the drama of her life. The only thing we really had in common was the skin torn from our wrists, and ankles, and necks, in our attempts to escape Youngstown, and lives of rented furniture, high fructose corn syrup, bad backs from the factory, and toxic debt buildup from the layoffs. In San Francisco, I could drown myself in women. Catholic schoolgirls turned pagan sluts, dykes into dick on alternate Thursdays, hippie chicks with hairy armpits, older women in old man bars . . . anyone who'd have me, really.

So I bought a ticket, via Southwest. Four hundred bucks got me a cramped seat and two layovers. At Midway Airport, in a little bakery called Let Them Eat Cake, I had a slice of tres leches cake. It was the single best piece of solid food that had ever passed through my lips. How many people still alive have ever had that soft cake melt on their tongue? How many would still treasure that mayfly sensation over the other experiences of their lives? The army of the dead didn't just destroy civilization, it ruined the very nature of the everyday. Every sober moment is a crisis—how to get food, who to trust, what's worth trading. I suppose some things never change. Now there are so few sober moments, and little need for there to be any.

There are times—times like now—that I think the reanimates are the lucky ones. They have another chance to get it right, but with no social obligations and only a single appetite. The living have it a little better in some ways now than in the days before reanimation—the huge databases of demographic information and debt records and legal histories and property deeds have been destroyed, so it's just whatever street hustles one finds oneself wrapped up in that weigh heavily—but the dead have evolved beyond caring about anything but the quick-moving, screaming blurs before them.

"There are no dead people." I can imagine Alexa's childhood priest matter-of-factly making such a declaration. I was told the same exact thing. Nobody is dead, and hell is empty until the Day of Judgment. Somewhere in Constantinople, a bearded old man is laughing his ass off. All the other branches of Christianity have to try to explain human suffering—Eastern Orthodoxy just wallows in it. At a loss my whole life, when the zombies came and Jaffe woke me up, a part of me was, finally, well-prepared for the world beyond the walls of my apartment. There are no dead people, so the shuffling footsteps I hear in the hallway outside my door do not belong to the dead. The reanimates are as alive as I am. It's just that I'm not so very alive.

On the last leg of my flight to California, after a lengthy delay in Denver where I had to stay on the plane while other passengers disembarked and a new troupe boarded, I was seated next to an older woman. She was eager to chat. So eager that she complimented my selection of orange juice during beverage service. I'd never been afraid to fly, and needed to save every dime for the struggles ahead, so I was pleased to select a free drink. Burying my nose in the book I was reading at the time—some horrifically boring thriller I'd found in the seatback pocket—didn't help either. She knew she was more interesting than the high-stakes nonsense in my hands.

"Do you know what someone should come up with?" she told me. "A sort of map, or chart, that explains whatever it is we see when we're flying over America. Did you notice those round patterns back before the Rockies? Are those crops? I wonder why they were planted as circles within the squares of the property lines."

I shouldn't have told her, but I did. So rarely did I actually have a definitive answer to anything. "Circle irrigation. A long moving pipe waters all the crops, so it describes the radius of the circle. You only see it in flat parts of the country." I did a little maneuver with my forearms and table tray to illustrate.

"Are you from a flat part of the country?" she said. She touched my arm. A wrinkled old auntie, just a few years from grandma, the brush of her fingers was entirely asexual, but it was the only warm, meaningful contact with another human I'd had in weeks. She had me.

"Not especially. I'm coming from Boston, but I'm really from Ohio."

"And what brings you to the Bay?" she asked. "Vacation?"

"Relocating. I'm . . ." I'm planning on drinking myself to death in a transient hotel where the bunks are surrounded in chicken wire. I have no idea what I'm going to do, because I'm too stupid to plan ahead, and because my mother spent twenty years cooking my meals and ironing pleats in my blue jeans because she thought they were to be worn like trousers. I'm beyond help, so I figured I may as well throw myself in the middle of a big crazy mess of a city and see if somehow something good happens to me, like falling and tripping over a broken jar of mayonnaise in the supermarket, and settling out of court. There was no hope in truth. This was my moment, my chance to declare something before another human being, and in front of the lower echelons of the heavens themselves.

"I'm going to be a writer," I said. "I've already published one story." Of course I didn't mention that it was in some dopey sci-fi webzine. Maybe she'd think I'd been in the *New Yorker*, my old enemy. "California seems like the place to be to get some serious work done. It's like America's Paris—full of vitality. Full of life. That's where I want to be."

The woman, who didn't ever introduce herself or offer any *quid pro quo* personal information, smiled at me. "How do you plan on paying your rent till you make it big?"

"Oh, I have some money saved." One hundred-fifty dollars, actually. A little leftover from Colin's payout, augmented by the proceeds from selling sperm and blood and some hardcovers to a sympathetic clerk at Rodney's Bookstore in Cambridge. Enough for a week in the worst room in a dumpy residency hotel in the worst neighborhood in the city. My only plan, and it was half-baked, was to find the Californian version of Papatheofanis and talk my way into a job washing dishes or running a bread and pastry route servicing the local restaurants. Little did I know that the Greek diner, or Greek-run pizzeria, was virtually unknown out west. My gig, ultimately, was picking up odd jobs via Craigslist—moving furniture and writing term papers for Chinese college students at Berkeley were my twin specialties. "And I can write anything. Fiction, journalism. Copy for websites. Maybe even a piece for an in-flight magazine," I told her. A wrinkled copy of the airline's rag, *Spirit*, mocked me, the torn corner of the front cover a permanent wink. But I made a note to take the magazine with me, just in case.

"Good luck to you. Maybe I'll see your name on the spine of a book one day. What is it?" I told her, and she made a face, as normal white people do when they hear a Greek name, but she recovered quickly and made me write it down for her on a scrap of paper she fashioned from her seatback's barf bag. For a moment, my father's paranoia roared to the forefront of my brain. *She's a cop! CIA! This is a trap set by the airline because they don't like people flying one-way after 9/11!* She still may have been, actually, but it didn't matter. My ears popped, and the pilot told us to fasten our seat belts as we were beginning our final approach.

A few months later she was dead, and I got an email from her son. He'd Googled me, and wanted to know how my name, written in my handwriting, ended up on a piece of paper in his mother's only partially unpacked luggage. Her name was Mary Beth. She had taught school in the South Bay somewhere for thirty years, then retired. Her husband had died the year before, and she had taken a flight out to Chicago to visit a sister who lived in nearby Lake Forest. Then a stroke took her suddenly, and it was sonny's job to pick through her belongings. He was as chatty as his damn mother was in his friggin' email.

I was curious, and wrote back. "She didn't happen to have any other names written down anywhere, did she?" I pictured great snowy piles of scraps of paper atop a coffee table, spilling forth from her pocketbook, stuffed into the pockets of a sensible coat with a breadcrumb trail leading back to the front door.

"She did, actually," he wrote back. "Mom liked talking to people. But only your name was easy to Google. Sorry to bother you." It hadn't been a bother. In fact, the email kept me from cutting my belly open with a kitchen knife, an action I had been seriously entertaining, even though it meant finding a dollar store and buying a kitchen knife. Dollar store cutlery ain't an easy way to check out. A little human contact was enough to keep drinking rather than bleeding that day.

San Francisco had not been good to me that first month. How could it have been? It was a city of artists, of sexual adventurers, of intellectuals and mathematical geniuses. Nobody here cared whether I was alive or dead. Hell, nobody here knew *that* I was alive and not dead, except for Mary Beth's very thorough first born son. San Francisco had only given me one thing ever, just as I got off the airplane and walked out from the terminal.

My little card table desk and laptop face south. There's a window on my left. Saturday has become Sunday, and the cold steel night sky is melting into bright day. In my peripheral vision, I caught a shambling reanimate moving down the sidewalk across the street, then another. Maybe I saw a third too, or maybe it's the drink, and the long hours of squinting and typing. There are more dead than I've ever seen at once, though of course I slept through the initial uprising. I don't hear the ones out in the hallway, surely loitering by my door, but if they're not moving and jostling one another, not scratching at the knob, there's nothing much to hear. No breathing, no impatient sighs. I think I know who they are, regardless. The girls, Alexa and Thunder. Whatever's out there fills space, displaces air, in the way those two do. *Eureka!* They found me. I don't want to know what they look like now. If one another's flesh is under their fight-ruined cuticles. If Alexa died smiling. Maybe behind them, still climbing the steps, is poor, loyal Junior, or crazy Tolbert with a scam to sell me some new skin. Or it could even be long lost Aishwarya, a skeleton with a name tag pinned to a pitted, crumbling rib. Only Yvette is truly dead and buried to me, forever.

Something terrible must have happened when the video hit the net. A rash of suicides, or a crazed power struggle outside City Hall. Why not both? The dead walked alone. Only the living hunted in packs, until now. Some faction or other has lost for winning. A brace of cops versus a coterie of drillers. Garbage men versus sewer workers. Fags versus breeders. Draw the line any way you like, someone will step over it. One set wiped out the other, but even in death the passions and desires of the losers have reanimated their limbs, compelled them to keep working together to fill the power vacuum, to take the city. There's a stream of ambulant dead now, little lives on scraps of skin scattered like Mary Beth's paper slips across the streets. The message of these last few paragraphs isn't the street corner prophet cliché *The End Is Near!* but *The Beginning Is Near!*

That's what the city gave me, on the first day. I walked out into a new beginning. A new world, rising forth from the ashes of the old. The sun was rising on my left, as it is now. I turned to the orange-painted sky, saw the sun boiling away the Northeast—evaporating frigid Boston, melting rusted

Youngstown, consuming all of old America—and I smiled. In that one moment, I was happy, and I was free. That moment, I'll remember forever. This next one too. For now I see another new dawn, and I'm here to greet it. The notes on my foolscaps and pads have all been keyed in. The printer is humming. The text file has been uploaded. There's a number of solicitors standing just outside my door with a great new deal, and I'm ready to take it.

The germ of this book started with an email from my friend R.J. Sevin, who had what seemed like the surefire idea of launching an imprint of zombie fiction, and then getting George A. Romero to lend his name to the concern. Well anyway, it didn't work out, as these things rarely do, but I kept writing anyway out of sheer pique despite the howls of protest from publishers and my agent about the sheer number of zombie books—as if I'd been publishing them all. I do agree though; this should be the last zombie novel ever published. I'd also like to thank Erica Satifka for her keen eye, and Jeremy Lassen and Cory Allyn at Night Shade for bringing this book to the United States.

Nick Mamatas is the author of six and a half novels and several collections. His work has been translated into German, Italian, and Greek. Nick is also an anthologist and editor of short fiction, including the Locus Award–nominated *The Future Is Japanese* (co-edited with Masumi Washington) and the Bram Stoker Award–winning *Haunted Legends* (co-edited with Ellen Datlow). Nick's own short fiction has appeared in genre publications such as *Asimov's Science Fiction* and Tor.com, lit journals including *New Haven Review* and *subTERRAIN*, and anthologies such as *Hint Fiction* and *Best American Mystery Stories 2013*. His fiction and editorial work has been nominated for the Bram Stoker Award five times, the Hugo Award twice, the World Fantasy Award twice, and the Shirley Jackson, International Horror Guild, and Locus awards.